The Road to SHAMBHALA

GERALD R. STANEK

SHIVER HILL BOOKS

ISBN: 978-0-9747417-9-6

Published by Shiver Hill Books
Printed by Lulu.com

for Alice

Acknowledgements

I would like to thank my friends in Sedona and Ojai for their support, in particular everyone at the Sedona Creative Life Center, The Symphony of Life, and Meditation Mount. This book would not have been possible without the assistance of Joyce, Zachariah, Aldo, the Abuelito, A.A.B, and D.K. A special thank you goes to Randee Vasilakos and her posse for technical assistance with my broadband connection.

Lovers

O lovers, lovers it is time
to set out from the world.
I hear a drum in my soul's ear
coming from the depths of the stars.

Our camel driver is at work;
the caravan is being readied.
He asks that we forgive him
for the disturbance he has caused us,
He asks why we travelers are asleep.

Everywhere the murmur of departure;
the stars, like candles
thrust at us from behind blue veils,
and as if to make the invisible plain,
a wondrous people have come forth.

Rumi

translation: James Cowan

CHAPTER ONE

THEY sat on the stone, on the word, and looked out over the valley. As he leaned back, bracing himself with his arms behind, his fingers found the letters chiseled there in authoritative capitals, spelling out UNANIMITY. They had passed other boulders, placed carefully along the path, on which were engraved the phrases SPIRITUAL APPROACH, ESSENTIAL DIVINITY, GOODWILL, GROUP ENDEAVOR, and RIGHT HUMAN RELATIONS. Probably, they weren't supposed to be sitting on the rock, it was like sitting on a gravestone or an altar in a way. There were benches nearby where they could have sat, but this schoolboy bit of rebellion had seemed necessary to complete the experience, and could only serve to aid the stated aim, UNANIMITY, – to become one with nature, or some god or spirit of the place. It seemed to be working; Brendon didn't want to leave. The view below them was awesome, not awe inspiring like the Grand Canyon, more storybook or perfect postcard.

"Idyllic," he said, the appropriate word coming to him. She didn't respond, being equally captivated by the day. A sign at the beginning of the short path had proclaimed *International Garden of Peace*. 'International' seemed a bit extravagant, like Fargo International Airport, but the landscaping was well thought-out, and it certainly was peaceful. Comforting, he thought, as if the mountains were arms shielding all within their embrace; the gently sloping green hills, the groves of citrus trees laid out in rolling grids, the hint of red tile roofs in the distance, the diffuse

1

sunlight gilding everything with an etheric honey. A soft breeze and the sibilant pulse of devoted bees quieted his thoughts by turns, anchoring him to the stone, the valley, and the moment, inducing a kind of self-hypnotic state. He had a déjà vu feeling, or rather a *simul view*, as if by sitting on this spot he was simultaneously sitting on a rock in Tuscany, or a hillside in Spain, a moment of 1475, an afternoon in 1890. He took a deep breath, relaxing and surrendering to this feeling of connection with the earth and eternity. Perhaps it was an international garden after all.

Cassidy began to fidget. The boulder wasn't exactly comfortable. She got off and scuffed her feet in the reddish gravel. She always had too much energy, Brendon thought. This motive quality was typical of her, she repeatedly approached things with unbridled enthusiasm, failed to find them as exciting as she had hoped, and quickly moved to the next item on her list. And he knew there had been a list, if only mental, when she had casually suggested that morning that they drive up to Ojai. She had a habit of slipping her agenda in before he got his first cup of coffee, before he had wits enough about him to calculate a feasible reason why he should be excused from whatever it was she had cooked up and spent irrational amounts of time contriving some justification for, which would make it all for *his* benefit.

"Where's that?" he had asked.

"Up the coast a little way. It's a little town in the mountains. Supposed to be very arty. You'll love it. It'll do you good to get out of the apartment."

He had taken another sip of morning and thought about sitting in his room all day, staring alternately at his laptop and the block wall five feet from his window.

"Sure, why not," he said.

'A little way up the coast' turned into two hours and twenty minutes, no big surprise. They walked along the picturesque arched arcade and perused a few galleries. A cute cafe provided an overpriced sandwich at a table by the window, through which they watched people doing what *they* had done, wandering in and out of shops full of nondescript pretty *stuff*, as if that new dress or scarf or photo or book would keep the moment from passing, as if acquiring a plein-air painting which simulated a sunset or a mountain or the ocean would provide endless days of youth and California sun.

He likewise was not surprised when she had nonchalantly turned down a side street and they had found themselves in a little metaphysical bookshop, where she went gaga over the tarot cards and crystals. As if she hadn't known, via Google, all about the place, including its location and hours. She had probably been planning this little jaunt for weeks. He had purchased some incense and a paperback entitled *Developing a Spiritual Practice.*

"Let's go back this way," she had suggested when they returned to the car. She pointed in the opposite direction from which they had come. He didn't hesitate. She was a great planner, list maker, manipulator. He generally played along. It seemed to make her feel more important. Just when they were about to climb out of the valley, she told him to turn left, clearly away from the highway and any route which might take them home, down a winding road where orange groves were interspersed with immaculate front lawns of modest multimillion-dollar homes. After a mile or two they came to a sign that read *DEAD END.*

"Keep going," she had ordered.

"I thought we were going home," he had grumbled, rubbing the back of his neck.

"Have a little sense of adventure. Enjoy the drive."

Grumbling was a bad habit of his. She always wanted him to be open to the moment. He knew she was right about that, so he tried again.

"It is beautiful," he had admitted. Here and there overarching oaks shaded the narrowing pavement, their massive trunks blocking the view past the next twist in the road. He couldn't escape the sensation of *entering into* – something, some mystery; hidden, charmed, expectant. Another slow mile passed, another sign: *END OF ROAD*. He had stopped, though the asphalt continued.

"Keep going," Cass had urged again. With a shrug he had stepped on the gas. Then the oaks closed overhead and they were in a tunnel woven of roots, greenery, and privilege. He had been anxious, and allowed Cass's planned adventure to excite him, just a little. They were trespassers, spies, those courageous fools in every fable who ignore the signs to *Turn Back Now!* He wondered whose father's castle loomed on the other side. Then the trees parted, the sky opened up again, the light engulfed them, and they began their ascent of Meditation Mount. At times the hairpin turns switched them completely around to face the valley, and it seemed they would drive off into nothingness, but with resolute compassion the way led inevitably to the summit. A few steps from their car they had found the International Garden of Peace.

Now, after briefly taking in the view, Cass was ready to go again. He pushed himself off the rock, out of long ago Tuscany, and followed her up the gently curving path. As they pulled out of the parking lot and started down the winding drive, he had the definite sense that she was not done yet, there was something else on her secret agenda for the day, otherwise she would have stayed there with him in the Andalusian hills for a few more years. Back on the highway, they drove for about ten minutes before she began to look hard at every building they passed by. He slowed a bit, anticipating a quick stop. Just off the shoulder ahead he spotted a rustic sign with faded blue letters: ART. He gently applied the brakes.

"Oh, let's stop here," she finally blurted, trying to make it seem as though she had just this moment had the idea. He pulled into a gravel lot, past a sandwich board that promised *Spirit Paintings*. The place was an old ranch house, probably built in the 20's or 30's; white stucco, broad overhang, mullioned windows. Brendon parked a few feet away from what must have been, at one time, the living room or front parlor. Weathered wood hanging from the fascia named the place *ORANGE GROVE GALLERY*. It was unclear whether it was used as a residence as well.

"What the hell, Cass," Brendon muttered to himself as he got out of the car. The entrance had been altered; a concrete ramp had been installed, along with a glass shop door. Credit card decals were stuck in its bottom corner, and a hand written poster offered *Intuitive Sessions*. Dressed in spattered work clothes, a grizzled, paunchy man wobbled on a ladder nearby, squinting into the eaves, apparently repairing an exterior light fixture. Fingers of wire twisted about his head. He looked down and grunted a greeting as they walked past.

"Beautiful day," Cassidy exclaimed, as if the guy couldn't see that for himself, as if that made any difference to his task. She pushed open the door, causing a strand of Tibetan yak bells to ding dully.

Inside, the place made a handsome gallery, Brendon thought, with its saltillo tile floors, open beamed ceilings and skylights. Colorful paintings glowed and vibrated against the old white walls. Numerous arched doorways and niches drew one's eyes ever upward. A simple desk, two teal barrel chairs, and a print bin completed the furnishings. The art had a religious feel about it. It seemed to him this was not just due to the subject matter, although there were several paintings of angels.

"Kind of Renaissance-y," he said quietly.

"Aren't they incredible?" Cass sighed. "Look, this is the view from the Mount."

"Oh, yeah," he agreed, recognizing it as well. The way it had been painted, it looked even more like Tuscany. He gazed long at it, wishing it could somehow return him there, to 1475, to a simpler, happier, or truer life. It did not, which was just as well because he was having second thoughts over hygiene issues. Cass had wandered across the room and was peering through a doorway. He followed. In what might have been a dining room sixty years prior, a woman in a wheelchair was positioned in front of an easel. Although the two of them were standing there peering in at her, she remained lost in the painting, her brush in midair, her head tilted slightly, considering the next stroke. She was older, arthritis, or some degenerative disease had twisted the hand that gripped the brush. Her other hand was limp in her lap. She was a tiny thing, looking crumpled in her seat. The painting she studied so intently had only been started; a bright blue triangle blocked in over a swirl of warm tones.

"Hello," said Brendon. She quickly turned her head; the look of surprise melted into a broad smile.

"Oh, I've been expecting you," she said, dropping her brush in a bottle of turpentine, nearly bouncing out of her seat with excitement, like a little girl greeting a favorite uncle. Then, looking directly at Brendon, she stated, "You're here for a reading."

"No, I'm the one who wanted the reading," Cassidy corrected, stepping forward.

"Of course," the woman replied, but still beamed her smile at Brendon. Why was there laughter behind those eyes, he wondered. And where did she, of all people, find joy? With that gnarled hand, the one that still gripped, she wheeled herself slowly forward, turning awkwardly toward a doorway opposite the easel.

"We'll go in this room," she explained, pulling on the jamb to leverage her wheels over the threshold. Cassidy followed her into the small space, where there was a coffee table and a couple of armchairs. Brendon returned to the gallery area.

"Oh, Cass," he sighed under his breath. He paced the space, taking in the images, realizing now they had all been done by the same hand. Did it hurt, he wondered, holding the brush with knotted knuckles? Was she pushing the paint through the pain? One certainly wouldn't know it by viewing the art; it was nothing if not exuberant. He was about to sit and wait, but found himself drawn to one painting in particular, a small thing tucked away in a niche on the far wall, framed, as it were, by the arch of light descending from a bulb hidden in the roof of the recess.

The image was a woman's face, looking out and down at the viewer, but set at an angle, diagonally across the top right corner. The stylized, bejeweled headdress she wore was too tall to fit on the canvas, and gave her an exalted, Asian air. Her supple hands and bangled bent wrists were pointedly posed on the same side of her face, as if she had four or eight arms but the others were out of the picture. He might have assumed she had been taken from a statuette of some goddess, were it not for the incredibly realistic expression on her face. The rest of the canvas was taken up with clouds, which did not look real at all, as if the artist had given all her time to the face and none to the background; each cloud was virtually the same size, same shape, same color – primitive in comparison with the exquisitely captured woman in the corner. Her eyes were so real he could hardly meet them; her mouth was gently turned in... resignation? No – understanding.

7

Yes, wisdom was portrayed there, and infinite kindness it seemed to him. Her look was attentive yet relaxed, in contemplation, as if seeing eternity, as if she were feeling the same thing he had experienced sitting on UNANIMITY.

"Miraculous," he whispered to himself, or to her, and wondered why, and why the corner? Is she floating away, this wisdom goddess in the sky? Is she falling? Was she coming into, or out of the space? He began to fall, to drift into those eyes that gazed at him as if they knew him, yet received him with his many faults. That was the miracle, not that she came warm and alive out of the paint, but that she embraced him with informed acceptance. Now that sensation returned in earnest, the queer impression of being in another time, somewhere else, some*one* else. *In addition to.* What language has a word for this sense, this capacity to be more than one, he asked her, knowing if anyone spoke such a language, she did. He began to feel that not only did she know and accept him, but that he knew her as well, somewhere, sometime.

"She's sweet, isn't she?"

"Yes," Brendon returned coolly, managing not to jump at the intrusion of the voice into his reverie. It was the bearded workman they had seen outside on the ladder. He was standing at Brendon's shoulder, smelling of sweat and sunshine, smiling. "Yes," Brendon repeated, "she's remarkable. Could you tell me who posed for it?"

The man laughed, raised a burly arm, and pointed a soiled finger at the goddess. "She did," he said.

"Brendon," Cassidy's voice called quietly. He turned and saw her coming across the tile toward him. She looked as if she'd been crying. "Come on, she wants to talk to you," she explained.

"What?" That ringing in his ears had drowned out the end of her sentence. Tinnitus, the doctor called it. It had been bothering him off and on for two or three years, that and a pulsing hum. Sometimes in the quiet of the early morning it kept him awake, going on for hours. More often, it rose very loudly and faded as quick as it came. There was nothing they could do about it.

"Come on," Cass urged, motioning him to follow. The ringing stopped. "She says there's someone here for you."

"What do you mean there's someone here," he mumbled, following her into the dim room. The thick incense made him cough. The flame of a purple candle on the coffee table lit the artist from below. Her deep-set eyes were closed. Cass pushed him into a chair.

"There is someone here for you, Brendon." Her voice was quiet, quavering. Brendon raised his brow and glanced about the room in mock search. Cass thumped his shoulder.

"Very high energy. Very clear. Very beautiful. Female." Brendon wiggled his eyebrows suggestively. Again Cass struck.

"Oh?" he managed to utter with sincere curiosity.

"She wants me to say... it is time for you to *wake up*," the seer declared, snapping the last two words, as if her eyes were not really closed and she had seen his irreverent behavior. "She wants you to know that you are needed..." here she paused as if listening, "...for the forward progression of events. Time for you to be present and take an active role."

"Well thank you. I appreci..."

"You must raise your vibration." Now the artist's crooked fingers reached out and grasped Brendon's wrist in a surprisingly tight grip, holding him there in the chair. Her eyes opened and hesitated a moment to be sure she had his gaze. "Open your heart," she said. It sounded part plea, part advice, and part command. He wanted very much to leave. It seemed the quickest way was to acquiesce.

9

"Okay," he said, as though an agreement had been reached. She released his arm. He mustered a smile and stood.

"Thank you *so* much," Cassidy said tearfully. The woman nodded and sank back in her chair, as if she had been exerting herself. They stepped back through the bright studio; Brendon couldn't wait to get out of the place.

"Oh, wait," she called after them, painstakingly wheeling herself out into the gallery. "She wanted me to give you this." She pulled a small print from the bin and held it out. Cassidy went to take it, but was waved off. "No, for you," she said to Brendon.

He wanted to ignore it, wanted to just get in the car and drive, but how does one refuse such earnestness? He went back to her and took it. It was a landscape full of red and tan striated rock formations, scrubby twisted evergreens, blazing blue sky.

The grubby workman crossed the room, squeezed the artist familiarly on the shoulder, and kissed her on the top of the head. "I think he would rather have the *dakini,* hon," he chuckled.

"No," she answered, her face perfectly serious. "He is to have this one. That was definite."

Brendon reached for his credit card.

"It's a gift, Brendon," she said, that broad smile now returning to her face, "from Spirit." He looked doubtful. Cass pulled his hand down, returning the wallet to his pocket.

"Thank you," he managed, and looking again at it asked, "Is this Utah?"

"I'm afraid I have no idea. It was a vision. I painted it several years ago."

"In one day," the workman said, "I practically had to pry the brush from her hand. She was in a daze that day, didn't realize she'd been at if for six hours."

10

"It was a very strongly guided painting, I felt like they were pushing my hand. I never knew why. Until today."

This information seemed to make Cass light up. "Wow, that's incredible," she said, "This is such a blessing!"

"Yes, thank you for this," Brendon repeated as he turned toward the door again, "Bye now."

Safely back on the highway with the foisted print tossed in the backseat, Brendon tried to laugh it off.

"What the hell was that?" he chuckled, but try as he might, he could not quite keep the anger out of his voice. He didn't enjoy being put in awkward positions, and this counted as one of the most awkward of his life.

"It was a gift from Spirit," reiterated Cass. She was not amused. "And if you had any sense, you would see it that way."

"Felt more like an ambush to me," he protested. The knot in his neck was going to drive him insane. "Do you have any Advil?"

"No. You take too much of that stuff anyway. You might try opening your mind for once. I don't hold out much hope for your heart."

"Thanks for the vote of confidence," he laughed.

"Do you have any idea how lucky you are? Your spirit guide actually showed up for you, with a specific message, and you're pissed off? What the hell is wrong with you?"

"Oh come off it, they say that shit to everybody."

"No, they do not say 'very high energy' to everybody. They do not say 'needed for the progression of events' to everybody. They don't even say 'needed', you moron."

Brendon was silent. He had forgotten that Cass took this stuff seriously.

"In case you didn't notice, Spirit did not give *me* a free print, and I'm the one who paid for the reading."

"Sorry."

"You owe me 70 bucks," she barked, but the fake frown was a sign that her good humor was returning.

"Well you can have the print, it makes no difference to me."

"No, I don't want the print, you idiot, it's for you, and it will damn well make a difference to you if you let it. Don't you get it? They're trying to help you. It's a message of some kind. You're supposed to learn something from it. You have to keep it and look at it until you get it."

"Ohhh, I see. We're all here to learn and all that. I keep forgetting."

"Jesus. You're hopeless. You ought to be grateful."

"I guess that's just another one of those things I haven't quite learned yet," he concluded, and turned on the radio. They drove without speaking for a bit, while he searched for a station worth listening to. Eventually he turned it off again. Curiosity had gotten the better of him.

"So what did she say to you?"

"What difference does it make, she says the same thing to everyone."

Brendon did not respond, he deserved it, and would let it pass. After another silent mile, Cassidy spoke again.

"You have to move out."

"Hh... what?" he chuckled, thinking this was supposed to be amusing. But a second glance made it clear she was again in serious mode. She had that pre-pout expression on her face, which she reverted to whenever it was imperative for her to get her way. The mothering disappeared and the prepubescent child reemerged. She didn't respond, didn't even turn to look at him.

"The psychic said I have to move out," he repeated, wanting clarification.

"No. No, she said I'm going to meet someone in the next month."

"So... I have to move out."

"You know, *meet* someone. I can't have you in the apartment if I'm... it'll never happen if you're there."

"Well shit, sis, you didn't have to invent something this elaborate to kick me out, you want me to move out, I'll move out! Jesus, just say so."

"I want you to move out."

"Fine," he laughed.

"But for your information, I did not invent anything. She's known to be very accurate. You should listen to her. And you should listen to me. I know you can't stand to take advice from your little sister, but..."

"That's not true. That's not true at all. I've always respected your opinion."

"Bullshit."

"Well, sometimes. When you're lucid."

"Up yours. You just can't stand the idea that I might know more than you, about anything."

"You could be right about that, but it makes me uncomfortable to think about it, so... we'll never know for sure," he chuckled.

"Ugh. Why can't you ever have a serious conversation? You can pretend all you want, but underneath, subconsciously, you know that was a meaningful experience. You know what she said is true.

"Hmm. It was certainly an experience, I'll give you that. So who's this someone you're going to meet, is he tall, dark, and handsome?"

"She didn't say what he looked like."

"But she said it was a he."

13

"No... but what else could she have meant? Look you have to move out, regardless. You heard her; it's time for you to take an active role. I know you've been going through this mid-life thing or whatever, but you're supposed to wake up to the *rest* of your life now. And I need to get my space back."

"You need to get laid, that's what you need."

"That, too," she agreed, smiling.

CHAPTER TWO

THE swirling red rock formations and twisted evergreens were resting on the nightstand, leaning against the wall, as they had been since that day in Ojai. Every time he looked at the print, Brendon saw a bed of clouds instead of rocks, bangles instead of trees, a tiara and headdress reaching off the canvas. The memory of that face haunted him; the eternal look in those eyes, the sheer kindness of her expression, the promise of utter acceptance. How had that odd little artist contrived to capture something that could move him so much, yet which he had never encountered before? A portrait of someone lost in love, or maybe found in love, but not the love of this world.

He would reprimand himself for making too much of nothing, for fantasizing, for procrastinating, then go back to his laptop where he could properly pretend to be searching for a job. Naturally there was nothing. Then he would look for an apartment, a room he might somehow afford. There was little worth going to look at, nowhere he could see himself living. And so a week passed.

Of course, Cass was right, it was time for him to move out, move on somehow. They didn't need a psychic to tell them that. It had been two years since he had lost his job, and nearly eighteen months since he had moved in with his little sister. It wasn't fair to her, and it wasn't good for him. But he was stuck, in that midlife thing, as she put it.

There had been an incident, just after his breakup with Sharon two years earlier; he had gone to the emergency room for chest pains and been told it was anxiety. Their breakup had been amicable, and he had considered it his idea, yet it proved difficult to recover from. He harbored no regrets and seldom thought about her, so it wasn't as though Sharon was 'the one', or that there was only one. His 'midlife thing' was due to a rudimentary understanding of statistics. In all likelihood, given his age and prospects, he could not do better, and might well spend the rest of his days alone. Even though he had been aware of this, he had tired of putting in the effort to make it work. That was essentially how he felt about every aspect of his life; he knew he could only expect to get out what he put into something, but in the immortal words of Bartleby the Scrivener, he 'preferred not to'. He was grateful for his time with Sharon, and had nothing really to complain of in her or her treatment of him. It was more himself he was disappointed in, disillusioned with, bored with. He was unable to brush aside the knowledge that the best part of his journey was past, that he was on the return trip, the way *down* the hill, in which the field of view – the options – could only narrow. He couldn't get motivated, didn't care to get up in the morning. It wasn't as though he was really pessimistic, just uninterested, and unconcerned about that lack of interest. Cass said he had too much money, that was his problem, and not enough. Not enough to feel like he could waste it on some extravagant gesture like traveling the world, but enough to get by, if the rent was low. He split everything with Cass, and that had really helped her out, but the place was too small for her to have her own life, and because of his input, she had now saved enough to be comfortable kicking him out. If he had had less in the bank, he might have taken some hideous job waiting tables or parking cars, but since he had managed to get by this long hardly lifting a finger, it seemed a shame to sign up for something demoralizing just to get his own place. Regardless, he had to now, at least, he had to get out of his sister's little apartment, so he went about his panicked scouring of craigslist.

At least twice a day he felt sure Cass had hired that crazy artist to say all that stuff. She could have set it up right then, while he was in the gallery looking at the art, at the bejeweled goddess. A part of him had fallen for the spiel immediately, embarrassingly, but he refused to admit it to Cass, refused to give her the satisfaction. Who wouldn't be flattered by 'very high energy', it was like saying some bigwig had seen your work and wanted you, 'needed' you for a job, like Steve Jobs himself was requesting Mr. Pearce to design a website – as if he remembered how. If he were honest with himself, he had to acknowledge that part of the reason he had stopped trying to get a job was that he had let his skills go. He wasn't up on the latest code, he didn't own the latest gadgets, and the worst of it was, he didn't care. It no longer intrigued him. He still spent time at the computer, certainly, but only on amusements, and simple, outdated ones at that. He did jigsaws, crosswords, Sudoku. He watched dog clips on YouTube; he played Tetris because it was an old friend. If he ran across a site with some app or flash which was new and different, it failed to peak his curiosity as it once had. It turned out he could sleep just fine without learning the secret of what the webmaster had done. It was hard for him to believe he had devoted so much of his life to making pixels wink and blink their way across a screen. What an incredible waste of time it had all been.

So in a way, he dreaded going back to work. He didn't feel up to it. Not in LA, anyway. Maybe that realization is what made things click, or maybe it was staring at the print he had been given and finally realizing it represented a *place*. Why not live somewhere else entirely? What about Monument Valley, if that's where the red rocks were supposed to be, were there any towns there? What about Sedona? Brendon googled it, decided it looked like the print, and pulled up sedona craigslist > jobs > art / media / design.

> Looking for a graphics designer with print, label, web design and marketing experience. SEO work and web master capabilities. Numerous web sites in place that need weekly updates and marketing, co-ordination etc. hourly pay work at home or from your own office. $18-25 per hour depending on capabilities. Send resume and references to email address.

Yes, he decided, he would do that, send the resume, why not. A change of scene would do him good. He clicked back and scanned 'aprts / housing'. Less expensive than what he had found locally, but still more than he was paying Cass. And did he really want to live alone? Under 'rooms / shared' there were many items below $400, some below $300. That was definitely doable. With that small a commitment, he wouldn't have to obsess about work, he could freelance. There was one in particular which struck a chord.

> A dream environment to live and work, set in the beautiful red rocks near Soldier's Pass in Sedona. Join a lifestyle community for Artists, Writers and Healers and as part of this private compound perched just above Sedona on 3 acres, you will have your own private room and full bathroom. Rooms with views available. Shared space includes a beautiful great room, dining room, fully equipped kitchen, swimming pool, Jacuzzi and stunning views from 14-foot floor to ceiling windows.

The pictures of the place were incredible. Would they take him, was a graphic artist an artist? He had written ad copy, did that count? He sure as hell was not a healer. He could feel himself diving into that pool. It sounded and looked too good to be true, then he remembered a phrase from the book he had picked up in

Ojai: *Miracles are not dispensed, or found, or created, they are allowed.*

"It sounds like a great idea," Cass agreed, without deliberation, when he told her about his plan.

"You just can't wait for me to get out of your hair."

"No. Well yes, but that has nothing to do with where you go. I think Sedona is just the place. It will be very healing for you. Just moving to a new place will help you let go of this unhealthy pattern you're stuck in."

"What unhealthy pattern?"

"The one where you pretend to be thick," she needled, "the one where you pretend you don't care about anything, the one where you pretend you're above it all, when what you really are is afraid."

"And what is it I'm afraid of, O Wise One?" he scoffed. She sighed and shook her head, not having a ready answer. The answer came to him, much to his surprise; he was afraid of joy. Why, he wondered, and that came to him too; because it doesn't last. But he didn't say it.

"You just don't have to think of things the way you do," she insisted, "It *is* possible to change your thought patterns."

"I know. I'll try."

"Do or do not," Cass croaked in her Yoda voice, "There is no try."

"Yes, swami. I will go to the holy land of Sedona and become a new old man."

"And get a job. Then when I come visit you can take me to all the best places to eat."

"Ah-ha! The *real* Cass makes her appearance."

"Don't be rude. I am going to miss you. It's been great having you here."

19

"For a while," he chuckled.

"For a while," she echoed, and hugged him.

"Well let's see if I get a response before we get all maudlin about it."

"What do you mean? I thought it was settled."

"Well, they might not take me, at this 'artist' house. Not sure I'd want to go otherwise."

"Of course they'll take you, why wouldn't they take you?"

"It's just... I'm not really... they wanted to see some of my work first. Not sure what to send them. I don't think..."

"You think too much. Just do it."

"For a short, puny woman, you're awfully bossy."

"For a mature, a *very* mature-looking man, you're awfully insecure."

"So helpful. I feel all better now."

Brendon went back to his room and prepared another email. He attached a few things he had actually done, a logo or two, some 3D models, some industrial illustrations. But he knew that was not what they wanted. Whoever owned the house wanted to create a modern *salon* or something. They were looking for poets, seers, *artistes.* They wanted a new Bohemia – 1920's Paris in 2010's Sedona. So he searched the more obscure corners of the web and borrowed some images of abstract paintings, shifted the hues, cropped them, and sent those instead, along with a modified artist's statement he had appropriated. It worked. Three days later he was on the road.

The print he had received in Ojai, still wrapped in wrinkly plastic, rested in the passenger seat, where he could see it. He saw the landscape now; the image of the goddess had all but faded from his memory, yet her presence lingered. Those few minutes spent viewing a woman created in paint had primed him for a true encounter. For the first time in years, he felt excited, truly interested in what the future might bring. He was high on that most dangerous of drugs – hope, and in relenting, in relaxing his habitual guard against possibilities, he allowed a cowering desire to creep from its hiding place in the back of his chest. He was forced to acknowledge this secret wish: to find someone, a new love for the new town, someone who might share what remained of his miserable life. He was old enough to know it was damned unlikely, but it was a dream he had been unable to stamp out. He took his time, driving under the limit, stopping frequently, as if to keep the obvious truth (that there was no one new waiting for him) at bay as long as possible.

His mother had wanted him to stop in Phoenix to visit Aunt Karen who had lupus or possibly lymphoma – something with an 'L' – but he'd only met her twice, and that was at least fifteen years ago. He couldn't imagine anything more awkward for either of them, so he took the 60 from Quartzite and wound his way up through piney Prescott, keeping his mind focused on the new landscape; the sprawling desert and expansive sky. When at last he turned onto Rt. 179, and the color of the scenery began to match the reds in the print beside him, he felt a shiver run down his spine.

As he rounded the corner coming into the Village of Oak Creek, with Castle Rock looming on one side of the road, majestic Courthouse Butte on the other and Bell Rock straight ahead, he was awestruck. How was it he could have lived within driving distance of this place most of his life, and never been there before? Continuing on into Sedona proper, he realized he hadn't been this excited in years, possibly decades. Being away from LA felt great. He had loved California from the minute he had arrived. It had allowed him to reinvent himself. Now, for the first

21

time in twenty years, he felt that again, a chance to stop being Brendon.

A wave of gratitude welled up in his chest, gratitude for the print, the artist who painted it, and even for the supposed spirit who "told" her to give him that print. He would not have been there without it, might never have seen the place. A second, deeper wave followed the first as he wound his way through the maze of mesas, spires and buttes, many emotions he found difficult to comprehend shifting from his chest to his throat to his eyes. He actually shed a few tears. He felt a need to thank the very rocks themselves for existing, but how nutty was that? What the hell's wrong with me, he wondered.

"Right turn ahead," Victoria, the GPS girl said. The voice was always a surprise, but Brendon found it soothing nonetheless. He saw the sign for Soldier's Pass Road and pulled into the right lane.

"Turn right," she said. Obediently, he turned and drove toward towering cliffs. Victoria guided him higher and higher over the valley as the road wound its way up the hilly terrain, then to the end of a little drive which rose sharply from the main road, parting a community of cypress, juniper and pinyon pine. Spread out over the hillside was a sprawling adobe style house, surrounding its demesne with rounded arms of sorrel-colored stucco wall. Rough wood and wrought iron adorned its gates, light fixtures, windows and doors. The parking area was laid in large terracotta pavers that blended with the enormous pots standing on either side of the entry, from which tendrils of aged succulents depended to the ground. Three vehicles were already stabled there: a cherry red Prius, a blindingly white Lexus, and a pre-millennium pickup caked with reddish mud. The Prius had Arizona plates, the Lexus, California, and the pickup, Ohio.

Brendon parked his sapphire Hyundai beside them and went to the door.

"Hello, Crystal?" he asked the woman who answered. She was pretty, though not young; her face, tanned nearly to the shade of the red earth around them, glowed with vitality. She was dressed in loose jeans and a shirt that looked like it had been made of flax or hemp. It hung on her ample chest like a burlap bag full of cantaloupes. Her long brown hair was pulled back in a single braid. Her feet were bare against the tile floor.

"No, I'm Harmony. Are you Mitch?"

"No, Brendon. I'm supposed to meet Crystal here at five. I guess I'm a little early."

"Oh. Are you moving in?"

"Yes, I just drove through from LA."

"Well come on in," she said, holding the door open and gesturing for him to enter. "Crystal's around here somewhere I think. I'm expecting a client; I thought you were him." He took in her scent as he passed her in the threshold. It was earthy and exotic.

"Should I come back later?" he asked, noticing her eyes were the color of the sky.

"No, no. Make yourself at home. Have a look around. I'm not sure which room she had you down for or I'd say bring in your stuff."

"Wow," he said, looking through to the living room, its huge wall of glass, and the view beyond.

"Isn't it incredible?" Harmony remarked, leading the way into the round space. There was a sunken floor with curved sectional sofas forming an almost complete ring. They crossed to stand in front of the windows. Through the glass you could see all of Sedona laid out below, like little mole tracks in a bed of moss. Across the valley, the enormous hills and buttes looked

23

like lichen covered boulders or the unshaven faces of long lost mountain men.

"I mean, how lucky are we to live here?" she said, touching a slim hand to his shoulder, her face just beaming with joy.

"Very. I agree," he mumbled, moving back to the plush beige sofas. One section had been left free to enter the circle. "Mind if I sit? I'm feeling a little woozy." A round coffee table was positioned in the center, with a giant cream-colored candle on it, beside an impressive amethyst geode.

"Oh, it's the energy," Harmony said. Brendon looked at her quizzically, rubbing the back of his neck.

"It takes a while to get used to. I'll get you some water." She went through a doorway. He looked around the broad, sparsely furnished space. A huge fireplace dominated the wall opposite the windows. Around the perimeter there were built in planters, holes in the tile floor from which various palms, philodendrons, ferns and umbrella trees stretched toward the skylights and leaned toward the windows. Several of these appeared to be long established residents, and were considerably taller than Brendon's six feet. Buddha was to be seen in several attitudes and mediums, placed carefully underneath their branches as if beneath the Bodhi Tree. Guanyin looked on him with compassion from her niche in the wall, St. Francis of Assisi gurgled away in a corner, trickling holy water on stone birds and bunnies, while potted bromeliads patiently awaited stray drops and splashes. Other, more exotic deities which he did not recognize or could not remember the names of were also observing him from their stations, such as that Indian elephant god, who returned his gaze from high above the mantle. While the atmosphere was peaceful and pleasing, it seemed to contribute to his dizzy feeling.

Harmony returned with a glass of water. He took it and sipped.

"You should drink as much water as you can for the first few days. It's very dry here." The doorbell rang and she went to it. This time her expected client, the aforementioned Mitch, had indeed arrived. They disappeared down a hallway. Perhaps in response to the bell, another woman entered the great room from a different wing of the rambling house. Her neck was ensconced in white silk, and she walked with her chin held high. As she passed the circle of seating, she saw Brendon out of the corner of her eye, took a step or two more, glanced at the front door, and came back to him.

"Hello, I don't believe we've met."

"Brendon Pearce," he said, rising, "You must be Crystal."

"Yes, so happy to meet you." She was an older woman, rather plump, a big head of graying blonde hair that had been volumized and extended and blown up to thrice the size of her skull. She had huge gold earrings, a monstrous diamond on her ring finger and rubies on both pinkies. Her white pantsuit had more layers than an onion, and was surmounted by three strands of pearls. Her makeup looked as if it had been applied with a trowel. She was the direct opposite of Harmony in style and manner. It occurred to him that Crystal was just the sort of woman the word *flounce* was invented for.

"So you made it across the desert alright. Fabulous."

"Yeah, it was faster than I expected actually."

"You must be exhausted."

"I am feeling a little light-headed," he admitted.

"It's the vortexes. The entire valley is an energy well, you know. And this house amplifies it magnificently. You will acclimate in a few days." Brendon gave her the same blank look he had given Harmony. Yes, he had heard of the Sedona vortexes, but he hadn't expected to be sharing living quarters with people who actually believed in their 'energy'.

25

"I'll drink plenty of water," he assured his hostess.

"Do. And orange juice is good. NO alcohol," she commanded, "At least not for the first week. And I do prefer not on the premises, if you don't mind." Brendon looked incredulous, but nodded agreement.

"Don't worry, I'm not much of a party animal," he assured her. She smiled.

"Tell you what, let me find the paperwork, and take your payment, then you can get settled in. You should probably just get right to bed. You'll feel better in the morning. Maybe there's something in the kitchen for you."

"Oh, I can go get a burger or something, don't worry about me."

Crystal frowned at him. "You really shouldn't dear. I do hope you take advantage of this opportunity." Then she floated out of the room, wings of silk fluttering behind her.

CHAPTER THREE

BRENDON'S room was nicer than he had expected. There was a skylight, a huge closet, quality furnishings, and an attached bath with its own, smaller skylight. Beside the bathroom door hung an odd photo of half a dozen people outside at night, surrounded by fuzzy white circles or bubbles. It looked like a mistake – a flawed negative or a bunch of somethings on the lens – except that the people were holding their arms out to the sky, as if welcoming the luminous floating balls. There was a caption written on the mat: *Orbs, Sedona, 2002.* On the wall behind the bed was a large picture of rocks arranged in a circular pattern on the red desert floor – some kind of medicine wheel. A small Buddha rested on the nightstand, beside a pointy rock specimen about a foot in length labeled *Tibetan Black Quartz.* Near the window from a planter set in the floor, several trunks twined their way up to a bushy green head. On the other side of the window was a seven-drawer chest. He set the print from Ojai on top of this, beside a card already propped there, which read *Goodwill is the touchstone that will change the world.* As he did so, he noticed that there was a title written in faint pencil on the back of his print: *View from the Gate.* How very odd, he thought. There was not a single building depicted in the scene. Maybe the backing board had been left over from a different print.

Opening the blinds made the place even brighter. The view (sparkling pool, soft garden wall, scattered evergreens, and the reddish bulk of some butte beyond) was far more restricted than that from the great room, but the landscape was so new, and such an improvement over the concrete block he had lived with through his window in Cassidy's apartment, that he just stared, drinking it in. After a minute or two, he turned back to his open suitcase, and was startled to see someone leaning in the doorway looking at him.

"Hey, how's it goin'?" an easy baritone asked.

"Oh, okay," Brendon quickly replied, trying not to give away how surprised he was and wondering if he had really left the door open. "Just starting to unpack," he added, and crossed the room with his hand extended. "Brendon Pearce."

"Dennis. LeRose. Good to meet you," the guy said, shaking Brendon's hand while his head bobbed an acknowledgment. It was not a deferential nod, but the sort that began with a preliminary uptick, and said at best 'what's up', and at worst 'what are you going to do about it?' They were about the same age, he looked to be late 30's to mid 40's, average height, seemed fit. His copious curly hair was beginning to gray, while that deep Sedona tan brought out the crows feet and laugh lines of his clean-shaven face. There was an ever-present smile around his eyes, as if he and only he were privy to a rich inside joke, which he might have shared if only the setup required less effort. A little more control was exercised over his mouth, but it too tended to smirks and smears of humor. Brendon liked him right away.

"How long are you in for?" Dennis asked. Brendon chuckled, but wondered what he was implying underneath the jest.

"Well I just signed a six month lease. After that we'll see."

Dennis whistled. "Six months, wow, what did you do to deserve that, break someone's heart?"

"No. Got kicked out of my sister's place. She's expecting a new lover."

"Oh yeah? Hasn't met him yet though, huh? That's funny."

"So you're in the room next door?" Brendon asked.

"Yeah. I've been here since January. It's...uh... it's been an interesting experience, let's put it that way," he laughed. A muffled sound like a farting elephant came down the hall at them. Brendon took a step to look out the door. The noise continued, a long, drawn out rumbling raspberry, which seemed to have no intention of ceasing.

Dennis gave him another one of those amused looks. "Didgeridoo," he explained. The other nodded and went back to his suitcase.

"Hope you don't find it distracting. It's pretty much all day every day."

"Every..."

"No, not really. Just whenever you're really trying to concentrate. It's this girl Harmony. She does sound healing therapy. Pretty powerful stuff, or so I'm told."

"Oh, I met Harmony earlier."

"Yeah?" Dennis said with a leer in his voice, if such a thing were possible. "What did you think? Nice piece there, eh?"

Brendon smiled broadly. "She *is* attractive," he readily agreed.

"Still working on her."

Brendon chose to let the subject slide. "And what was your crime?" he asked.

"Mm?" Dennis suddenly looked guilty.

"That got you sentenced to this particular prison?"

"Right. Yeah, I'd rather not say, what with Homeland Security listening in," he laughed.

"Do they have a particular interest in this house?" Brendon asked with a smile. Dennis nodded and grinned while he thought of a suitable rejoinder.

"Let's just say I wouldn't be surprised. And I figure I'm on enough lists already."

"Why's that?"

The humor faded from Dennis's face. He looked both ways down the hall, and through the window as if checking who might be within earshot. He opened his mouth, closed it again. The smile returned and he mumbled, "Maybe when we get to know each other better."

Brendon shrugged. "You've been here since January, you say. Then you can fill me in on the arrangements, you know, kitchen etiquette, laundry, parking, that sort of thing? Crystal had something to do, I guess."

"Don't tell me, she disappeared as soon as she got your check, right?" Dennis surmised.

"Yeah, pretty much."

"That's Crystal all right. Sure, I can fill you in on the way things work around here," he conceded with a chuckle. Brendon waited expectantly for further information, maybe some unflattering comment on their hostess or one of the other residents, but as none was forthcoming, he prompted him.

"Oh? What do you mean?"

"Well," he drew out, nodding and smirking. "As I say, it's been an interesting experience. Maybe I'll elaborate some day."

"When we get to know each other better?" Brendon guessed, taking another pair of jeans out of his suitcase.

"Yeah. But sure, I can show you the ropes. You can park wherever you want, as far as that goes, just don't dent Crystal's Lexus. Did she get you a key yet?"

"Yeah, I'm all set. I think. No locks on the individual rooms, then?"

"No, of course not," he chuckled. "No one here has anything to hide, Pearce, we're all enlightened beings." And he blinked. On one side of his face. Did he just *wink* at me, Brendon wondered, what the hell? Then he *does* have something to hide?

"So, what's your particular... talent, or *modus operandi?* Are you another healer? Blind acupuncturist maybe?"

"No," he laughed with a shake of his head.

"No? So you're not going to try and sell me on inverse spectrum magnotherapy or ionized coffee enemas? No? No desire to cleanse my aural cavity?"

"Not even a little."

"So what then, artist? Seer? Or are you a scribbler like me?"

"Um... sometimes." Brendon cleared his throat. "Right now I'm a little more focused on painting."

"I can't wait to see your work."

"Well, yeah, me neither, to tell you the truth," Brendon laughed, "I'll be trying out some new techniques while I'm here. So what do you write?"

"This and that. Working on my magnum opus even as we speak," he said with a sly grin.

"Wow. When do you expect to finish it?"

"One can't put timetables on these things. But I promise, you'll be the first to know when I'm done."

"Looking forward to it." The didgeridoo had stopped and now a new, softer, clearer sound was ringing through the house.

"Stage two of the healing," Dennis commented. "She has these crystal singing bowls. Supposed to balance your chakras or something."

"It's a beautiful sound."

"Yeah, I wouldn't mind having her work on me," he said, winking again, "but I don't have the extra 200 bucks right now."

"Ouch."

"Have you met Rune?"

"*Rune?* Seriously? Are we the only ones here who haven't changed our names?" Brendon chuckled.

"What makes you think I haven't changed my name?" he returned, "Used to be Rainbow."

"I wonder if it's too late to get my check back," he sighed. Dennis laughed.

"Well, you know what they say about Sedona."

"What?"

"You have to be the real you – true to yourself, or it'll spit you out like a bad penny. Six months is just about long enough to find out if you like it here, and if it likes you."

"So I should change my name, and let my true self out?"

"Well, if you want to stick around here I guess."

"Right. I'm not sure about that yet. So what about Rune, what kind of therapy does she do?"

"Not she, he. Or maybe you're right, maybe 'she' *is* more appropriate," Dennis joked. "No, he's a good guy. He does whatever he can get someone to pay for, like most people around here. God knows what goes on in that room when he's with a client, could be anything. He gave me a business card once, all it says is *Channel*, and his phone number. He says he's a Reike Master. He teaches yoga on the weekends over by the cinema. Makes jewelry too, I think."

"Wow, a man of eclectic talents."

"Yeah, he's alright. Anyway, that's his room down there, across from the art studio," he said, pointing down to the end of the hall. Crystal had shown Brendon the airy studio briefly, and told him which area he could use to set up his easel and things. She didn't want anyone painting in the bedrooms. He hadn't brought any art 'things', since he didn't have any; his work had always been completely digital. He had planned to pick up some things after he arrived, now he realized it looked bad

32

not having his car jammed with art supplies and canvases. But she had taken his check and he had signed the lease, so what did it matter now.

"Dennis, I'm pretty hungry, I think I'll go get something to eat. And how's it work with the fridge? I mean if I want to get some things, how do we keep them separate?"

"Good luck with that. There's supposed to be assigned shelves for everyone, but certain people don't cooperate. I won't name any names," he added accusingly yet without losing his good humor, "but let's just say don't put any caviar in there and expect it to be around when you want it."

"Right. So I can just go in the kitchen and find something to eat?"

"No, I wouldn't do that either," he laughed. He looked both ways down the hall and lowered his voice. "I keep stuff in my room, even though Crystal would shit bricks if she found out. Just dry stuff, snacks. Fruit. Otherwise it gets eaten. She likes to have a group meal every Monday night, but I'm not usually there. Vegan stuff."

"Then everyone else in the house is vegetarian or whatever?"

"Pretty much. I mean I usually stay away from red meat, except for steak and pork chops." There was that wink again. Was the wink meant to confirm his words, or cancel them, Brendon wondered.

"Well I'll probably eat out most of the time," he decided, picking up his keys. "So where's the nearest grocery store?"

"Sure. If you go back to the highway and turn right, there's two of them, both on the right side of the road."

"Great. I guess I'll see you around, then," Brendon concluded, stepping into the hall and pulling his door closed.

"Yeah. Look, if you like to hike, I know all the trails around. I try to go every morning. You're welcome to join me, anytime."

"Sounds good."

* * *

Brendon sat in his car with a burger, fries, and chocolate shake keeping him company, wondering what the hell he was doing there, and yet feeling glad about it. The scenery alone would make the entire experience worthwhile. There he was in a parking lot, gazing up at some of the most majestic peaks and cliffs he had ever seen. They really were so unusual, so odd, jutting out of the earth that way. He knew they had been formed by erosion, not upward thrust, yet they gave the feeling of vertical movement nonetheless; great sentient beings rising up to meet the heavens, as if to say, 'erode *this,* I dare you'. It was humbling to be among them.

After finishing his meal, he went into the grocery store to stock up on crackers, cereal, nuts, Hoho's and other healthy snacks. He took his time. Something in him didn't really want to return to the house, exquisite as it was. He hadn't really counted on personality issues when he had made his decision to come to Sedona. Then again, maybe it was only Dennis who had the issues. He couldn't quite make that guy out. There were so many things he wasn't saying.

When he came out of the store, the sun was setting through a breathtaking array of stratocumulus clouds, spreading like an orange and pink quilt across the desert sky, turning the tips of the red rock spires bright orange, then rose, then copper. The skirr of cicadas swelled behind him as the clouds played, reaching its crescendo when the sky was most radiant. The drone seemed to pass over him as it died away. He stood leaning against his car, a refreshing breeze tickling his hair, watching the colors shift until only a dull blue remained.

He realized, unexpectedly, that he was *thankful,* in that place, at that moment at any rate, to be alive.

When he returned to the house, the only spot left to park was beside Crystal's spotless Lexus. He pulled in carefully and gathered his munchies. Considering how many cars were there, the place seemed awfully dark; no lights shone in any of the windows, only the sidewalk lights and an overhead by the front door. The great bulk of cliffs loomed behind him. Stars were out in force; it seemed they had appeared that night just for him, he wondered how many years it had been since he had been in a place so free of city glare. Groceries in hand, head tipped back, he stood staring up in wonder.

There was a flash. It was quite small, it was extremely brief, if he had blinked he would have missed it, but he was certain that he had witnessed something unusual. Its afterimage remained fixed on his retina as he continued to stare, waiting for it to reoccur. It had been a tiny turn of something, a star, a quasar, or pulsar; its rays had rotated as it flashed. It was just the sort of thing which he would have completely discounted, had someone else (like Cassidy) seen it and described it, yet he was left with the distinct impression of contact, as if a heavenly being had winked at him. It did not come again.

He let himself in with the key Crystal had provided. A golden glow reached him from the great room. The susurrus of his swaying bag of groceries, and his footsteps on the tile were surprisingly noisy as he went toward the light. Several people were seated around the circular sofa, silent and still. The giant candle in the center of the table had been lit, but its three wicks flickered weakly from the individual hollows they had formed in the wax. In the dimness he thought he recognized Crystal, still in her white silk, and Harmony sitting with her long braid drawn forward across her shoulder. Perhaps that was Dennis with his

35

back to him. The light was just enough to reveal the presence of other figures in the room, those watchful Buddhas and elephants and gods with multiple arms in the shadows of the palms. It was an eerie sight. He surmised they were engaged in some form of meditation, so he turned away toward his room.

"Please join us," Crystal's voice suggested, almost in a whisper. After a moment's hesitation, Brendon slid his bag to the floor, made his way around the circle and sat beside Harmony on the end. She had her legs crossed beneath her, but she was the only one of the six to manage it. Her hands were resting palms up on her knees. She gave no indication that she was in any way aware of him. He folded his hands on his lap, briefly closed his eyes, then opened them again. He scanned the others, but in the dim light he couldn't be sure they weren't looking at him looking at them. Out the window the city lights were visible below, the moon above, and the bulk of Airport Mesa made a black shadow against the deepening night sky, sprinkled with yellow porch lights.

Good God, how long are they going to sit here, he wondered. Eventually he settled on watching the flickering flame play about the amethyst geode. As he became more comfortable and sank into the cushions, his eyes drooped and closed. He shivered; it was not cold. He became aware of intense warmth on his right side. He dozed.

"As we begin to return our awareness to the body..." The sound of Crystal's voice, though soft and slow, jolted Brendon awake. He blinked at the candle flames. "Let us be thankful for this time together," she continued, "and for all that Spirit has bestowed this evening."

Brendon looked across the circle at Dennis, who was looking back at him, smiling a slightly superior smile, sitting now with his hands behind his head and his elbows in the air. He wondered how long he had been observed.

"We open our hearts in gratitude for life and this place of peace and creativity. We welcome Brandon, our new family member, and know that he too is grateful for the love in which we live and move and have our being." Dennis grinned when she said 'Brandon' instead of 'Brendon'. The latter couldn't keep an amused puff of air from sounding out his nose. Harmony had not yet stirred.

"Wiggle your toes and fingers, returning to the physical realm, feeling the floor beneath your feet once more, feeling grateful that the earth supports you. We bring back to the room the peace of the eternal."

Now everyone was shifting in their seats, save Harmony, who remained motionless beside him, her head bowed slightly, her palms still on her knees. Crystal rose and stepped toward him, reaching out her hand.

"I'm so glad you sat with us, Brandon." She grasped his hand and squeezed it, holding it as she spoke. "I'm sorry I forgot to mention it earlier, as you can see, we gather for meditation every Thursday evening, if possible."

"Actually, it's Brendon," he corrected, freeing his hand and rising from the couch.

"Oh, I'm so sorry. Please forgive me. Of course you're free to use this room for meditation at any time, but as a group every Thursday evening at seven. It's all about habit, you see – building the *antahkarana* – just like repatterning the neural pathways. The plasticity of the subtle bodies is even greater than that of the brain, you know."

"I don't really know what..." Someone turned on the lights. He squinted at his hostess, who continued as if he was interested.

"Habit forms the structure through which thought, love – everything – flows. Habit will crystallize the sacred geometry. Think of it as constructing the nadis, the spiritual pathways, of the group," Crystal concluded, looking to see if he was on board. He nodded meaninglessly.

"I'll be sure and remember next Thursday at seven."

"You must be Brandon," another woman interrupted, "I hear you'll be joining me in the studio."

"It's Brendon, actually," he repeated to this second woman. He heard Dennis laugh out loud and saw him retreating down the hall.

"I'm Carol. I'm not in the studio that often anyway, I prefer to work *en plein air*." Carol was older, whitish hair, a kind, fleshy face, slightly stooped.

"I may be doing a bit of that myself," Brendon said. Everyone was speaking at once, he felt unable to ascertain who might have addressed him and who hadn't.

"Michael, good to meet you Brandon," a man said, thrusting a burly hand toward him. He noticed Harmony finally unfolded her long legs.

"Actually, it's Brandon. I mean Brendon. Now you've got me so I don't know my own name," he laughed. Michael was black, tall, round, maybe mid 50's. He was dressed in a white button-down shirt, white jeans and a big warm smile.

"Glad to have you here," he said.

"Well, I'm glad to be here," Brendon replied, though he wasn't sure about it. Michael was undeniably sincere, and made him feel very welcome. Everyone was smiling and patting one another, all so friendly, so accepting of him, treating him like family. He felt guilty for not quite being able to reciprocate, but they were strangers, weren't they? He wanted to be comfortable with their demonstrative reception, but it made him uneasy.

Harmony rose from the couch, turned to him and embraced him. It was not a cursory arm-on-the-shoulder greeting, but a full hug; she pulled him to her giving chest and reached her chin up over his shoulder. He leaned forward and returned her grasp with equal pressure, allowing his head to rest against hers, taking in the scent of her hair, feeling the flesh of her ear on his, the turn of her back under his palms, the fullness of her pressing on him. They stood that way for a full twenty or thirty seconds, his amazement growing, his eyes beginning to well up with gratitude. As she pulled away she looked him in the eye, squeezed his arm, and said soothingly, "You're going to be all right." He nodded, thankful for her kindness, yet thinking nonetheless that it was a strange thing for her to say. Had he given the impression that he was *not* all right? Did he look ill? He had admitted to being woozy, but somehow it seemed she was implying something more. Was the midlife thing Cass kept harping on that obvious? Did his body language say 'unemployed, brokenhearted, homeless'? Was there a big L tattooed on his forehead?

Crystal had gone. The others said good night to each other and went about their business, either toward the kitchen or down one hallway or another, leaving only the slender little man who had been sitting beside Dennis. This time Brendon took the initiative.

"You must be Rune," he said, extending his hand.

"Yes."

"Brendon Pearce." Rune had a slim mustache and thinning hair. He was of indeterminate age, and with an air both frail and vital. He gripped Brendon's hand very tightly and stepped into his space.

"There was someone here for you tonight," Rune declared quietly. "A woman. I saw her very clearly; she just walked right in and sat down beside you, just there on your right side.

39

Absolutely stunning, just shining like the sun. Is this someone you're familiar with?"

"Uh... no."

"Native American maybe, I was getting the name Skydancer. I think she's been with you for a few months."

"Well, that's interesting."

"You haven't felt her around you? Because I'll tell you, she is on you like a dog on a bone, just watching your every move."

Brendon chuckled, "No, I haven't felt anyone around," he said, and as he said it he remembered the feeling of warmth he had noticed during the meditation, but dismissed it as irrelevant. Yet the idea of any woman, even an ethereal one, taking an interest in him piqued his curiosity.

"Well she said she's glad you made it to Sedona, and that you are..." here he paused and closed his eyes again, as if still listening to this supposed spirit, "needed for the forward progression of events. That was how she put it."

A shudder went through him. "Huh," he grunted. He had heard those exact words in Ojai, 'forward progression of events'. Was this psychic's common catchphrase? He had no way of knowing, but refused to admit to Rune or himself that it was more than a coincidence. Instead, he quipped, "So there were *two* angels sitting next to me."

"Two?"

"Yeah, this 'Skydancer', and Harmony."

Rune's small eyes became even smaller; a furrow appeared in the thin skin of his forehead. "You don't believe me, do you Mr. Pearce," he stated accusingly.

"Well... it's not that I think you're lying. I believe you saw what you saw."

"But *you* didn't see it?"

Brendon nodded helplessly. What could a rational person expect him to say?

"For the life of me I don't know what she sees in you," the little man blurted, taking a step back and putting his hands on his hips. "You don't deserve her, that's certain. She has *very* high energy. *Very* high."

"And I'm very flattered. I guess... I just don't know what to do with this information."

"Well you can start by making an effort," he said, a little less harshly. "You are on a spiritual journey, young man, you must take responsibility for that, at least."

"Then please tell her, this Skydancer, that I will endeavor to... um... be more spiritual."

"You don't get it, do you? I don't need to tell her. She's with you all the time. She knows exactly how far along the Path you are. You need to open your mind and acknowledge her existence. You need to show a little gratitude for her assistance. But most of all," he concluded, putting his hand on Brendon's chest, "you need to open your heart. Don't waste this opportunity."

This tirade left Brendon quite speechless. His immediate reaction was to calculate the effect defaulting on the lease would have on his finances and his credit. These people were a little too far out for him. He rubbed the back of his neck and remembered the feeling of warmth on his side during the meditation. Surely that was just Harmony's body heat reaching him. It wasn't possible for anyone to *feel* an angel or spirit, was it? A rush ran up his arm to his head, he felt himself blushing, and dying to know what this Skydancer might look like. Absolutely stunning, he had said, but then, she was dead, right?

"And about Harmony," Rune added as he left the room, "You're barking up the wrong tree there, I'm afraid. She's celibate."

41

CHAPTER FOUR

THE sunlight streamed through the blinds making buttery stripes on the dull white wall. One ray of morning struck Brendon's eyelid, turning the surface of his dream screen tomato red. He had a hold of himself, and had been enjoying a very realistic encounter with an Indian maiden, who was wearing a very sexy feathered headband, soft beaded moccasins, and nothing else. Her long black braids had led him all the way down her back. Her curves gave under his hands; her smooth skin gleamed in the sun. He was left with a sweet feeling of acceptance and devotion, as though she were there for him completely, almost as if she existed only for him, and as he continued to wake, he remembered where he was, and what that bizarre little man had said the night before, and he married in his mind the image of the goddess painting, the eros of the dream, and the name of Skydancer. His chest felt warm and shaky, he was sad that the dream was gone, but incredibly grateful it had come.

He opened his eyes to the brilliant blue rectangle skylight. The sounds of birds came through the window, which he had left open a crack. The air was delightfully cool. Despite the long drive of the previous day, he realized that he was eager to get up, and noted how unusual that was. He stretched, rose, and opened the blinds, letting the full force of the desert sun into his room. The leaves of his little tree became translucent with golden light.

On the patio by the pool, Harmony and Rune were each standing on one leg with the other held out behind them and their backs arched. From there they tipped forward, dropping their heads down and swinging that extended leg straight up in the air, doing perfect splits without losing their balance. Yoga is insane, Brendon thought, how could they do that? He watched them for a while, slowly shifting their poses in unison, performing their obeisance to the sun. Rune was shorter, slimmer, and more flexible than Harmony, but she looked far better in spandex. He couldn't see her face; he tried to recall if there was anything native about it. Her long braid was brown – more Scandinavian than Indian, he decided. But the Indian maiden was only a dream, and Harmony was real, and at that moment he wanted her desperately. He wondered if she were really celibate, or if Rune had simply told him that to keep her to himself, or if she had told Rune that to keep *him* at a distance. But surely he was gay, and surely she knew it, which made a ruse of celibacy unnecessary. Why would she have hugged him that way if she were not interested?

'Very high energy' and 'open your heart' Rune had said, in addition to 'progression of events'. *Was* his heart closed, he wondered, then realized he could not argue the point. It had not slammed shut at any particular moment, but had rusted solid from disuse. Getting it open now would require far too much effort. He might have put in the effort for Harmony, but apparently that was pointless. He thought about joining them out there, maybe taking a swim, but saw himself in the bathroom mirror and reconsidered. Maybe a little health food would be a good idea.

After a long shower Brendon realized he didn't know the wireless password and so couldn't check his email. He threw on some clothes and went in search of Crystal, crossing the great room and venturing down the hall whence she had come the day before. The first door he came to was open to a cluttered, almost chaotic space, which seemed to be an office or study. A large desk was positioned across the left corner; a row of blue bound books ran neatly along its edge. File drawers and shelves lined the wall to the right. The sliding glass door offered yet another view of red earth and hardy trees. It was certainly Crystal's office; the entire perimeter was lined with varied specimens of her namesake. There were large geodes of chalcedony, agate, and amethyst, lopsided lumps of aquamarine, tourmaline, and azurite, polished spheres of red and green jasper, clusters of celestite, citrine, zincite, calcite, etc, all carefully labeled. One hulking example of clear quartz, perfectly terminated, stood on guard in front of her desk.

The walls were plastered with posters and photos, odd charts and diagrams. He recognized Leonardo's Vitruvian Man, tacked up beside an anatomical poster with the title *Meridians of the Human Body*. This was overlapped by what looked like an air traffic map, but was captioned *North American Ley Lines*. Beside this was a print of a Byzantine icon, Christ with an enormous gilt halo. Written in the white border was the phrase 'accretion disc', with an arrow pointing at the halo. A photo purporting to depict the north pole of Saturn had been marked with a highlighter outlining a hexagon in the swirling clouds of that planet's surface. There were amazing satellite pictures of Earth at night, in which city lights, thunderstorms, and auroras were clearly visible. The highlighter had been used again on a glossy poster of a sun flare titled *Coronal Mass Ejection*, this time to add the words *Rod of Initiation*. There were many images of celestial origin; merging galaxies, constellations, nebula. One showed the Earth, nested inside a series of semi-transparent spheres of different colors, like force fields or additional atmospheres. An intricate crop circle clipped from a magazine had been notated *vibratory inducement of 4th globe.* A poster of the Great Pyramid had been marked with a small circle at its peak and the words *above meets below, critical point of manifold.* There were mineral charts, sky charts, mandalas, the zodiac, the Kabbalah, something titled *The Seven Rays*, and a map of *Vortexes of Sedona*.

Brendon's eye came to rest on a diagram which seemed to have been hand done in colored pencil: a figure in profile, sitting cross-legged as Harmony had been during the meditation, circles of color placed along the spine. He took these to be the chakras. He had seen this type of diagram before, however this one included a sphere surrounding the entire figure, like a bubble, only above the head there was a funnel shaped depression, a similar one was below the figure. Small arrows were positioned in an attempt to indicate a direction of flow, in and out of these funnels.

Carol quietly entered the room and stood beside him.

"It's all about the spin ratio," she said, "poloidal to toroidal." The mathematical terms seemed incongruous with her dowdy appearance. As if to make herself clear, she held her index finger up and made little circles in the air, then she tipped her hand horizontally while continuing to make the circles.

"Or planes to rays, you could say," she threw in offhandedly, as if it were obvious. He looked at her blankly, completely mystified. She seemed surprised by his utter confusion. "Inducing the vortex," she added, nodding at the wall, but not, he thought, at the chakra poster he had been studying, rather at a photo tacked up beside it, of a huge piece of machinery, taken from high on a catwalk, showing the skeletal mass of support beams, the bound serpents of wires and conduits feeding it, the winding stairways its minders used to attend or flee. Printed over this intimidating monster of industrial exertion was the label: JAEA JT-60 Tokamak Reactor.

"I taught physics for thirty years," she revealed, a quiet smile on her face.

He returned his attention to the diagram, smiling in return.

"What is spinning?" he inquired. Her face betrayed a hint of surprise, which quickly turned to kind condescension, like a grandmother toward an ignorant child.

"Everything," she said, her voice full of love for the word spoken.

"You don't say," he chuckled.

"Oh yes. Do you know the surface of a torus may be divided into as many as seven equal regions yet each be in contact with the other six?"

"I did not know that," he admitted.

"The rotation of one force from pole to pole," (here she illustrated by rotating her fingers again) "in combination with a second force, rotating around the circumference, you see, creates the helical field lines which maintain the shape of the torus."

"Uh-huh. Well that's not something you hear everyday."

"The parameters of the central flow produced – depth, torsion, velocity – depend entirely on the spin ratio."

"Naturally."

"It's of prime importance to the work."

"It would have to be, wouldn't it?"

"Good morning my darlings," Crystal blurted as she swept into the room, her flounces following, "Looking for me?"

"Yes, I was wondering if I might borrow one of the blue books," Carol replied.

"Certainly, dear, any you like, no need to ask."

Carol selected the desired text from Crystal's desk, then turned with a little girl's glee and flashed the front of it at the newcomer so he could share said glee. He noted its title, *The Consciousness of the Atom,* and nodded appreciatively. She then clutched it to her chest, as if she had just been presented with a favorite doll, sighed, and padded out of the room.

What the hell have I gotten myself into, he muttered to himself silently.

"And how are you this morning, Brandon, settling in all right?"

"Brendon."

"Of course, I'm so sorry. I've never been very good with names."

"That's okay. Could you give me the wireless password, so I can get online?" He wondered how she didn't get a stiff neck, holding her head that way, her chin thrust out and up, as if she were above all mundane concerns, and only the heavens could command her attention.

"Didn't I give you that yesterday? Oh dear. I have it here somewhere," she sighed, whirling around her desk, flipping papers in the air. Brendon was patient, he continued scanning the wall and noticed a second drawing done in colored pencil, with those directional arrows indicating flow or spin. Here the shape depicted was more of a doughnut than a bubble. It was not surrounding a single meditating figure, rather it had been sketched to encompass a circle of people sitting much as they had been the previous night, with the hole, or vortex coming through the center of the group. The artist had filled this space with many strokes of white and yellow pencil, as if to depict some kind of energy streaming down. Scrawled below the illustration was the caption *Toroidal Flow of Group Consciousness.* Beside this drawing was an aerial view of Stonehenge, overlaid with a semi-transparent depiction of that same innertube shape, suggesting the stones had been arranged to match or create a large vortex. Another print showed the black Ka'aba in Mecca, the hub of a seething gyre of Hajj pilgrims, and over the top of this image someone had written *omphalos*.

"Oh, I know what it is," Crystal exclaimed, "How could I forget? It's seven planes, seven rays. Only don't spell the sevens."

"Seven planes, seven rays," Brendon echoed, wondering what that was about. "Got it." He turned to leave but his hostess was not through with him just yet.

"Wait, I wanted to loan you this, to put in your room while you're here," she said, taking a large cluster of ruby-red crystals from a shelf.

"Oh, that's not necessary."

"Yes. It's rhodochrosite, it will ground you. Take it."

"But I'm not... there's already the black one on my nightstand."

"That one's important too, but now that we have met I can see... there is much new here, for you. You're feeling lost, uprooted. It's only natural. Sleep with it beside you, it will help."

The very fact that this stranger *knew* how lost he felt was exactly the sort of thing which was making him feel lost. All his housemates seemed to think they knew him, what he was going through or thinking about, or the quality of 'energy' that surrounded him. It was unnerving, particularly when they were right.

"But I don't really bel..."

"I'm afraid I must insist." He looked her in the eye. She seemed to know he thought her rocks were stupid, yet she took no offense.

"I would consider it a personal favor," she added, placing the stone in his hands. It *was* extraordinarily beautiful; the pinkish red columns appeared to glow with an inner light. He somehow felt undeserving of it.

49

"And let me say again how pleased I am, we all are, that you sat with us last evening. I am so glad you have come. Really." Then taking another step, so her face was quite close to his, she said, as if imparting a state secret, "You're the seventh, you know."

Due to an instinctive fear that it would be unable to compute the answer, Brendon's mind shied away from asking 'seventh what'.

"Well, I'm glad to be here, it's a great house."

"It's perfect, isn't it? Now I can't wait to see how your art progresses!"

"Oh, me too," he assured her, wondering how he was going to come up with any art at all, or if he would get evicted when he was 'found out', when that inevitable day came for him to admit he was a fraud, and not a real artist at all. He thanked Crystal again, and headed back to his room.

As he crossed through the great room, he saw the thick figure of Michael on a ladder, using a spray bottle to mist the top of one of the taller indoor palms. He was wearing a green polo shirt, which accentuated both the size of his arms and the bronze sheen of his skin.

"...beautiful, mm, hmm. You are just gorgeous, aren't you?" he was saying, "We are so happy to have you here with us, gracing this room with your presence. So green, baby." He saw Brendon out of the corner of his eye, and smiled broadly.

"They do better if you talk to them."

"Uh-huh."

"You know, show a little appreciation." Brendon nodded and walked on down the hall. Michael continued spritzing the palm leaves, and showering them with compliments.

The door to the studio was open. He entered and looked around. There were shelves and print drawers for storing art, a sink and cabinets for supplies and cleanup, north facing glass doors opening to the courtyard, and two skylights. There was one easel on which a landscape in progress rested, presumably Carol's. It was respectable, for a retired physics teacher. Better than he would be able to do, no doubt. On the walls hung several others, desert sunsets, buttes, red rock vistas. He noticed something odd in the sky of one of them, a darkness which didn't quite belong to the surrounding clouds, and moved closer to get a better look. It was pinkish gray, disc shaped, with a little bulge on top. There were smears descending from its edges, which made it look a bit like the hat of an invisible head. The whole thing was tipped about 30 degrees. He decided it was supposed to be a flying saucer. A closer inspection of the other paintings on the wall revealed similar incongruities, indistinct suggestions of things not quite manifest, most reminding him of UFOs or ETs.

"Pretty wild, huh?" Dennis asked, right at his ear, making him jump.

"Shit, don't sneak up on people like that," Brendon protested. Being 'caught' snooping made him feel guilty, even though he knew he had done nothing wrong. He immediately moved toward the door.

"Sorry, didn't mean to scare you." His grin belied his apology. His brow and his shirt were moist with sweat. "Whoa, whatcha got there?" he asked, pointing to the ruby red treasure in Brendon's hands.

"Crystal insisted I keep it on my nightstand," he explained, holding up the specimen for Dennis to see, but still walking out of the room and down the hall.

"Holy shit, Pearce, you lucked out. I've never even *seen* that one."

"She says it'll ground me. Whatever that means."

"Is it rhodochrosite?"

"I think that's what she said. You know about rocks?"

"I know that one's gotta be worth about ten grand. Do you have any idea how rare that is?"

"Jeez, I told her it was completely unnecessary," Brendon asserted, shaking his head. He took a few more steps, entered his room, and set it on the nightstand beside the Tibetan quartz.

"Yeah, but you can't argue with Crystal," said Dennis, following him, uninvited, into the room. "She... she has her own agenda, shall we say. She's always trying to..." here he paused and gestured with both hands in sort of mixing motion, "... balance things. She's switched out the specimens in my room twice since I've been here. First there was a rose quartz heart, now there's a cheesy selenite candleholder. So I'd say you're *in* with the landlady, there, big boy."

"Maybe she can tell I'm more unbalanced than you."

Dennis chuckled, looked like he was about to make a comment, but he didn't.

"So you've already been hiking?"

"Yeah, just got back. Gotta get out early in the desert, before it gets too hot. You want me to wake you up tomorrow?" Something about the slight smile on his face made Brendon hesitate.

"Uh, what time would that be?"

"I usually get out by six."

"Maybe next week. Hey, do you know where this might be?" he asked, showing Dennis the print of red rocks, twisted juniper and valley below.

"Well this," he said, putting his finger over a spire far in the background, "looks like it *could* be Kachina Rock." He studied it thoughtfully for a minute. "You might get this view from the back of Secret Canyon area, if you were high enough, which would not be easy to get to. But I can't say for sure. Didn't the artist provide any information on where it's supposed to be?" he asked, turning it over to look on the back for a blurb.

"No."

"*View from the Gate,*" Dennis read. "Huh."

"She said it was a vision. She's never been there."

"That's bullshit. It's gotta be from an aerial photograph. Definitely looks like Sedona. You should take one of those helicopter tours."

"Yeah, maybe."

"You're going to be here all summer, so we've got plenty of time to scout it out. We could try all the canyons, if you want. I'm game."

"Well I was just wondering if it looked familiar to you."

"Not really. But there's a lot of territory out there, it's not like I've been everywhere."

"Have any recommendations for an easy hike? In case I get out in the afternoon sometime?"

"Well, you could go to Crescent Moon Park and walk along the creek. It's cool enough there, even in the middle in the summer. And if you get too hot, you can always take a dip. It's off of 89; you turn where the high school is, then wind down and around. There are signs." As he left the room, he added "But if you're serious, you gotta get up early."

Brendon nodded, and shut the door. His neck was killing him. He opened his laptop and entered the bizarre wireless password, 7planes7rays. Success. He scanned his email and sent one to Cass:

Hey Sis,

Boy, would you love this place. I think I should keep your apartment and you should come live here. I wasn't here six hours before they had me in group meditation. There are big crystals in my room, sound healing going on down the hall, everyone speaking Cryptic Newage tongue. I have no idea what they're talking about half the time. The scenery is incredible. I'll try and get some pics to you in a couple days. Hope you're doing well. Did Mr. Dark T. Handsome turn up yet? ;)

B

He spent the next few hours munching on a box of Lucky Charms and finalizing his resume. He had found three possibilities in the area, and was proud of himself for sending it out on his first full day in town. Then he decided he absolutely had to go for a walk. After downing a couple Advil he slipped out the front door. It was quite warm, but he was glad to get away from the Crystal's crystal palace, and the great room of gods and the talking plants. He headed up the lane, rolling his neck, trying to work out the kinks. A short way down the road he saw a small parking lot and trail signs, and so marched into the desert, scuffing up red dust, squinting at the bright blue sky, and berating himself for not bringing his sunglasses. Oh well, he thought, I won't go that far.

His mind reviewed the previous day, the thrill of arrival, the good humor of Dennis, the general acceptance he had received, Harmony's hug, and the good intentions of everyone. He had always thought of himself as pretty open minded, but this household was testing him. Here, he failed by comparison; *he* was the intolerant one, the uptight one, the skeptical, suspicious, negative one. It was not the way he usually saw himself. It had always been so easy to dismiss crystals, psychics, and 'energy' as crazy ideas because it was only his little sister who championed them, but with the exception of Dennis, everyone in the house seemed to believe in all kinds of stuff. Perhaps Cass is right, he thought, maybe I do need to work on opening my mind.

A pile of stones, stacked about five feet high, marked a fork in the trail. He chose left and quickly came to a huge opening in the terrain, a couple hundred feet across, just to the right of the path. A sign read *Devil's Kitchen Sinkhole*. It was an impressive feature; great chunks of rock had simply fallen in on themselves. The area across from him was in shadow. He peered into its dim depths for a minute or two, until vertigo crept up on him, then he continued on the trail.

A short while later another sign pointed out *Seven Pools*. He veered off the way again to see seven hollows in the surface of a red rock streambed. The stream was only a trickle, but there was water in the basins. He ascended the incline slowly, winding his way in between the circular depressions, which must have been formed, he thought, by the swirling action of water in some previous era of more abundant rain. There was something hypnotic in following the same path that the runoff followed when it came after a thunderstorm, the channel eons of flow had made, grooved into the stone by force of habit, leaving this eternal record of its whirling, wheeling passage. Some day, perhaps, a greater sink would develop there, or a quake would come, a jolt out of the blue. Only then would the water be free to follow a different course.

He returned to the trail and wound himself deeper into the enveloping canyon. A few squirrels scampered here and there, the occasional lizard twitched away, a family of Gambel's quail pattered comically across the path. Flies buzzed him, and infrequent bird calls broke the air, but for the most part it was incredibly quiet. Quiet was a difficult thing to find in Los Angeles. He felt very appreciative, very fortunate to be there. How many millions or billions came and went without ever having the opportunity to walk free from noise pollution, air pollution, light pollution, to say nothing of the rare beauty of the geology and the hi-res bluest blue above.

His artist's eye noted the negative space in the desert; the absence of clouds, the absence of canopy, the absence of flora on the spires and buttes, the sparseness of ground cover. Little clumps of various grasses shared the desiccated soil with bushes and shrubs he would eventually learn the names of; creosote, desert broom, catclaw and cliffrose, yucca, hedgehog cactus, century plants, and dozens of others, yet there remained a lot of empty places. Then he wondered who he might be insulting by thinking the soil was empty, what microscopic life toiled there, storing up nutrients, preparing the way for larger, more evolved beings.

Sometimes the way became vague, when the area worn by feet appeared nearly indistinguishable from the surrounding desert, or when it crossed undulating strips of bare rock that looked like sunburnt knees and dimpled midriffs, but without fail these areas were marked with more little stacks of stones. Whether this was a sign of guiding human intelligence, or interference, he could not decide.

The farther he hiked, the better he felt; freer, clearer, and lighter than he'd felt in years. The old self was left behind, in the critical thoughts and judgments that fell from him like droppings on the red dirt. None of it mattered there; it was blown away by the slightest of breezes. All that remained was the gravelly trail, the sky, and the breath.

Into this clear silence came a sound – low, rhythmic, accentuated. It was a beat, faint, yet resonating through him. At first he thought it was his own heart, pulsing in his ear, but it was not. He folded his ears over themselves and the sound became muffled rather than louder, so he knew that it was external. It sounded like Native American drumming, straightforward, resolute, and significant. As he walked, it became slightly louder, although still quiet. But for the bodily sensation of vibration that accompanied it, he would have thought it was coming to him from far away. He stopped walking and sat on a boulder, quieting his breath. The sound dissipated.

"What the hell," he mumbled, now I'm hearing things. Since he was quite thirsty, but had no water with him, he decided it was time to head back to the house.

CHAPTER FIVE

"BRENDON, come join us," Michael invited. He and Carol were sitting at the bar in the kitchen while Rune was fixing a plate for himself. There were bowls of salad, some suspicious looking thin, flat bread, and a plate of crudités.

"Are there any glasses?" he asked.

"Left of the sink," was the reply. Brendon drank a full glass of water, then dished himself a little salad.

"You should wear a hat when you're out walking," Carol suggested, "And be sure you take plenty of water. In the desert, it's so dry you sweat without even noticing."

Brendon chuckled. "I don't think I'll make that mistake again. Man it gets hot quick out there." He sat beside Michael at the end of the bar and took a mouthful of salad. Michael's open palm appeared beside Brendon's plate. He looked over and saw that Rune, Carol, and Michael were holding hands and had their eyes closed. Good grief, thought Brendon. He put down his fork and placed his hand on Michael's, which grasped it firmly.

"In gratitude we bless this food that it may fortify our flesh," Michael intoned. "We thank the beings who have given this gift of eternal light which we are about to receive. And so it is."

"And so it is," Carol and Rune echoed.

Rune, noticing the stunned look on Brendon's face, said, "The blessing is a time to connect with the food before consuming it, to align with it so that the maximum life force is released. True

59

gratitude never fails to calm the vibrations, which allows proper enmeshing of the fields."

"Okay," Brendon said, although what Rune had said meant nothing to him.

"The vessel must always be conditioned prior to receiving, just as before meditation," Carol put in. "It's a matter of synchronizing wavelengths."

Brendon nodded. They began to eat. He took a few mouthfuls of the salad, but it was very bitter.

"So you guys are all vegetarian?" he asked, knowing what the answer would be but still feeling a little surprised.

"We seek to conquer the lower three worlds," Rune said, motioning from his belly downward.

"What?"

"Ambition, greed, lust," he elucidated, again gesturing down his body, this time with three distinct pauses.

"We work to incorporate them, to make the baser energies subservient to the higher," Carol said quietly, placing her hand gently on his arm and nodding, as if she were a Victorian chaperone explaining a sophisticated table setting to her charge.

"Of course," Brendon acquiesced.

"You've got to give it up to God," Michael grinned, filling his big mouth with greens.

"Allow me to apologize for my hasty remarks of the other evening," said Rune. "I assumed you were on the occult path, I see now you follow as yet the mystic way."

"Uh, no problem." Brendon tried not to laugh, because the others were so serious about whatever it was they were talking about, and he didn't want to open another can of worms by admitting he had know idea what they were getting at.

"Did you enjoy your walk?" asked Michael.

"Yes, very much. The rock formations are just spectacular. I can't quite get over it."

"Why would you want to get over it?" Carol giggled.

"You never will," Michael assured him, "I've been in Sedona for fifteen years, and I still can't believe how lucky I am to live here."

"Let me ask you guys something... is there a school or a... campground nearby, or..." Brendon began. They looked at him blankly. "I was on the trail, heading up the canyon, and I heard this drumming. Have any of you ever heard anything like that up there?" They shook their heads, chewing.

"Maybe someone hiked up there this morning with a drum, and it echoed back to you." Rune suggested, smiling slightly.

"Maybe. It didn't sound like that though."

"Did it sound like it was coming from below, from the ground?" Michael asked.

"Yeah. That's exactly what it sounded like. Sort of from above and below at the same time. I thought it was just in my head at first, but it was vibrating up my legs."

Michael nodded.

"When the demand and the response are lost in one great Sound, move outward from the desert, leave the seas behind and know that God is Fire," Rune said cryptically, apparently quoting from something he thought Brendon should be familiar with.

"First you see the star, then you hear the sound," Michael said, as if agreeing with him.

"How exciting!" Carol exclaimed, "this is such a special time for you!"

Brendon was quite bewildered.

"He doesn't know what you're talking about," Rune told her with a resigned, slightly smug air.

"Oh. Well that's all right, dear," she said, patting his hand. "Understanding will come. The most important thing to remember is to remain open."

"She's right," Rune agreed, "If one attempts the lower route, the road to Shambhala is tortuous and full of sorrow. One will not see progress until the critical point is reached, and eversion is achieved. It's like passing through the bowels of the earth. Better to remain open to guidance; that is the high way. If one consciously works to build the *antahkarana*, the bridge, success is guaranteed and the passage is made clear. Then it is like flying."

"Initiation can be very confusing," Michael consoled, patting him on the shoulder. Brendon tried to laugh the whole thing off.

"Exactly *what* am I being initiated into?" he chuckled.

"Don't confuse him with your mumbo jumbo," Dennis jovially reprimanded. He had entered the kitchen and had overheard just enough. Brendon looked at him and rolled his eyes.

"I feel like there's something I'm missing," he said.

With that sly smile, Dennis suggested, "It's all on a need to know basis." Brendon chuckled.

"LeRose rescues us from the slippery slope of gravity," Rune deadpanned.

Dennis shuffled about in the open fridge, inspecting and smelling things from every shelf to see if there was anything to tempt him. After a while he withdrew his head and closed it, empty-handed.

"Yeah, I'm the clown around here," he boasted, fingering the spoon in the fruit salad, "Now all we need is a cook."

"But Dennis, you forget that cooking leaches the light from the food," Carol objected earnestly, and continued munching on a radish.

"Oh, yeah, I did forget," he replied, shooting a quick wink Brendon's way.

"Why don't you join us, there's plenty," invited Michael.

"I was going to, but all the stools are taken."

"Here, I'm finished," Brendon said, standing.

"No, no," Dennis protested, "You don't need to do that."

"Actually I've got to run a few errands, so please, take my spot. Thanks again for lunch, everyone."

Ten minutes later, as Brendon was pulling out of the driveway, Dennis came jogging toward the car. Brendon lowered his window.

"You going to get some real food?" Dennis asked.

"Uh... I'm not sure where I'm going actually, just had to get out of there for a while."

"Mind if I come with?"

"No, sure, hop in." Dennis went around and got in the passenger side.

"Thanks. My truck isn't real trustworthy right now. Or truckworthy," he chuckled.

"No?"

"I can get it started, but it's been stalling on me in traffic, so I haven't driven it in a couple days."

"Did you get it checked out?" Brendon asked.

"That's not really in the budget until next month, maybe. I haven't driven it in a week. You think we could swing by a supermarket on the way back from... wherever?"

"Sure. So where should we go? Know any good places to eat?"

"Well, we could go to Tlaquepaque, there's some nice places there. Sit under the sycamores. Or there's a KFC if you turn right."

Fried chicken sounded great, but Brendon had a suspicion that somehow it would get back to the vegans at the house – back to Harmony, and that didn't seem like a good play.

"How do we get to Tella... whatever it was you said the first time."

"Take a left. So where are you from?"

"Baraboo Wisconsin. But I've been in LA for twenty years."

"No kidding? I'm from Tomah." Brendon raised his eyebrows to indicate he had never heard of it.

"At the junction of I 90 and I 94?"

"Oh, right. We didn't get up that way much. Mostly we went to Madison, and once in a while Milwaukee. Isn't Tomah near Fort McCoy?"

"Yeah. Actually, we were only in Wisconsin for a couple years. We moved around a lot. "

"Your dad was in the Army?"

"Well... not exactly."

"What does that mean?" Brendon chuckled, "Did he work at the base?"

"Maybe we should change the subject," Dennis suggested, his face unusually sober.

"What, was he Special Forces or something?"

"Something."

"CIA? NSA?"

"No comment."

"You're telling me your dad was in the CIA."

"No, I'm just messin' with you," Dennis chuckled, adding, "Probably."

"Have you ever *been* to Wisconsin?"

"Yes, I've even been to Baraboo. I spent some time there with your mother."

"Jesus," Brendon laughed, "I think I was wrong, you are definitely more unbalanced than I am. *You* should sleep with the rhododendronite."

"Rhodochrosite," Dennis corrected.

"Whatever. I mean, what is it with the friggin' crystals? Does she really think it's going to make any difference to anyone? Do you?"

"Well, I've never noticed anything particular from hanging out with pretty rocks, but I'm not really one to pick up on 'vibes'. You can bet your ass Crystal believes in them, so she must have felt something from them at some point, I guess."

"My sister is into that stuff. I don't know. I just don't get it."

"I reserve the right to keep an open mind. It couldn't hurt, right? And the specimens she's got are incredible."

"I guess. But God, I had no idea..." he laughed, "What I was letting myself in for when I signed that damn lease. And the séance the other night? Christ, I didn't know I'd be joining a damn cult. And what the hell were they talking about in the kitchen? Some kind of bizarre hazing ritual?"

"No, nothing like that. It's not really a cult. I don't think. They're well meaning enough, just... living in a different frame of reference."

"That's an understatement. They should've put something in about that when they posted on craigslist – Oh, by the way, we all speak in tongues and levitate on Thursday nights."

"Well, it *is* Sedona," Dennis chuckled.

They came to a roundabout. Brendon intended to continue on in the same direction, which, he thought, would lead them toward shopping and dining areas.

"Oh, you missed it."

"What?"

"Keep going, keep going, go around again."

Brendon veered back into the lane he had been exiting, and drove around the circle.

"Here, the first right there, it's a shortcut."

"Why is it this whole town makes me dizzy?" he chuckled, "and *don't* tell me it's the energy."

Dennis laughed. "Okay, it's the heat."

"Did *you* know what you were getting into when you moved in?"

"No. No, it's definitely been interesting. But I figured I wouldn't be here if I wasn't supposed to be."

"Now you sound like Cass. Is anyone *supposed* to be anywhere?"

"Well, you may not be conscious of it, but a part of you intended to be here."

"If I'm not conscious of it, how can I intend it?"

"That's a good point. But you have to admit," he insisted with a wink and a smile, "you're not really here to make art, anymore than I'm here to write." This took Brendon back a bit. Did Dennis know he wasn't really a painter? Was Dennis really a writer? He could never quite read the guy. On the one hand, he seemed the most normal person in the house, but on the other, the least trustworthy, always saying one thing and thinking another, as if he were hiding something, as if he knew *way* more than he was telling.

"So what are you here for," he countered, "if not to write?"

"I'm here to wake up. I'm here to see the world as it really is."

"That's what Rune said to me last night, I should 'wake up'." *And* the woman in Ojai, Brendon remembered. "I have no idea what that guy is talking about, 'God is fire, first you see the star... And what is all this about 'initiation'? Is this some kind of secret society or something?" Suddenly he remembered seeing that little twinkle in the sky the night before, standing with his groceries in front of the darkened house.

"I'm afraid I can't answer that at this time," Dennis chuckled, hitting Brendon with another of those trademark winks. "No, you don't have to get into all that. I say I'm here to wake up because it's the best analogy I know of. This world is a dream. We're all asleep. The place we all think we are is illusion; it's not reality. It's a mind event, okay? Everything I see or experience is coming out of my own head, it's not out there, it's in here," he said, poking his finger at his temple, "or in the ether," he qualified, "or where ever it is consciousness is contained. Turn here."

Brendon turned and parked under an aged giant sycamore. These enormous trees overshadowed the shopping center built to exploit them, the beauty of Oak Creek, and the majesty of the red rock formations. The place pretended to be an old Mexican village, where the humble residents just happened to have been replaced by hawkers of overpriced clothing, paintings, sculpture, glassware, kitsch, and food. Dennis led the way down cobbled alleys to the seating patio of a modest looking eatery.

They were quiet, reading the menu. Brendon listened to the birds, and couldn't help admiring the massive sycamores. They had such a presence. He felt proud just seeing them. Surely Dennis was wrong to think *they* were illusion, they seemed more real to him than he did to himself just then. The ringing in his ears came up, then gently faded. A stray idea struck him that the trees had sprung up there, centuries ago, just to provide shade to them in that moment, that all their years of growing culminated continuously in a moment of service, diffusing the sun, harboring birds, announcing the wind.

The waiter came; he ordered grilled salmon, Dennis, a steak.

"This certainly feels like a dream," Brendon posed, taking up the conversation again. He gazed meaningfully at the sunlight glinting green and gold through the broad leaves gently swaying overhead, "Entirely too civilized."

"I don't mean like a dream come true, I mean everything you see is generated by your senses, you're creating it. So in every situation, I ask myself, what is this dream about. What am I trying to tell myself, what is this person that calls himself Brendon doing in my dream. If I write something, I ask myself, why am I writing this. If I'm teaching a class, you know, I ask myself, what are my students trying to tell me. Because that person or people or thing in any given relationship or situation is your guru. It's your higher self, your superconscious showing up where you called it, to let you know, 'hey, this isn't real'. There's something beyond this. This is only the mask."

"That's all well and good," Brendon responded, "but this world is all we really have to go on. I mean, you can't actually get to that 'real' reality until you're dead."

"I think that's where you're wrong. You can experience the universe differently; you can wake up from this. It's a matter of retraining your senses. It's what all the prophets do; they realize they *are* the universe. I'm going to share something that happened to me several years ago, which I haven't told very many people about, because it's kind of hard to explain, but you have to promise not to think I'm crazy."

"Okay," Brendon agreed, smiling.

"I was in Idaho, hiking in the Sawtooth Wilderness, by myself, which probably wasn't very smart, it's like one of the most isolated places in the country, but the weather was good, and nothing bad happened. So I was out there for a few days, sleeping under the stars, and just really getting away from it all, you know, really emptying my head of all the day-to-day crap. It was great. I don't know if you ever camp out or anything, but it... it really helps clear away all the stuff you accumulate from living in the modern world. You get down to the bare essentials of what it means to be alive. I mean maybe that had something to do with it, I don't know. So on the third day out, I was walking along the shore of Little Redfish Lake, not really thinking of anything, just enjoying the air, you know, it was picture perfect, sunny and cool. I was just walking along, then it was like... everything sort of went white, and... I mean the only accurate words are... everything, everywhere." Here Dennis paused, with that little smile on his face, and looked to see if Brendon was getting it.

"The Oneness," Brendon surmised.

"Yeah, I guess that's one way to say it. Thank you," he said to the waitress, who had arrived with their meals. Brendon waited to see if Dennis would give his plate a blessing, but he did not. They began to eat.

"But that's so overused," Dennis objected, his mouth full of meat. "This was not just a concept of the One being, it was experiential. I mean, I wasn't just *connected* to it all, I *was that.* It only lasted a moment probably, I don't even know for sure, because that moment was eternal, you know? And I came away from it knowing without a doubt that time, *and* space are just manufactured illusions, this is all a dream. I didn't tell anyone for a while, and after a year or so I came up with a good analogy." He paused again to swallow and free his hands so they could assist him in getting his point across. He posed them over the table as if he were holding something.

"It's like we're all contained, like water balloons in the ocean, and sometimes you can see through your boundary and recognize that there's a whole ocean out there, and maybe you can tell that you are made of the same thing as that ocean, but it's out there and you're in here in your bubble or balloon, right? But that day, in that moment by Little Redfish Lake... it's like the balloon burst. So that thing, whatever it is, that contained me, or what my mind tells me is me, just evaporated for a minute, so there was no edge between me and the whole ocean." Again he paused to gauge Brendon's reaction.

"So you became aware of the One."

"But more than that," Dennis argued. "If you break a water balloon in the ocean, you can't separate that water out again, it becomes the ocean, see?"

"Except that it *did* separate out again. You're just you again, right?"

"Right. But I'm awake now. I know what's really going on."

"We're all dreaming."

"It's an analogy, but yeah. This is all a mind event," Dennis concluded, attacking his steak with renewed vigor. "Have you ever experienced anything like that? Anything that... took you out of the dream for a minute?"

"No, not really. But I did hear a weird drumming this morning on the trail by the house."

"Oh yeah?"

"That's what I was telling them in the kitchen when they started with their mumbo jumbo."

"Right. Well they're just trying to get you to see that... something which impresses your mind like that, anything which you take notice of, has meaning."

"What is that drumming doing in my dream?"

"Exactly. They would probably say someone is trying to communicate with you. I would say you're trying to communicate with yourself."

"So what does the drumming mean?"

"Only you can know for sure, it's *your* dream."

"Thanks for nothin'," he chuckled, "But what's your official CIA opinion; am I hearing things, or was there someone in the canyon drumming?"

70

"I have heard there are certain... installations in the canyons, which might be emitting certain sounds. But my guess is the natives are getting restless," Dennis replied, winking again, "and what you heard is a war dance. Drums along the Mogollon. Probably coming to you from a hundred years ago through a wormhole."

"Very funny."

"Well if I told you the truth," he laughed, "I'd have to kill you."

"God you're so full of shit," Brendon chuckled.

"Look, I have no idea what you heard, obviously. I've never heard any drumming in the canyon, so..."

"Then what was all the stuff about the 'mystic path', and 'initiation', and the 'lower three worlds'?"

He shrugged and nodded knowingly, taking time to prepare a careful answer while he finished a mouthful of steak.

"As far as I can make out," he began, "that comes mostly from Crystal. Although the others go right along. It's all about the seven rays..." Brendon looked blankly at him. "Well, it's complicated, but basically they talk about seven frequencies of cosmic energy, and the seven major chakras being receivers of them. If you follow the Path your chakras are activated and you are initiated to higher realms of consciousness or something. I don't know. Ask Crystal about it, she'll talk your ear off."

"Okay."

"Course, she doesn't make much sense. I just take it as another metaphor. Another way to say it's time to wake up from the dream."

"Right."

"Like there are seven veils between you and reality, seven stages to waking up."

"I thought *you* got there in one stage."

71

"Yeah, but I'm not there all the time. I have to keep reminding myself that it's a dream. Maybe, if I work at it, I can get to a place where it happens automatically, where I'm more fully conscious of reality."

"More awake."

"Exactly. Maybe I'm at the first stage, maybe at the sixth. I don't know. Maybe it's all crap, but I figure it's in my dream for a reason, and I ask myself, 'what is the me that is Crystal trying to tell me in my dream?'"

"And what *is* she doing in your dream?"

Dennis laughed. "Still working on that one. Crystal's a piece of work, for sure. She's not really concerned with... she's all about the group. If you have a problem, it doesn't really matter unless it's going to affect your presence in the group. I mean, she'll do almost anything to keep you in the house, except maybe behave rationally," he laughed, "but little personal problems, like... running water, not really her problem."

"Is she that bad off, financially?"

"No... well, maybe. But that really has nothing to do with it one way or another. If she likes you, you can get away with just about anything I think. I'm not even sure some of the others are paying anything, actually. Basically if you don't show up at the weekly meditations, you're on her naughty list."

"Oh. Well I don't mind napping once a week."

Dennis chuckled. "You might get more out of it than you expect."

"Yeah."

"What she's trying to do is create a group mind in the great room. That's really what the whole house is about, for her."

"Group mind? Like collective unconscious?"

"Collective *conscious*," Dennis corrected, "Ideally with each of those seven rays, those seven frequencies represented."

72

"*That's* what she was talking about," Brendon realized. Dennis raised an eyebrow. "She said to me, all quiet and mysterious, 'you're the seventh'."

"Yeah, that's it. Of course I was the seventh before you. Someone else got fed up with it all and left, and then there were six again."

"Hmm. Then why does she advertise for artists? Why not people who are already into meditation?"

"I don't know, maybe it would be too easy? She wants to mold us, teach us. She gets off on it."

"So we're *her* art."

"You're not as thick as you look, Brendon," Dennis chuckled.

CHAPTER SIX

HEAVY silence, a dull hum only, as much in his head as out of it. There were no markings, no corners, no shadows; all was smooth pale blue. Gliding this deep it was difficult to discern where the bottom became the side, though the water was clear as crystal. Clearer, he thought, than any of the crystals Crystal kept about the house. He took another stroke, pulsing forward, and was forced to arch his back and push off the rising pool floor, which pitched abruptly up from the deep end to the shallow. He noticed the lightness, the subtle change in pressure, the silence less dead in his ears. As he approached the wall he rotated slowly, releasing a bubble from his nose. He watched it rapidly rise, and thought of Dennis's water balloon moment.

Was there really so little between 'I' and all, one tenuous membrane, the merest concept of boundary, nothing more than 'I am air and you are water', or as in Dennis's example, 'I am inside, and universe is outside'? Did the membrane exist first, making its contents different, or did the difference create the membrane? Was there truly nothing more to it than discrimination, that thought of self vs. other, the *intent* to be separate?

And all this flushed through the plane of his mind before he emerged to take a breath. Then down again into the muted blue, thrusting away from the edge, skimming over pale shadows of ripples he had created, racing these disturbances to the opposite edge of the wave's world. What if I don't want to be separate anymore, he wondered, how does one dissolve the membrane, pop the bubble without jarring the contents?

This time, when he came up for air, he saw Rune and Harmony unrolling their yoga mats on the pool deck. For some reason, when he had looked out his window after waking, he had assumed that yoga time was over, that they had come and gone. He had wanted to get away from the house and all the jibber jabber unnoticed that morning, to get back to himself, if that were possible. He thought the exercise would clear his head, and it had been helping, but now Harmony's presence was throwing him. He couldn't help but want her; she radiated health and kindness. He knew, however, that *he* did not. Now he would have to walk past her (and Rune's bronzed, sinewy form) with his gut bulging out, looking flabby and useless. If she was indeed celibate, he could hardly furnish a reason for her to change her lifestyle, yet he wanted her to have a good opinion of him. He wanted her to like him on some level, if at all possible. He took a few more laps, brooding on his longing and loneliness before climbing out of the pool, choosing a moment when they were bent over, facing the ground. He quickly dried his hair, then wrapped the towel around his midriff, rather than his shoulders as he would normally have done, thinking first that it would distract from his spare tire, then that perhaps it was drawing attention to it, but knowing either way it was too late because they had returned to an upright pose and if he changed the position of the towel now he would certainly look foolish. Blushing with embarrassment, he began walking into the house.

"Good morning Mr. Pearce," Rune's strident voice shot at him. Both of them were now standing on one leg, holding their other foot behind their backs with their hands.

"Morning."

"Don't stop on our account," the little man added.

"Oh, no. I was done."

Harmony smiled at him. "Join us for yoga?"

"Thanks for the invitation, but I don't really uh... yoag," he declined, smiling back.

"Well if you change your mind, we're out here most mornings. Do you climb?"

"Climb?"

"Oh, I guess not. Rock climbing? There are some amazing routes around here, so many awesome spires. You should come sometime, even if you've never done it. We'll get you up to speed." The little cropped top draped over her bra left her flat belly exposed. He failed to keep his eyes diverted.

"Well maybe I will," he said, unconvincingly. It sounded like a lot of effort in this kind of heat. As he passed by, he inhaled her earthy perfume.

"Hey Brendon," she called after him, forcing him to turn his gut toward her again, "I've had a cancellation for this afternoon, would you be interested in a healing session? It'll help you align with the local vibration."

"Great idea," Rune concurred, "You look like you could use it." So many reasons to dislike that guy, Brendon thought.

"On the house," she added, which seemed to him unnecessary, and gave rise to a glimmer of hope.

"In that case, sure, why not," he answered, smiling, hoping his enthusiasm was not too obvious. Spending an hour alone with Harmony was just about the best thing he could imagine at that moment.

"Come to the therapy room at three."

"Thank you. I'll be there."

∗ ∗ ∗

12 x 16, 16 x 20, relatively small, that was good, he thought, they would take less paint, less time, and be easier to dispose of if they were as horrible as he suspected they would be. He threw some acrylics in the basket; cad red, cerulean, viridian, hooker's green, alizarin crimson, cobalt, burnt umber, cad yellow, two tubes of white. He didn't want to invest in more colors than that at this point. He chose the cheapest brushes. At the last minute he grabbed a 24 x 36 canvas, just for kicks. The big expense was the French box easel, which folded down compactly for carting around in the great outdoors, yet had a place to keep all the paints. It had to be done, if he were going to keep up the pretense of being an *artiste* for Crystal's amusement. Dennis was lucky, he thought, to have no equipment but the computer he would have had regardless. He probably never wrote a word anyway, like Jack Nicholson in *The Shining,* 'all work and no play makes Dennis a dull boy'. He wouldn't even have to type it out more than once, just copy and paste, page after page. With a smile, Brendon handed his credit card over to the cashier.

From the art supply store, he drove to Crescent Moon Park. He had no intention of painting that day, or of returning to the house before evening. He walked around the campsites, past the old mill, and found himself beneath a widespread cottonwood along yet another section of rambling Oak Creek. The creek bed and bank were formed of the now familiar red rock that the current had worn smooth. He sat with his feet dangling in the cool water. To his left was a view of Cathedral Rock, perfectly framed by the tree branches. The sound of the water soothed him. He sighed, and felt his body really relaxing for the first time in weeks. How long had it been since he'd had his feet in a stream, since he had felt the current of the natural world pulling on him, swirling around him? A decade had passed since he had even been in the ocean; it was always too cold, filthy, and public for him. Nothing matched the pleasure of sitting alone watching leaves and twigs riding on to their destination, quietly communing with the water as it passed by, knowing it for only a moment before it was gone. Yet it was always there, unchanging, ever changing. The last time he had dangled his feet that way was in Wisconsin, a lifetime ago. He remembered vividly the thrill of water play, digging and stomping in marsh mud. He had loved to create bridges between puddles and pools, and watch them flow into each other. In his freeform, preschooled mind, those water connections he had gouged out with sticks and stones were bridges, because the leaves used them to cross from one body to another. By this method of extending the boundaries and giving the water a place to flow, he would coax floating things to move into ever-larger bodies until they at last reached the lake.

More hours of his youth than he could calculate had been spent along, in, or on creeks, rivers, lakes and marshes, watching life emerge from them in the spring, as if from nothing, growing, blossoming, procreating, expanding all summer, only to wither, freeze, desiccate, and blow away. In biology class he had been made aware of the incredibly complex interdependency of life involved in this annual explosion; the layers of cooperation across species, kingdoms, and states of matter. He had been taken with it at the time, exalted by the notion of regeneration, that in a way, immortality was a given, every part of everything was redeemed and reassigned. Today's leaves were tomorrow's soil, all things equally important in their way, all necessary to each other and the whole. He had seen the treasure in the muck of the marsh, the green fire of life woven through it all. A little of that feeling returned now, as if carried to him on the water, infusing his feet and calves with a connection he had lost. Surely that was seeing the One. Is that what Dennis had meant, or had he been talking about something else entirely? Had Dennis truly *experienced* something others only glimpse; could a person really *be* all things?

Remembering the waters and trees of Wisconsin grieved him, and that was surprising. He was not normally one to look back. He had never once regretted leaving that frigid state, as far as he was concerned, the winter made the place uninhabitable. But just now he missed the big maples of home, the sweetness of soft grass underfoot, the call of the geese, the whoop of the cranes, the swish of leaves while tramping through autumn woods. This longing for his childhood landscape flew as quickly as it had alighted, yet something of that sense of connection to nature remained, and filled him with a sense of regret for time spent without it, on the highways and in the office buildings of LA, where the living things of the earth were entombed, sequestered, and estranged. Nature in LA was segregated, and as a result was on life support, despite extensive plastic surgery. There was an undeniable difference between a waterway created by the water itself and one coerced by civic or Disney engineers. Surely it was more than an aesthetic preference; there was an empirical difference in the effect it had on one's mind, if not body. He fancied for a moment that he could sense a force, an energy coming into him, not *from* the cottonwood or the water or the rocks, but *through* them, flowing up from the earth. Why then, sitting there looking at the towering solidity of Cathedral Rock, strongly aware of the vitality surrounding him, did he feel that he was dying? Not then and there, but soon. That which he knew as himself was leaching downstream, being extracted somehow. He did his best to let go. It was simultaneously unsettling and relieving.

His focus softened.

He inhaled and exhaled fully.

His body entered a deeper stage of relaxation.

He became quite still; motion ceased.

He entered peace; emotion ceased.

He became aware that he was smiling, then let the awareness go.

Words went silent; thought ceased.

The purling of the water.

Expansion.

Light.

Laughter.

Voices. Where? On the path behind. Fading away. Awareness of detachment. He did not feel his legs, did not want to feel them. Tingles increased from the crown of the head down. He inhaled sharply. He was frightened and elated that he had left sensation. His butt hurt, his feet were freezing. How long had he been sitting there? Another deep breath, he pulled his feet from the water.

Brendon didn't know what to make of this experience. He felt excited about it, surprised by it, but what had happened, really? He had sat with his feet in the water and almost fallen asleep.

He had lost track of time. The big difference, the new thing, was that he had been sort of awake, aware, while *not* aware of his body. He had been aware, while *not* thinking – stacking thoughts on thoughts as he had been before, and resumed after. He was proud of this for some reason.

* * *

When he got back to the house, he found the door to his room open. He felt a twinge of trepidation, then irritation at seeing the large figure of Michael inside, uninvited to his personal space. His automatic reaction was to object loudly to this invasion of his privacy, but he checked his voice and observed for a second, processing the situation, taking the time to respond rather than react. Michael's back was to the door; he was in the corner with a spray bottle in his hand, spritzing the little twined tree that grew from the planter in the floor by the window. His deep voice was rumbling quietly; good humor, gentleness, and love radiated from his being. For a moment it seemed to Brendon that the leaves were reaching out to the big man, but it must have been the breeze from the open window. He turned and saw Brendon; his smile deepened. There was not the slightest hint of self-reproach on his face, no thought that he was in breach of any boundary by being there.

"Brendon, there you are," he said warmly. "You've got to look around you, man, Phil here was in need."

"Phil?"

"Well that's what I call him," he chuckled, "Phil the fabulous ficus."

"Okay."

"I heard him all the way out in the hall, he was so thirsty, weren't you Phil," he said, looking at the plant as if for acknowledgment.

Brendon had no idea how to respond to this, or what Michael or Crystal expected from him in regards to plant care.

"You need to speak to him once in a while, bro. It's not all about you, you know. You need to step out of yourself. Phil needs your light. Phil is living in your light while you're here, and you are living in Phil's light, see? You've got to live for others. You've got to raise your vibration."

"Sure," he agreed, as noncommittally as possible. It seemed like a lot to ask of him for a houseplant.

"That's what keeps you healthy, that's what keeps them healthy. If you get down, and you stay down for a while, you get sick, right? But if you raise your vibration, the pathogen is forced out. Same as with a plant. Because that germ only exists in the lower frequency, see?"

Brendon nodded.

"If you bring down Phil with your low vibe, you leave him exposed, because now he's where someone else lives, the frequency of a foreign body, a certain type of bug or germ. Earth is the same way. One of these days it's going to up its energy and those of us who can't raise ours to match will be thrown off like a dog shakes off fleas. That's why you've got to conquer the lower three worlds. Live in the Light. That's the way to raise your vibration."

"Right. What are they again? Greed? Lust?"

"Ambition, greed, lust. But those are just the more obvious symptoms of someone who's been conquered by those worlds, rather than the other way around. That's why some people say 'he's got demons', you know? It's not always that easy. Some people just say you're ruled by your subconscious, by the ego, by the personality. However you call it, you've got to let the soul take charge. Keep the bodies clear. And you've got to look out for this fabulous ficus," he chuckled, "Or I'm gonna come looking for you."

"Well how often should I water it, then?" Brendon asked, almost in a panic because he realized that even though Michael was joking, Michael was not joking, and he, Brendon, had never had a houseplant that didn't die on him.

"Check the soil, if it's moist, don't water it. But Phil loves the mist. Especially in the summer, he's gotta have it couple times a day. And keep the blinds turned halfway this time of year, you know, at least when you're out. Open your heart, man," he said, patting Brendon on the chest and smiling broadly, "and he'll tell you exactly what he needs. You are he and he is you. Don't be afraid of him." He took Brendon's hand and placed the spray bottle in it. "You know, if you take care of someone, it doesn't mean you throw food and water at them. It means you *care* for them, you know?"

"Right," Brendon nodded, although he had never thought of taking care of a plant in that way before, as a relationship, not just a chore.

"So how are you enjoying it so far?" Michael asked as he moved toward the door. "Been seeing the sights?"

"I went to Crescent Moon Park this morning. Sat with my feet in the creek for a while. That was nice, kind of lost track of time."

"Yeah, that's a beautiful spot. There's a vortex right there, between the park and Cathedral Rock."

"Oh yeah? Maybe that's why. I couldn't feel my body for a while," he said proudly.

Michael smiled at him and nodded. "Have you been to the Chapel yet?"

"Which? No."

"You gotta go. Chapel of the Holy Cross? Down 179, turn on Chapel Rd. You can't miss it. Just an incredible view. Great place to meditate, if it's not too hot."

"Cool. I'll check it out."

"Oh, and I left you a tincture, on the dresser there," he said, moving to the door. Brendon picked up the small brown bottle and looked suspiciously at it. There was only a plain white label on which his name had been hand written.

"It'll help you through it," Michael offered uselessly. "Just a dropper full in a little water every morning."

"What's in it?"

"Little of this and that. The botanical names aren't going to mean anything to you. Don't worry. It's what I do. Trust me," he grinned.

"I'll give it a shot," the other agreed reluctantly.

Then the smile was gone, and the big man with it, down the hall. God, I really like him, thought Brendon, he's such a nice guy. He closed the door and turned back around. There was the plant, a ficus apparently, suddenly more than a bit of decoration. He sat on the bed and looked at it, it's twined trunks, the deep green of its small leaves, now glistening with the mist Michael had applied. A relationship, an interaction, he thought; the plant is acting on me as much as I am acting on the plant. For a minute he felt awkward, as if thrust together with a stranger, stuck in an elevator or sharing the last available hotel room. The greeting 'hello Phil' was on his lips, but he couldn't bring himself to utter it. He nodded slightly. The breeze helped Phil flutter a reply.

CHAPTER SEVEN

BRENDON didn't know what to expect when he went to the therapy room for his appointment with Harmony. He was glad when he saw the massage table set up in the center of the room.

"Hi, right on time," she said. Gone were the spandex pants and crop top, replaced by the baggy jeans and nature girl shirt, but he knew the yoga figure that was under them. The space smelled of incense; now he realized Harmony's intoxicating perfume was nothing more than a fog of *nag champa* clinging to her hair and clothes. Several didgeridoos were leaning against the wall, and a table with strange glass bowls arranged according to size. They were set upside down on the table, because rather than being flat on the bottom, they each had a handle protruding from their base. She saw him looking at them.

"Aren't these awesome? They're called walkabout bowls."

"Very cool."

"Have you ever had sound therapy?"

"No, this will be a first."

"Ooo, a virgin," she teased, "Well you're in for a treat. You're going to love it. And it will really help you adjust to the Sedona energy."

"Great."

"Go ahead and get up on the table, on your back, hands at your sides. You should take off your sandals."

"Okay."

"So where are you from, Brendon?"

"Baraboo, Wisconsin. But I've been in LA for twenty years."

"Oh. Never been to Wisconsin, and I can't tolerate the traffic in LA."

"Are you a native Arizonan?"

"No, I was raised in Portland, but I've lived all over; Mexico, Peru, Australia, India." While she spoke, she put a bolster under his knees, and lit more incense.

"Wow, you really get around."

"I go where Spirit sends me."

"How long have you been here?"

"About five years. Before that I was in Australia, which was great, and I thought I would never find any place I liked as much, but the moment I got here, I just fell in love with the land, and I promised to never leave it."

This struck Brendon as an odd way to put it; promised whom, he wondered.

"It is pretty amazing," he agreed

"You should see the valley from on top of Earth Angel Spire! It's incredible. And the energy here is so powerful. I just feel so good here. Loved."

"That's great."

"Okay, so I'm going to start with the didgeridoo, to ground you. Then we'll work on the chakras with the bowls."

"And should I be, like, visualizing anything, or..."

"No, that's not necessary. Just relax. It's best to close your eyes. You will feel the vibration of the different tones in your body; notice how they make you feel. You want to go with the new tones as they move. Allow the sounds to shift your vibration."

"What if I'm not vibrating?" he chuckled.

"Of course you're vibrating. We're all vibrating. In fact, we're nothing *but* vibration, fields of energy in motion, you know?" Brendon said nothing, trying to grasp what she was saying.

"Yeah, I guess. I mean, I know molecules and atoms vibrate. But it's not like you can *feel* the atoms in your body vibrating."

"Maybe not the atoms, but your body as a whole has a vibration. Each chakra has a vibration; your consciousness has a vibration. It *can* be felt, with practice. But it's not necessary for you to feel anything for this to work, believe me."

"That's very reassuring," Brendon said with a smile. Harmony chose a didgeridoo, raised it to her lips, and began to blow. Its unmistakable rumble shook his torso. He laughed at first; he felt so silly lying there while she huffed and puffed the droning aboriginal tones. She waved its bell end over his body and under the table as she blew, surrounding him with a blanket of sound. He watched her for a while, out of the corner of his eye, her cheeks bulging, her chest heaving with each breath. Then he closed his eyes and gave himself over to the sensation, attending to it, focusing on it. He noticed he could feel it *inside* his chest. It did not bounce completely off of him. Of course not, he realized, sound goes through flesh, how else do you get ultra-sound pictures? But he had never really sought to identify or qualify the sensation of sound traveling through his body. The sheer power of the didgeridoo seemed to even him out. Was that what she meant by 'grounding'? It did feel like it was flattening him to the table, to the ground. She kept it up for a surprisingly long time, perhaps ten minutes or more, now sweeping it around him, now holding it over his chest or the top of his head. All manner of growls and barks seemed to emerge from her instrument at times. There was something very primordial about it. He found himself becoming emotional; a sadness rose up his throat and welled in his eyes, as if it were shaking some forgotten grief out of him. When the noise finally faded, and she turned to set the didge back against the wall, he quickly wiped away a tear. It embarrassed him for some reason, to have been moved by her playing, not dramatic or beautiful music, but sound alone. He didn't want to appear weak or unstable.

"I'm just going to check your chakras for a minute," she said. With her eyes closed, she slowly moved her hands over his body, about three inches away from him, pausing occasionally, breathing steadily.

"You're definitely out of alignment," she said confidently.

"What, my spine?"

"Well, that too, probably. But I'm talking about the subtle bodies. You're out of tune."

"Why does that not surprise me," he chuckled.

"When the chakras are not vibrating cleanly, at the right frequencies, the bodies slip out of alignment. Here, just below your neck, the green is bulging out."

"Okay."

"Do you understand what I'm referring to, what we're trying to do here?" she asked, ceasing her hand movements, looking down at him with a soft smile.

"Not really," he admitted.

"You are more than this physical body," she told him, grabbing his wrist and lifting his forearm off the table. He didn't know quite how to respond, what she was getting at.

"You mean my mind," he suggested, thinking of Dennis's mind event.

"Yes, the concrete mind, the abstract mind, but also other frequencies; the emotional body, the causal body, there are several to consider. They overlap and interpenetrate one another, cohering according to their harmonic. The dense body issues from a network of meridians which is in turn formed by the intersection of fractalized waves in the subtle bodies and the alignment of these energies in perfectly resonating multiples."

"Okay, now I'm really lost," he laughed.

"Well that's alright," she assured him, "you don't need to understand it. Or even believe it, for that matter," she added, picking up one of the walkabout bowls. "Just stay open to it. It's all about willingness. As long as you're willing to change the wave pattern, I can help you. What I'm going to do now is use the tone of the bowls to induce the proper vibration into your chakras." Then she began running a baton around the rim of the bowl as she held it upside down over his belly. In a way the vibration was stronger than the didgeridoo, although not as loud or low. It was purer, clearer, more focused. He felt it ringing into his body; he thought he could even feel it circling, spiraling or pulsing as it moved into him. After a few minutes, she set that one down and chose another.

"Try to hold the vibration after I stop," she instructed. This time she aimed the bowl over his chest. He watched her moving her hand around the bowl, watched her shirt sway with the motion, felt her warmth, inhaled her scent. Surely she knows what would really make me feel better, he thought, surely she knows what I need. She kept her attention on the bowl, and never once turned to see his face. Eventually he relaxed and closed his eyes. She continued to ring it for several minutes. It seemed to him there was a soft sound other than the tone of the bowl; he lifted his eyelid slightly and confirmed that she was whispering. Her eyes were closed, her right hand continued to run the baton around the rim of the glass, and all the while her lips were moving.

"Do you feel it vibrating?" she asked, in a normal voice, opening her eyes.

"Yes."

"Hold that frequency."

"What are you whispering?"

She seemed a bit startled, then smiled and looked at him.

91

"You're supposed to keep your eyes closed," she scolded. "It's just like a mantra. I call for Light to descend on Earth."

"Light?"

"The Christ consciousness. The Light of pure love," she explained, smiling at him with incredible warmth.

Brendon reached out and put his hand on her waist. Harmony very quickly, but gently, took his wrist and placed his arm back on the table, with a firmness and detachment that indicated she had dealt with the situation before.

"No," she said, disappointment showing behind her (now forced) smile. Instantly, he blushed with shame at his mistake. He had made a fool of himself. He expected her to freak out, and kick him out of the room, but she did not.

"I should explain that I'm celibate. To say nothing of professional standards. It's nothing against you, you're a perfectly attractive man, okay, but I found a number of years ago that I do better without... entanglements."

"That's what Rune said," he acknowledged, feeling relieved, "but I figured he just wanted you for himself."

"Hah! You more like it," she laughed. He laughed too. He was glad she was not offended and could laugh it off so easily. It made him less embarrassed to have done something so inappropriate. He was grateful to have been forgiven.

"Well, I had to try."

"Actually, you didn't," she countered, "That's what I've learned. You don't have to be driven by old patterns. You can find fulfillment through other channels. For me, the desert is my beloved. It's all I need to feel love and to give love. It connects me to the One. If you want, I can help you to learn what I've learned."

"I don't think I'm ready to give up sex, no matter how much quicker I get to heaven," he chuckled. "I'm not motivated to conquer that particular world."

"But I'm not actually giving anything up. I mean, sex, yes. But not the energies involved. I get the same satisfaction and joy by opening up other chakras. Besides, conquering the lower three worlds has nothing to do with heaven."

"So what *does* it have to do with? Everyone around here keeps yammering on about the three worlds. Are you talking about sex?"

"Well yes and no. Celibacy is not required, poverty is not required, fasting is not required, but in order to bring in the highest energies, one must be free of the lowest. You can think of it as learning to control your physical desires, your emotional desires, and your mental desires. It's not necessary to shut them off, just to divert those desires to a higher cause. The goal is to enlist those powerful energies in the work of the soul, not just feed the insatiable personality. That's one way to think about it. A more detached way is to focus on the vibrations, not the thoughts. Don't try to suppress your desires, but try to move the vibrations from the lower chakras to the higher."

"Sure," he laughed, "like I can control this energy that I can't even feel. How do you know I even have any energy to control?"

"Of course you do. I can prove it. If I hold my hand here," she said, with her palm hovering over his groin, "what do you feel?"

"Uh, aroused," he admitted, "Which is not really cool if you're claiming celibacy. I mean I don't have a lot of options in this house."

"Don't be a pig," she scolded. "My hand is no where near making contact, but you feel something. What do you feel, in terms of sensation?"

93

"Well, sort of tingly I guess. Warm."

"Exactly. That tingle is a change in *vibration*, that is what it feels like when a chakra is activated."

"But that tingling is just because of increased blood flow, because a certain someone is anticipating closer contact," he argued.

"No. Increased blood flow, yes, but that's not all. There is also increased flow of prana or chi, and increased flow of emotional energy, and anticipation is itself an increase in the flow of mental energy."

"Well, if you say so."

"I do say so. Energy flows where attention goes. Now if I move my hand over your navel, what happens? What can you feel?"

"I guess there's a little tingle there," Brendon decided, "but it's nothing like the other."

"That's because you haven't been using it," Harmony argued. "The energy of your higher chakras is not weaker, just less familiar. In order to conquer the lower three worlds you need to become familiar with all the chakras, with the multiples, not just the fundamental, then you can learn to control the flow of your energy, and raise your vibration from the frequency of these lower centers to those of the higher. It's not that hard, with a little practice, because they're related. It's like music, like the heart chakra is an octave higher than the root, and the throat chakra is an octave higher than the sacral. Do you know anything about music?"

"Not really."

Harmony went to a corner of the room and returned with a Native American flute.

"Here, I'll show you." She blew into the flute, a low note, then a high note. "See, I didn't change any fingering. It's just a matter of increasing the air pressure to go from the low octave to the high. And if you practice with it, you don't even think about how hard you're blowing after a while, it's just a matter of thinking whether you want to play high or low, and your breath adjusts automatically. It's the same with the energy of the chakras. It's really just a matter of intent, and repetition. It's like a quantum leap."

Brendon raised an eyebrow.

"Well that's what Carol says. Ask her about it. Something about energy potentials... or differentials or something. But that's what meditation is so good for, it gives you a chance to really feel the higher vibrations and get accustomed to them. You try." She handed the flute to him. He blew into it and made a low tone.

"Now blow harder," she prompted. He did, and the tone modulated to a higher one.

"So that's really all you need to do. You need to step it up to the next octave. We are all vibratory beings. Your body resonates to a series of multiples. They obey the laws of harmonics. Keep them in tune, and focus on the higher ones. Then overtones will appear. Healing will happen."

"That would be welcome," he said, he handed back the flute.

"Let's try it again," she suggested, "with the bowls. Your heart chakra needs attention. While I'm ringing it, try to hold the vibration up, just like you would with a high note on the flute. *Intend* to keep the energy up, and it will remain in the higher register. Your lower centers get plenty of use, let's try to get the higher ones initiated."

Brendon lay back down. This time he closed his eyes, and tried to forget Harmony was in the room while she sounded the bowl. All her words churned in his head, mixing with bits and pieces of residue from other voices of Sedona and Ojai. *Raise your vibration. Open your heart. It's all about willingness.* He

95

focused on the sensation of sound meeting his body, and tried to imagine it turning in his chest.

* * *

A few days later Brendon visited the Chapel of the Holy Cross. It was south of Sedona proper; he must have seen it as he came into town, but for some reason it had escaped his attention. As he approached, he was already glad he had taken Michael's suggestion; the mere sight of it was impressive. The cross was huge, as tall as the natural spires nearby; it stood out bright and bold against the dark recess of the chapel itself. The building's sleek, sharp-edged form emerged in stark contrast to the softly eroded red sandstone, like a portal into the earth. It was set high on the hill, as if only heavenly creatures ever used it. He parked in the lowest lot and began the steep ascent up the drive, craning his neck to take in the enormity of the cliffs.

Once at the base of the structure, one reached the sanctuary itself by following a long ramp up and around the back. This ramp was freestanding, supported by columns like a bridge. Its left side hugged the curve of the rock, while the right hung in the open air. The entire approach was beautifully done, and effectively made one feel like a pilgrim, about to commune with something – a seeker about to find. Brendon silently congratulated the architect as he rose the last few feet to face the imposing chapel entrance, which stood out singularly against the intense blue Arizona sky. From this vantage point, the entire valley of Big Park was visible. Bell Rock and Castle Rock looked neighborly, as if each tall formation was an island above a sea of brush and pebbles. He felt like a member of an exclusive club, even though thousands of people visited the place every day. After circling the space and taking in the view for a while, he drew nearer the door, then stepped aside to allow an older man with a cane to exit. His white hair was pulled back in a ponytail, and a droopy mustache covered his upper lip. He smiled joyously.

"Heavenly day," he proclaimed, with a slight southern accent, before gingerly moving on. Brendon nodded, and sheepishly stepped inside. It did feel like a holy place somehow, despite the jostling tourists' flashing cameras. He sat for a moment, looking past the cross out the window. Maybe it was just the scent of the votives, but it felt stuffy and oppressive, as if one could not possibly hope to be penitent enough, selfless enough, or sorrowful enough. He went back out in the sun, brushing against the arm of a young woman with pink highlights in her hair, as she replaced him in the constant flow of pilgrims. Her fresh fragrance replaced that of a dead god. That little exchange of aromas begat a chain of vain remembrance; the smell of Harmony's hair, her soothing voice, her understanding smile, her brief touch, the purity of her rejection.

On the way down the ramp he again encountered the man with the white hair, who had come to a halt and was facing the petrous juncture of mountain and chapel, where cactus clung here and there. He threw something onto the rock and then saw Brendon, who only now noticed the coins collecting in the crevices and hollows of the hill. It was a wishing well of sorts, receptacle of orison and cantrip, pennyworth of thoughts to redeem one's soul.

"Here," the old fellow offered, reaching into his pocket. He placed a big Eisenhower dollar on Brendon's outstretched palm.

"You're not supposed to, but I figure no bird's going to be tempted by something that big," the gentleman explained. It struck Brendon as an odd boon to bestow on a stranger – a dollar coin. How long had the man been hanging on to them, only to fling them at the rocks now; how long had they been in that very pocket? He remembered Dennis's phrase 'what is this person doing in my dream'. I should accept, he thought, precisely because it is so unusual, there is more going on here than meets the eye. He held the heavy coin and fingered it, hesitating.

"Well go on, nobody's looking."

"Am I making a wish, or a prayer?" he asked.

"I'm not sure the big guy distinguishes between the two," he chuckled, the white mustache wriggling above his smile. "Just think of it as a tithe," he added.

Brendon looked at Eisenhower's profile; he hadn't seen one of those since he was a kid. He looked down at the coins others had flung beside the clumps of grass, the pads of prickly pear, the wiry survivors of the desert sun. He shut his eyes and closed his fingers around the hard metal in unintentional repetition of a universal gesture devised to implant intent. He did not wish for a job, he did not pray for Aunt Karen or his mother, or world peace, or an end to starvation in Africa, or the salvation of his soul. He wished for love – not the love of Christ or love for all humanity, but personal, solid, intimate love. He wished, from the center of his being, for prolonged, warm, womanly love, for blessed sexual congress with a female of reasonable attractiveness and sweet, wanton disposition – not in so many words, not in *any* words or with any forethought or consideration. He simply opened his heart in admission of earnest and honest need and tossed the dollar onto the cascade of red rock.

"That's the stuff," the old gentleman laughed. Then he continued his slow descent down the smooth spirallic ramp. The same young woman of the pink highlights passed them both by, bouncing her curves down the curling concrete. Brendon stood a moment watching after her, feeling slightly pathetic, but hoping the size of that coin might carry some weight with the powers that be, and wondering who *were* the powers that be, and if he truly had a beautiful female guide shining with high energy, would she, *could* she grant such a prayer?

* * *

Brendon hadn't painted, really painted with globs out of tubes, since college. He preferred the cleanliness of illustration, the lines and blocks of color, the pencils, markers, and airbrush, the exacting control. Switching to the computer had been easy for him; he thought in terms of composition and design rather than expression. The mess of the palette, the motley goo on the brush, the vagueness of the application of squirrel hair to canvas; all these made him uncomfortable, yet here he was standing in the desert with a ring of colored blobs and a blank white rectangle, trying to remember how to mix pigment rather than RGB values. Every time he looked at the sky he wanted to open the gradient dialogue box. The complexity of the striated cliffs and mesas made his head hurt. He kept trying to remember the keyboard shortcut to load a texture on a brush. He rubbed the back of his neck, where the knot was always tied. Sometimes he just wanted to cut it out, cut it off; he often thought the executioners ax must have brought great relief to its victims.

Carol had invited him to paint with her, but he was far too embarrassed to let her see that he had no skills. Instead, he took her recommendation and drove towards Cottonwood, finding Bill Grey Road, and had set up his kit facing back towards the rocky ridges of Sedona. He had placed the canvas horizontally, to best show the vastness of the landscape. There was nothing to do now but begin.

He filled his brush with cerulean and began laying in blue sky. Then he took another brush and blocked in the khaki foreground. It felt good to dab the color onto the blank field and smoosh it around; liberating, sensual. His neck loosened up a little. Focusing this way, moving his eye from scene to palette to canvas, from model to media to image, removed him from his concerns, from his habitual mental disputes. He was glad he had come.

A breeze tickled the top of his head; he brushed his hair down, and waved his hand at nonexistent flies. He felt hot, perhaps a little dizzy, and made a mental note to buy a hat. He squeezed more red onto the palette and took a long drink from his water bottle. The way the buttes changed through the shadows from salmon to rust to umber, and the rock layers jumped from red to tan to red again, required all his concentration. He mixed and matched, stroked, spread, scrubbed and scumbled and used all his brushes, forgot himself and forgot time until suddenly his water bottle was empty and a jolt of panic wrested him from the enthralling muse.

He took a step backward and was dumbfounded by what he saw on the easel. He had no memory of anything beyond laying in the blue, and trying to match the texture of the red rock. The painting in front of him was an enigma; it was as if he had never seen it before. He could recognize certain segments, remembered working in the green here, pushing out the line there, but where had the whole come from? When had he turned it vertical? The painting included a crude version of the scene, the buttes and the cactus and brush in front of him, but above them he had painted a towering storm, an immense dark thundercloud and curtain of rain streaming straight down on the desert. Brendon looked all around him; there was not a cloud in the sky. Even more bizarre was the upper part of the canvas. Here he had painted a reciprocal curtain streaming *up* from the cloud to the apex of the sky.

"What... the... hell," he muttered. He felt shaky; his legs were weak, his mouth dry, and his head woozy. He pulled out his phone and found that four hours had passed. "Jesus." As quickly as possible, he packed up and headed back to town, stopping at a taco place to cool off, replenish his fluids, and get his strength back with guacamole and sour cream on top. He didn't know what to make of it. It certainly wasn't a good painting; it was horribly done. But something *had* been done. Had it been done by him?

* * *

The touristy area of Sedona is referred to as Uptown. Brendon wandered through it one afternoon, partly to avoid contact with his roommates, whom he was still uncomfortable with for the most part. They were nice enough, but *too* interested in his welfare, only not *his* welfare, his *soul's* welfare, his spiritual growth. Yes, he did want to become a better human being, and he was even willing to concede that something more than mere chance had brought him there, but those people talked, ate, drank and slept nothing but spirit, spirit, spirit. He just wanted to feel normal for a few hours.

He rationalized this escape by halfheartedly looking for a postcard or something to send to his mother, and one for Cass. He tried on a few cowboy hats, and looked at some cowboy art. He thought of taking a jeep tour but was feeling cheap, and dried out. He had a soda on a balcony overlooking the creek bed and watched the tops of the aspens and oaks swaying below, their leaves twisting and glittering in the sun. They seemed to be laughing, because, of all the plants in Red Rock Park, they alone, with their feet in the water, had as much to drink as they wanted.

Ironically, while seeking solitude in the courtyard of Sinagua Plaza, he ran across Dennis. Half a dozen tourists were seated at wrought iron tables, cooling themselves with ice cream cones. His housemate was standing among them, with one foot on a chair, one arm braced on his thigh, his other hand gesturing casually, and the full glib charm evident on his face. They seemed attentive to him, as if they accepted his authority, or friendship. Brendon overheard him, holding forth on dreams, mind events, and the like. He walked past, smiling, gave Dennis a little wave, but the guru either did not see him, or did not deign to acknowledge his presence.

Still chuckling over swami LeRose and his captive audience, Brendon entered a bookstore. It was devoid of people and entirely New Age in content. He decided it was a perfect place to find a card for his woo woo sister. He spied racks in the back. There were the pixie/fairy cards, the Zen cards, the oriental goddess cards, the Buddha cards, the archangel cards, the wolf/coyote cards, the Native American goddess cards, photographic cards of crystals, sunsets, rainbows, red rocks, he went though them all, choosing for his mother a postcard of Coffee Pot Rock. An older, short, round woman came out from behind a curtain wielding a toothy smile. Her short cropped black hair stuck up at odd angles, adding a rumbustious cap to her warm face.

"Can I help you find anything?" she asked.

"No, I'm good."

She went behind the register. He could feel her watching him. Finally he spotted a card with a fanciful painting of a knight in shining armor astride a white unicorn. He chuckled. It would be perfect; he could ask Cass if she had met the prophesied 'someone' yet. He grabbed the envelope and turned toward the counter. The woman was grinning at him from ear to ear. He looked away, handed her his choices.

"Where are you from?" she asked, turning the cards over to scan the bar code.

"LA. But I'm living here now, at least for a while."

"Oh, good. I'm glad," she said happily. She finished poking the register screen, but did not inform him of the total, even though he stood there with his open wallet in his hand. "Isn't Sedona heavenly?"

"Yes. So far," he agreed. "Not sure what I'm doing here, but..."

"Oh, that's okay," she assured him, patting his arm, "You will. Believe me, you wouldn't be here if it weren't in perfect alignment, it's all about divine timing, don't you *feel* that?"

"Well..."

"You know, so many of us have been reassigned," she informed him conspiratorially. He looked blankly at her. She was still grinning that uncalled for grin. "To Sedona," she added, "in the last year or so. You're needed here."

"Uh-huh."

"Yeah," she affirmed enthusiastically, "the veils are getting thinner now. It's very important that you're here at this time." She nodded at him vigorously, as if the force of her assertion could fix this in his mind as undisputed truth. He pointed at his purchase.

"Oh, it's um... $7.87." He pulled a ten from his wallet and handed it to her. She took it, but rather than proceeding to make change, she leaned over the counter and whispered as quietly as her eagerness would allow, "I'm not supposed to say anything unless you pay for a session, but she's just so beautiful!" Brendon looked around to see who was behind him in the shop. There was no one.

"Who?" he asked, looking now through the window at shoppers on the sidewalk.

"No," she corrected, "I'm talking about your lady. Oh, I can see her so clearly! She's so happy you're here. You are right where you're supposed to be, she wants you to know that. And she says you are necessary... for the..."

"...forward progression of events, yes, so I've been told. I guess that line is standard the world over."

"No, no, you mustn't ignore her, Brenda. Is your name Brenda?" she asked, looking perplexed, realizing she had called him by a female name.

"Brendon. But how did you..."

"I'm sorry – Brendon. I just assumed you were aware of her, I've never seen anyone so *clear*."

"Look... maybe you could just give me my change?"

"Of course," the woman said, but stood gazing, then abruptly laughed loudly. Continuing to laugh, she got the change out of the drawer and handed it to him.

"Oh, my," she chuckled. "She has a message for you, I don't know what it's about, but she seems to think you'll know."

Brendon put his wallet in his pocket and picked up the card. He waited a moment, out of courtesy, for the woman to finish her thought.

"She says to tell you, *I like Ike*."

"I like Ike."

"Yeah," she chuckled, "does that mean anything to you?"

"Uhh..."

"Well, it will." Her laughter followed him out of the shop.

* * *

Back in his room, he wrote to his mother:

This is the view from poolside where I'm staying. Job hunting going well, many options. Sorry didn't have time to see Aunt Karen. Much love, Brendon.

Of course none of this was precisely true. He had received zero responses from the resumes, and had pretty much decided he didn't care, and wouldn't waste any more time looking. Apparently some of Dennis's lackadaisical or enlightened attitude had rubbed off; he might still wind up producing some art, but he definitely had not come to Sedona to continue work as usual. Just thinking about logos and headers and stylesheets made the back of his neck knot up. It was *his* dream, damn it, his mind event, and he didn't have to do anything he didn't want to.

When he wrote to Cass, he ran out of space and had to use the back of the card to finish telling her about the odd woman at the bookstore. There at the bottom was the insignia and name of the publisher 'skydancer designs'. Then and only then did it hit him, the connection between the dollar coin tossed at the chapel, and the cryptic message of 'I like Ike', and it stopped him cold, or rather, warm. He got warm all over, his belly heated up as if he'd had a bowl of soup. It was almost quivering with this realization; either it was the most unlikely of coincidences, or there was *something to it*. For the first time, at least since he was a child, Brendon began to believe, really *believe* in something he could not see. This woman, houri or angel, this Skydancer, *must* truly be there with him, at least some of the time, or how could she have known about the Eisenhower dollar? Perhaps she was in his room even then, perhaps sitting on his bed. A tear came to his eye, then a sob from his throat. He covered his mouth and wept hard for a full minute. What the hell's wrong with me, he wondered, recovering himself, chastising himself for being

105

so ridiculous. How could he be moved by someone who wasn't there, how pitiful was that? Except she was there, she had to be. And by all accounts she was incredibly beautiful, shining like the sun. He felt supremely blessed, grateful, unworthy, honored, privileged... loved. And because of her particular message, 'I like Ike', it felt not only like a divine love from a higher place, but also, because of what he had wished for with the coin, like an intimate love, like his most intimate desires were known *and accepted.*

CHAPTER EIGHT

"I'M GETTING too old for this," Brendon sighed, slumping to a sitting position with his back against the canyon wall, just a few feet from a precipitous drop. Dennis joined him; they took out their water bottles and drank, looking out at the chasm they had just conquered.

"Nonsense," he laughed. "If I can hack it, you can hack it." Hiking with Dennis had *seemed* more his speed than climbing with Harmony, but now that they had spent the day trekking the length of Secret Canyon, he realized that attempting the top of a spire with a beautiful woman would have been a quicker, more pleasant way to humiliate himself. They had worked every side path and every available upward course, all in hopes of finding that view which the artist in Ojai had painted. In that regard it had been an unsuccessful day, but they had enjoyed it nonetheless. They sat in silence a while, catching their breath, resting their feet, watching the shadows lengthen.

"I used to think the whole midlife crisis thing was bullshit," Brendon remarked, working the knot at the back of his neck with both hands.

"But then you hit midlife, right?"

"Yeah. And it's like, what the hell just happened? Suddenly I'm tired all the time, can't get up in the morning, all my muscles hurt if I lift a book. It's ridiculous. It seems like... like recovery is very questionable," he laughed.

"Is recovery ever feasible? Recovery implies returning to a previous state, which is impossible. And who wants that anyway? You want to move forward, you want evolution."

"Not if I can't feel better than this, I don't."

"Well... it's all about falling testosterone levels, you know that, right?"

"No, it's not that. I mean I haven't noticed any problem in that area."

"It affects all your bodily functions; metabolism, muscle tone, brain power..."

"Yeah? Well maybe that's it then," Brendon chuckled, "cause all of those are going to hell."

"You gotta get more exercise. Come run with me in the morning."

"More exercise than this? I'll think about it. I've been swimming a little. Running's not really my thing. How can you run in this heat?"

"You just have to recognize that it's all a mind event, including the heat. You know Crystal says 'the body is not a principle'."

"Meaning?"

"Well I take it to mean it's just part of my dream like everything else. It's not real. If the heat's not real, and the body's not real, why can't it perform in the heat? Don't get me wrong, I take plenty of water. And I won't be surprised when it fails, and I wind up sprawled in a cactus someplace. But I figure – push the envelope. Try something new. I'm determined to get back to that place."

"So you think getting sunstroke is going to make you enlightened."

"No. But I mean you can't always do the same things and expect different results, right? And at the very least I'll get in shape."

"I've certainly been trying a lot of new things lately, that's for sure," Brendon noted. "I'll let you know if I have any epiphanies. Except if I get to that place where I'm everywhere and everything, then I'll be you, and you'll be me and you'll know I'm there, so I won't have to tell you."

Dennis laughed. "Hey, how'd it go with Harmony? I understand you had a 'healing session'," he said, making quote marks in the air, "I don't know how you managed that, you lucky bastard, she never offered to do me."

"I guess I just give off a needier vibe, she's all about tuning your vibrations you know."

"I'd get her in tune, I'll tell you that."

"Except she's celibate."

"Or so she claims. I'm not buying it though."

"You think she's gay?"

"No. I think she's celibate, and she will be. Until she isn't," he chuckled, and winked.

"Yeah, we'll see," Brendon grunted skeptically. Inexplicably, he felt ready to defend Harmony's honor.

"I sort of made a pass at her," he confessed.

"No shit?"

"I was trying that trick you told be about – 'what's this person doing in my dream' – and it seemed pretty obvious to me what she was doing there, but... not so obvious to her."

Dennis burst out laughing.

"Now I'm wondering what the fuck *you're* doing in my dream," Brendon continued, "filling my head with bullshit about dreaming."

"You just haven't figured out what she's *really* doing in your dream," Dennis said with a wink, and laughed some more, "Or me."

"Yeah. Well... all that aside, it was good. She was talking about a lot of stuff I couldn't follow and conquering the lower three worlds, which seems to be the party line in that house. Then she was saying that the vibrations of the chakras are related, like octaves and harmonics in music. I've never heard anyone describe them like that. And I could kind of feel where they are, when she used those singing bowls on me."

"Oh yeah?"

"The way she put it was, she was *inducing* a new wave pattern. I thought that was a cool way to describe it. Made me think of thought patterns. Cass, my sister, has been trying to get me to change my thought patterns for years."

"Since you hit midlife, right?" Dennis surmised.

"Yeah. Says I'm stuck in self-defeating patterns, you know, seeing myself as old."

"And she's younger than you, right?" he chuckled.

"That pretty much sums it up."

"But she's right, though, you're not old. You got forty, fifty years ahead of you, which you could enjoy if you approach it right."

"I know, I know. Just not easy for me to do, usually. But when Harmony said *wave* pattern instead of thought pattern, you know, it made me think of it in a whole new light. Like the physics of it instead of the psychology of it. Makes me feel less... unstable, I guess, and more like I'm just, you know, like she said – in need of a tune up. Which is what Harmony basically said she was doing, tuning me like tuning a piano, which right there made me feel better about my thought patterns. It was pretty cool."

"So she was right, she *did* induce a new wave pattern, the one where you don't have to feel like any of it's your *fault*."

"Yeah. I gotta remember to thank her."

"I'll remind you. Or I could thank her for you," he suggested with that indolent charm, winking again.

"Good luck with that."

"Well at least now you know what she is doing in your dream. She's inducing new patterns."

"I guess so."

"Now I have to explain to her what she's doing in *my* dream," Dennis said slyly.

"You *are* dreaming, boy."

They sat quietly for a minute, enjoying the view, sharing the height they had reached, neither anxious to start down again.

"I feel like Butch Cassidy," Brendon mused, "I swear if there was water down there, I'd jump off."

"Well if you're Butch, then I'm Sundance. I can swim, but there's no way in hell I would jump voluntarily."

"Not even if you were being chased by a Pinkerton posse?"

"Pinkertons I could consider as a mind event. Drowning would be a little tougher to, uh... incorporate into my world view," Dennis admitted.

"Right, the mind event. But if you drowned, wouldn't that be like having your water balloon identity burst?" Brendon goaded, "You would immediately become the entire volume of oak creek."

"I'm sorry, have I given you the impression I was a Master of the mental plane?" he chuckled, "It was one brief experience about eight years ago."

"Just yanking your chain."

"Not that I wouldn't like to recreate it, but I don't think diving off a cliff would do it."

"So you haven't experienced anything like that again, huh? Not even with meditating every week at the house?"

"Actually, I meditate almost every day, at least for a few minutes. But no, I can't seem to get back to that timeless, omnipresent feeling. But I've been thinking about pushing the envelope there, too."

"Meaning?"

"You know, making the mind conducive to... alternative realities."

"How would you go about that, LSD?"

"No, and not by jumping off a cliff. But if you know anyone that can get hold of some peyote, that might be something to consider," Dennis chuckled. "It worked for Castaneda, right?"

"I'm afraid I don't know anything about the procurement of illegal substances," Brendon laughed. "I've got enough trouble making my mind conducive to this reality."

"Well, maybe we can revisit that another time. There's a guy Ben I know; he's Hopi, I'm thinking of asking him, he might know someone. One thing I've been seriously considering is spending a couple days and nights out in the desert someplace. You know, away from the city lights, away from any distractions. Maybe a fast. Just water."

"Yeah? Sounds intense."

"I was hoping you might join me. With a buddy it would be less risky. What do you say, are you up for it?"

"Uh..."

"Come on, it would be intense; just the thing to break through the veil of dreams. To be really out there in it, right, no pretense, sleep under the stars naked before God, not even a tent. Give you a chance to face your fears, and see that they're just part of your dream, coming out of your own mind. It's like when a child wakes in their darkened bedroom, you know, is that a monster, or a pile of clothes? I think it would be a good exercise to really force some issues... I mean, it wouldn't be a life and death situation, but the potential would be there. You'd come right up against your demons. It would be cathartic."

112

"Well I don't have any demons. That I know of. But I think I've had enough of catharsises. Catharsii?"

"Cathar-*sees*, I think."

"Well I've had enough catharses to last me a lifetime. I'm just hoping for a little peace and quiet."

"And a little piece of ass, right?"

"Amen. So how 'bout you, what's your monster? Are you afraid of the dark, or the stars?" Brendon chuckled.

"Ha ha, very funny. So you have no fears, huh? Rattlesnakes? Bears? Wolves?"

"Well I'm not going to seek them out. But I don't think they would seek me out either."

"So you'll do it then," Dennis stated with a smile.

"Um... except for the naked before God part, I guess. Do we get to use sleeping bags?"

"Well, I wasn't going to waste the experience by actually sleeping."

"But doesn't it get pretty cold at night?"

"Fine, if you're gonna be a pussy about it," Dennis grinned.

"I don't actually have a sleeping bag," Brendon noted.

"You can use mine," he offered conclusively. "We better get going if we're going to get back to the car before dark."

"I thought you weren't afraid of the dark, Denise," Brendon teased as they got to their feet and started the climb back down into the canyon.

"It's not the dark, Brenda, believe me. It's just not a good idea to be in the canyons at night."

"So this is not where you want to come face to face with God?"

"Hell no. I was thinking west, towards Cottonwood, where there's open ground and you can see what's coming."

"You're really scared of being out here, aren't you?"

Dennis paused and turned back towards him, an uncharacteristically grave look on his face.

"Listen, there are those who don't want anyone snooping around out here, especially at night. Don't think our movements today went unobserved." Then he continued down the path.

"Who? What are you getting at?" Brendon asked, but Dennis only waved the back of his hand and quickened his pace.

"You're so full of shit," he muttered, following.

It was quite dark by the time they got back to the car; they had to use their phones for light along the last part of the trail. They were very careful to observe the stacked rocks, or cairns, as Dennis referred to them, that marked the trail. His customary mischievous good humor did not return. They headed back to town along the curvy road in silence, until a sound like cicadas rose, hovered, and fell, as if they had driven through a nest of the things. Dennis lowered his window and leaned his head over, choosing an odd time, Brendon thought, to do some stargazing. Suddenly he noticed that all the dashboard maintenance lights had lit up, simultaneously. It was only for a split second, but he was sure he had seen them. Then the dash went dark; Brendon felt the power go dead under his foot. He couldn't hear if the engine had cut out or not, because of the loud cicadas. The car continued coasting down a long grade. Just as they were coming to a curve and he began to panic because the power steering was unresponsive, the lights flashed on again, then blinked out one by one, as if it were starting up. The clock said 7:58. Wasn't it just at 7:52?

"Shit, did you see that?"

"No, what?" Dennis asked, pulling his eyes away from the stars.

"All the engine lights lit up, then went black, then came on again. I think the engine quit."

"No, it's running."

"I mean it quit then started itself up again."

"Huh."

"Man, that was so weird."

"If you say so. I didn't notice anything."

* * *

The coarse clothes floating to the floor, the luxuriant hair at last spread free of its binding, immersing him in perfume that was not perfume but a passage to realms supernal, the round and responsive hips in his hands, the yoga body arching below him; by this glamour was he bound. He gripped her without restraint, pulling her to him; her eyes seemed eager, actually requesting all the thrust he could muster, yet incredibly loving, as if grateful *to him,* as if he were doing something for her, and not the other way around. There was a rush, a powerful flood of energy beyond anything he had ever known, spiraling up the column and out the top of his head, taking their being with it, until they were outside, above, free of the durance of ages, suddenly weightless, buoyed by utter joy. Seeing them coupled below, those dense forms of sorrow, he realized it was only a dream, and thoughts filed in, about sound, and celibacy, and Dennis and his mantra of waking up and making inquiry, so he asked her what she was doing in his dream, and she smiled, that was all, and he remembered the offering of silver and his earnest request at the chapel, and before in the car on his way from California, and a hundred thousand other iterations of desire, and he wept with gratitude, then remorse for the wasted theurgy he had squandered on selfish ends when he might have used it to heal Aunt Karen or the hole in the ozone or to transmute the ulcerous garbage gyres of the oceans, or even to fortify himself with enough courage to wish something for others, and she held him as he wept, placing a hand on his chest and another on his back, rocking him, singing *namastasyai namastasyai namastasyai namo namah,* until sleep overtook him again.

He woke with a presence in his chest, sorrow, or joy, he could not tell which. It was not yet morning. Diaphanous remnants of a dream were just out of reach; he felt as if he had been with a lover. He rose in the dark and found his way to the bathroom, feeling grateful, knowing he had been blessed. Her touch lingered, loving and tangible, hands holding his face, eyes seeking his out, sweet lips against his. He had always been deeply appreciative of nocturnal gifts from Eros or Venus or whoever was in charge of that particular heaven, but this one was different, almost more real than waking, as if his partner had truly been there and he were the one in *her* dream and he should be asking what he was doing there, what he had done to deserve such a gift, so that he might repeat the act and receive that gift again. He made a mental note to seek out Harmony in the morning and ask if she had dreamt any good dreams. It was silly, he knew, to be encouraged by a dream, but he went back to bed looking forward to the morrow.

In the morning, Brendon opened the blinds to the sun. Rune was out on the patio, standing in one of those nonhuman Gumby poses. Harmony was wearing her usual yoga attire, her mat was unrolled beside Rune's, but she was sitting on the edge of the pool with her feet in the water. The sight of her brought back his intention to seek her out, to ask about her dreams, and to a lesser extent, it brought back the dream itself, a wistful remembrance of luxuriant hair and sweet kisses. It was maddening that the trifling thoughts he had after waking should be more permanent in his mind than the delicious dream itself, that all he really was left with was a sense of it being intensely sexual, and loving, and that it somehow involved Harmony, else why would he have decided to seek her out. Beyond that, he couldn't clearly recall.

Dennis popped up out of the pool and sat beside her, his thick hair dripping down his back. He was leering at her, inducing her with his suasive speech, plying his indolent charm. It was clear that winks had been wielded. Harmony laughed, and kicked splashes at him. He grabbed her arm and forced her into the water; she pulled him in after her.

"Shit," Brendon said aloud. As he became more alert and his mind grasped for the pleasant release of the dream, he had the sinking feeling that he had failed some kind of test. Then a thought resurfaced, a wisp of hair, the feeling of her hands, the urging of her eyes, and a disturbing notion that the hands and the eyes were trying to get his attention, not his affection, that the sweet lips perhaps were not kissing, but had mouthed an admonition – *you're making a mistake.* This phrase had been forcefully placed in his head. Because she claims to be celibate, he reasoned, that the mistake, to think they would ever be together, to pin any expectations on her whatsoever. Or was the mistake to *want* her, to dream of, or pray for her love? He was supposed to be conquering the lower three worlds, bringing that energy up to the throat chakra or the heart chakra, or the crown. Yes, that must be the mistake – his wish at the chapel had been fulfilled, in a sense, by the dream, but prayer should never be squandered on personal desires, on the lower worlds. The *full* force of intention could only ever come into play when directed for the greater good, which is why only a dream, and not Harmony herself, was available to him.

117

* * *

They were sitting beside an old 40's style camper which looked like it had been parked in that spot, between an old stable cum crystal emporium and the creek embankment, since the last stable hand had slept in it. It now served as an office/bookshop for a local UFOlogist. The occasion was a UFO discussion group. Carol had invited him, and he had felt obligated to go because he had twice declined her invitation to paint *en plein air*. She was beside him listening intently, that kind smile lighting up her face. It was still difficult for Brendon to link her grandmotherly look with the paintings he had seen in the studio – the vehicles hiding in the sky, the faces lurking in the shadows of canyons.

Also present were the southern gentleman with the bushy white mustache and his genteel wife. He had nodded at Brendon when they arrived. Their presence, and Carol's, made him comfortable at a gathering that would, under other circumstances, have left him so ill at ease that Brendon would not have remained.

"I don't know if they're Men in Black, or Air Force, or shape-shifters, but they've been harassing me for months. I haven't been able to get a good night's sleep since I got here." The speaker was a young woman named Brittany. She wore a large men's plaid shirt, baggy jeans, and thick workboots. Her arms were crossed firmly across her chest. She was clearly disturbed, but then, Brendon rationalized, going without good sleep will do that to you. Beside her sat a soft looking man named Greg, still in baby fat, with thick glasses and that air which made one doubt he could catch a ball from two feet away.

"And when you say harass, what do you mean exactly?" This question came from the hostess of the group, the UFOlogist, a brassy woman with a big blonde wig named Debra. Nothing, it seemed, could faze her.

"I wish I could remember details. I can't. I've seen them following me, these guys wearing big sunglasses always driving white vans. I know they've taken me, but I can't remember what's actually happened."

"Well it's not uncommon for your memory to be erased after abduction," the hostess averred, "And it's a technology the Greys have shared with the military, so it could be anyone. Did you see any blue lights?"

"Blue? No. Not that I remember."

"What about noises, any unusual noises?"

"Yeah, I keep hearing this whirring, buzzing sound outside my window, only it sounds like it's passing overhead. Then I get this feeling like I can't move, and I fall asleep, only it doesn't feel like falling asleep, it feels like passing out, and I wake up with this awful feeling and I try to remember but I can't."

"Someone told me the sound they make is like cicadas," the mustached gentleman reported. Brendon got a sinking feeling in his stomach, remembering the whirring noise he had heard just before the dash lights went out, that night when he and Dennis were coming back from Secret Canyon.

"That's during take off or landing, while the vortex is changing frequencies," Carol noted.

"Yes, it can be similar. Others have reported no noise at all," Debra pointed out. "But tell me, Brittany, can you be more specific about the awful feeling? In what way awful?"

"Just... filthy, totally humiliating."

"You felt violated."

"Yes."

"Well, they could be harvesting your eggs."

"Oh my," the wife of the mustached gentleman exclaimed, "What would they do then, implant them back in?"

"They could. They have. The last time I was taken I was shown an infant, and made to understand that it had come from me. I didn't carry the creature, but I've known some who have."

"Oh, how awful!"

Brendon was inclined to disregard such outrageous statements, but he was curious what they thought about something Dennis had implied.

"I've heard there's an installation of some kind hidden in one of the canyons back here, do you know anything about that?" he asked.

"Yes, it's beneath Secret Mountain. Almost that entire mesa has been hollowed out. There are entrances in several canyons."

"So it's like a big ol' gopher nest," the southerner suggested with a smile.

"If the gophers were stealing your eggs and creating hybrids and plotting to take over the world," a young woman sitting next to Brittany said angrily.

"I was told it was beneath that fancy resort in Boynton Canyon," said Greg, "and that the rich people don't really stay there, what they're doing is paying to be transported to other planets through the stargate."

Brendon stifled a laugh, and felt sorry for being dismissive.

"I've seen the return flights landing just behind Kachina Rock," Debra agreed.

He tried not to think how weird and crazy it all was, but to ask himself what they were doing in his dream. He tried to open his heart, as had been suggested to him so many times recently, but a part of him was pretty sure it was all a set up to entertain tourists. Maybe this Brittany was an actress Debra paid to help sell books.

"The important thing to remember," Carol said quietly, "is to keep your vibration high, no matter what. You have to forgive them," she said to Brittany directly. "You can't stop them, you can't always control what happens, you can only control how you react. You mustn't let your emotions take over."

"Easy for you to say, have you ever been abducted?" Brittany barked.

"No," Carol admitted, "Not that I recall."

"Well I have," Debra declared, "several times. And I have to say Brittany, she's right. You're better off if you can just look at it as you would any other experience in life. If it's happening, it's happening, you can't fight them. If you cooperate, they might let you remember more."

"If you're vibrating fear, you're going to attract frightening things," the southern woman said slowly. Her husband nodded.

"Ezekiel was an abductee," he averred, and quoted from scripture: "...and their appearance and their work was as it were a wheel in the middle of a wheel."

"Yes, that's very much what some of the crafts look like, on the outside," Debra continued, "But you wouldn't know it from the inside. Nothing's moving on the inside. Once, they showed me all around the inside and let me see the power source."

"What was it?" Carol asked.

"Oh it was a fantastic blue light. The whole ship was like two pyramids stacked on top of each other. Only when it was spinning did it take on a disc like appearance. And in the center was this blue flame, but not like fire, more like electricity or something."

"Plasma," Carol suggested.

"Maybe so. It wasn't hot, but it was so powerful. I've never felt so good as when I came back from that. It's all in my book."

"Have you tried hypnosis to help you remember?" the southern woman asked Brittany.

"No. Look, why would I want to remember? I just want it to stop."

"I feel that way sometimes, but sometimes I think I can hardly wait for it to happen again," Debra admitted.

"You must say to them," Carol instructed Brittany, "I allow only beings of light. And use the prayer, 'The light of God surrounds me; the love of God enfolds me; the power of God protects me; the presence of God watches over me. Wherever I am, God is."

"Shit, you're so naive, lady," Brittany spat, "you think these fucking sadistic rapists are going to listen to fucking prayers? Jesus!"

"They are entities in the universe, and as such must obey spiritual law," Carol countered. "The prayer is not for *them* to hear, it is for you. It is not they who must change their vibration, it is you. You are entering their frequency. If you truly wish for it to stop, you must switch your polarization from fear to love. This prayer is a useful method to accomplish this."

"It's your fear that keeps you seeing them. If you want them to stop, you need to stop being afraid of them," Greg suggested.

"Screw this," Brittany cursed, rising.

"It's not spiritual," he assured her, "it's quantum mechanics. Things don't really exist until we observe them." But she had left the little gathering and was out of earshot.

"Oh, the poor dear," the gracious woman observed, "she's in such pain."

"Yes," Debra agreed. "She is not yet ready to release it."

Brendon sat without listening during the remainder of the meeting, as the others discussed optimal sighting locations, video techniques, avoiding government agencies, and similar issues. He was pondering too intensely what he had already heard to absorb more. He wondered if alien beings had really turned off his vehicle the other night. He wondered how Debra could be so nonchalant if she had really been abducted. He wondered if there was a reason *he* was in *Brittany's* dream, if there was anything he could have done or could still do to help her, and what, at this stage, would constitute help. He wondered if Skydancer was in his dream or if he were in hers, and if she was a shining angel or a beautiful dead woman or an alien life form playing with his mind, a shape-shifter showing itself to clairvoyants, whispering in their ears, biding its time. Was he saner than Brittany? Was he stronger?

"Do you think that things don't exist until we observe them, from a physics standpoint?" he asked Carol on the way home, "Dennis keeps trying to tell me everything is only a mind event."

"That's not entirely true," Carol argued, "Nor is it accurate to say that immaterial things don't exist. Observance, sensing of any kind, awareness itself, fixes the wave into particles, yes, but you must not forget that all entities can sense themselves in some way. The Earth, for instance, senses itself. That is what makes ordinary 'reality' so undeniable to most of us, so solid. We are part of the body of Earth, and as such *we* are being observed, sensed by the Earth itself. Our inability to perceive beings composed at lower or higher densities does not infringe on their eubstance."

"Their what?"

"Eubstance. The property of holding shape; their ability to maintain a waveform. Or, put another way, to believe in their own existence."

"So aliens are there whether we are afraid of them or not, whether we believe in them or not."

"Most likely, although the term 'alien' is probably not appropriate. Only the Earth decides what is alien to its being and what is not."

"But you've seen them, right? And the spacecraft they use?"

"What makes you say that?"

"Well, your paintings. The UFOs in your paintings."

"Perhaps that is what I've painted, perhaps not. I can't say for certain. Sometimes the anomalies seem like vehicles in the clouds, but more often when I look at them I think they are mere glimpses, portions of a larger whole. When I paint, it's as though a part of me is set free, expanded, and pushing the envelope of normal sensation. I believe I am seeing beings that are always there, they haven't arrived from some other planet, they exist all around us, in myriad forms from micro to macroscopic."

"So you don't believe in abduction?"

"I didn't say that. It's entirely possible. Spiritual laws are also laws of physics. Fear is a powerful attractive force. If you want to avoid abduction, fill your heart with love. Inclusion makes invasion impossible."

While Brendon mulled that over, they arrived back at the house and said goodnight.

CHAPTER NINE

"JUST relax," his authoritative voice directed. "Nothing is required of you now. Remain attentive, but relaxed."

Do I look that bad, Brendon wondered, or is there some sort of competition going on between them? He was back in the therapy room, sitting opposite Rune, who had insisted on giving him a full channeled reading and healing session, to facilitate his acclimation to the local energy, and spiritual growth in general. Having said yes to Harmony, he had found it difficult to decline the honor.

The thick drapes had been drawn, blocking the afternoon sun. Rune was sitting cross-legged on some kind of kimono or robe spread out on the floor. It was embroidered with gold symbols; sun and moon, yin yang, the ouroboros, the ankh, and many others. Brendon did his best to imitate his posture with the help of several large cushions. A lit candle was between them, along with a large clear quartz cluster. Ayurvedic chants played softly in the background.

"I don't need to touch you for healing to take place," he explained. "Once we invite the energy in, it will go where it's needed. If you feel nothing, don't worry, it's completely normal. You don't need to feel anything to receive. If you notice a feeling of warmth, or a tingle, just allow it. Say yes to it. Know you are safe. Only positive energy will come through. Okay?"

"Okay." Brendon was amused by this little speech, yet comforted by it. Rune's gaunt face had taken on a grave aspect; *he* at least was taking this very seriously.

"Then we will see if anyone wants to speak with you."

Brendon nodded. Rune closed his eyes and began breathing deeply. He scooped his arms up in the air, pulled them down in front of him, palms together, and repeated the process a few times.

"Relax your body. Relax your toes, and your feet. Your calves, your thighs, all are relaxing now."

Brendon smiled because they *were* relaxing; he could feel the tension leave the muscles as they were named. The little man had an unusually forceful, yet calming manner.

"Let your abdomen relax. Your chest, your arms, your neck, your fingers, are all quite happy to be still." Rune paused and scooped the air again. He stood and gestured over Brendon's head. "Relax your mind. Thoughts come and go. Let them go. Emotions come and go. Let them go. Be still."

Brendon might have fallen asleep, had he been lying down.

"I call upon the Light of pure love to descend," Rune invoked. "I call on all the cells in the physical body and the subtle bodies and all the parts of cells in these bodies to be activated... to cleanse and clear all channels... to rejuvenate... to move where they are needed... to assist the initiation of the body to higher frequencies..."

He said something else, but Brendon didn't catch it; he was busy noticing. He noticed a feeling of warmth at the back of his neck, and he noticed a phrase: *move where they are needed*. And his half dreaming mind matched this to a another phrase which had recently been deposited and had yet to be consigned to cold storage, *so many of us have been reassigned. You're needed here.* And he saw a map of Arizona, and fleets of platelets

126

streaming along I-17, and he decided he was dreaming and opened his eyes.

Rune had stopped speaking. He had his old body folded up cross-legged, a small pillow under his butt, his hands resting on his knees. His eyes were closed, chin in the air, the thin mustache quivering slightly as he breathed. It almost looked as if he were chanting, but there was no sound. Now his brow raised slightly, his head turned just a little to the left, as if he was listening or questioning some one or thing to that side. The small eyes opened and Rune smiled, except Brendon had the distinct impression it was not Rune at all, the expression wasn't familiar. This smile seemed to fill out his face in a rounder way; he seemed softer, kinder. He looked directly into Brendon's eyes in a way he had not done before. Brendon did not look away. A wave of something washed over him, warm, affectionate, soothing.

"Do you have a question for me?" It was Rune's voice, but not his manner. It was asked with the smile still in tact, with joy and sweetness in its timbre. Brendon chuckled.

"No," he said, "I didn't know... okay, what the hell am I doing here?" he laughed.

Rune's body jerked, his eyes closed and opened again. The smile disappeared, and so did the gentle manner. He glared for a second, then the eyelids slowly closed again.

"Wait... what just happened?"

"She popped out," the channel explained, without opening his eyes. His voice was flat and expressionless.

"Popped out?"

"They enter the bubble smoothly from the left, clockwise being the direction of Spirit into Matter. Frequently the method of exit is through the central jet, which moves rapidly counter-clockwise. Matter into Spirit. It can cause a spasm in the body. I'm alright."

"Did I do something wrong?"

"No," Rune sighed, his eyes still shut. "It was me. My shock and... annoyance with the rudeness of your question caused the vortex to squeeze closed and she was forced out. I apologize. I'm not sure I can become still enough to allow entrance again. But I can ask on your behalf."

Properly chastised, Brendon fell silent, and waited. After a few minutes, Rune began to speak again, in his normal, stern voice.

"She says you are to find something. Hidden knowledge. You know where. She has told you where. Shown you."

What? Brendon checked himself from blurting out loud. He didn't want to disturb the process any more than he already had.

"You have been looking, but you aren't ready yet..."

Now came to mind the print he had been given, presumably by this same spirit, this shining woman. Yes, he had looked for that view, with Dennis in Secret Canyon. But what if he had found the place? What then?

As if in answer to this unspoken question, Rune continued. "There is a baetyl. When you are ready it will be revealed, and it will reveal."

Again, Brendon kept his mouth shut and tried to focus on retaining what was said, but in the pauses of Rune's message Dennis's veiled warnings and tales about the canyons and Men in Black intruded on him.

"She wants to assure you of your safety. ' I've got your back', she says."

Once more the channel had responded to his exact concern. It was uncanny.

"Your role is of vital importance," he went on, "There is no other who can find it... in this window. It is difficult to reach... few have been there; all of those have passed it by. To the uninitiated, it is not meaningful... you must make your own path."

What the heck, he wanted to shout, it's not meaningful to *me*.

"Don't worry, when the time comes, it will be easy for you... and know always... you are loved."

This jarred something loose in Brendon's chest, which rose as water to his eyes. Immediately he felt like a fool who had fallen for a cheap trick, because who *doesn't* feel alone in this world, it was too easy for someone with the audacity to utter such phrases to convince a mark of their 'psychic' abilities. He hastened to wipe the tears away, but they recurred, because another part of him had come to believe that this shining woman was real. There had been too many coincidences, she had come to him through too many people, knew him too well to be nonexistent. In the last several minutes, she, or Rune, had known what he was thinking, answered every unasked question, allayed every unspoken fear. His old mental habits wanted to disregard it all, but the notion that someone with the capacity to traverse worlds, this angel or goddess, was in any way concerned for *him,* found value in him – loved him – was far more powerful than his old chains of cynicism, distrust, and apathy. It seemed no matter how many times he dried his eyes, they continued to leak.

Rune had paused a long while, as if waiting to hear if there were more to tell.

"Thank you," he said at last.

"No problem," Brendon muttered. Now the channel stirred, shifted his legs and opened his eyes, indicating that he was done meditating.

"I was thanking Spirit," he explained, "Gratitude is the key to progress."

"Yes, thank you. I'm sorry, I didn't mean to..." he couldn't finish this meaningless sentence, a lump crowded his vocal chords. Yes, there was a great deal of gratitude.

"How are you feeling?" Rune asked gently. Brendon did not meet his eyes, he found himself in the uncomfortable position of having powerful reciprocal feelings for the unseen woman, for Skydancer, yet having no available release but to transfer them, inappropriately, to the medium. He feared that if he looked him in the eye, this pent up emotion would discharge like an electrical pulse in Rune's direction, to where he had seen the other, the woman, shining through.

"Weird," he responded, eyes still moist.

"Well you are not yet accustomed to the influx of energy. As it moves through your system, things may come up. Emotions, memories. Just let them go. The Light does two things as it circulates the torus; first it cleanses, flushes out the old toxins, on the physical, emotional, and mental planes. Secondly, it repairs and restructures the etheric framework. Eventually, as the work continues, your new geometry will be stable enough to withstand a higher vibrational frequency."

"Shit," Brendon exclaimed, his voice cracking in a half-chuckle, finally looking at him, finally willing to let him see the tears, to admit his weakness, to admit that, at least in this unfamiliar world of energy, light, and invisible beings, Rune was the bigger man. "Why does everyone keep saying that? What the hell's wrong with my vibration?"

"No no no no no," he corrected with assurance, "there is no judgment. There is nothing *wrong* with any vibration. It is simply a matter of where you want to go, who you want to be. Clearly since you are here, in Sedona, in this house, whether your personality is aware of it or not, your soul wants to raise the vibration of your vehicle."

Brendon sighed and wiped his eyes.

"Your body, your emotional body, your mental body, this constitutes the threefold vehicle of the soul," Rune continued. "This is not philosophy, it's physics, ask Carol. What I understand from her is that we are made up of a series of nested standing waves; resonances that don't normally go anywhere, but sustain the information, the specific frequencies which separate you from the rest of the universe. Your awareness itself forms the waveguide that reflects the energy you consist of back upon itself, and keeps it contained. The soul desires more contact with the personality, more access to the vehicle. To achieve this, the vibration must be adjusted. Fluctuations in the vibrations are happening all the time, what you must learn is to control them. It's what I must do every time I give a reading. Its like when you're tuning a radio dial and you go past the clearest signal, just a little higher, to see if it will get clearer, but instead it gets fuzzier, or maybe you get two stations at once? Because to make contact, the entities must lower their vibration, you see, and I must raise mine, we meet in the margins, in the *in-between*. Eventually, through the practice of meditation, you will be tuned to an entirely new station. When a child has a growth spurt, the first step is to gain weight. They are preparing, absorbing nutrients, then they might grow four inches in a few months. It's the same with your consciousness. The energy builds, a new frequency is induced, and you are initiated into a new state of awareness. This changes the volume of the waveguide, of the etheric bubble or the egoic orb, if you will, so that more energy can be absorbed, embodied, and used for the benefit of the One. There is no judgment. There is only evolution, movement along the Path."

Brendon shook his head. It was too much to take in. He felt Rune studying him, judging him even as he said no judgment. Nothing was said for a few minutes while he processed.

"What does she look like?" he asked. There was a hint of disdain on Rune's face, as if he thought the question was unimportant, or inappropriate.

"Well, she might look one way to me, and another way to you, if you saw her, and a third way to another clairvoyant. She might look one way to me today, and quite different the next time I see her, *if* I see her again. In any case, it isn't the same as seeing someone here, in the dense physical. They have no dense physical; it is in part an image manufactured by the meeting of our minds for our mutual benefit, to aid in the transmission of information. They flow into me, I flow into them. So the image may change in accordance with what they need to get across, but at the same time it must hold true to their essential nature. In this case, her essential nature is very high. She appears as a woman of near perfect beauty. Her image is unusually clear, her dress is minimal, her hair is worn up, with gold combs, or a tiara of some sort. She has a great deal of gold and turquoise jewelry, bracelets, rings, and necklaces. And when she smiles she shines with the radiance of sunlight."

Brendon chuckled, believing, yet still in disbelief. "What does she want with *me*?"

"Though I have asked myself that question," Rune sighed, "There is no doubt whatever in her mind. And you have it backwards. She wants nothing from you. It is you who need her, your soul that has sought her out. She is with you to assist."

"Assist in what?"

"In finding the baetyl."

"And why do I want to find a beetle, is this like a scarab, some kind of special beetle? I don't get it."

132

"Not a bug, this is B A E T Y L. It's a sacred stone."

"Well, I'm not looking for one of those either."

"Oh, but you are," the little man insisted, standing. He put his hand on the other's shoulder. "Brendon, you are a *tertön*. She is your *dakini*."

Brendon rubbed his face and made a mouth noise of exasperation.

"Look, don't worry about it for now," Rune suggested, concluding the reading. "As she said, when you are ready, it will all make sense. We are not always prepared for what the soul contracts for us, but everything required is made available. You have already expanded in the short time you have been here. Sedona is a place where many things are accelerated."

"You can say that again, and I still won't know what the hell you're talking about," Brendon chuckled, walking to the door. But a part of him did know, he realized, a part of him had wanted to pinpoint the print locale from the moment he saw it.

"Well if anything comes up in the next couple days, that is if there's anything you want to talk about, or if you'd like another treatment, you know where I live," Rune said, with a rare smile. Brendon nodded and went back to his room.

He knew he had called for her, and not just his soul, he had consciously wished for a loving woman with all his heart and a silver dollar at the sacred well. To this she had responded, saying *I like Ike.* Of course he had had a fleshier woman in mind, yet he could not deny that he had already felt more love from Skydancer than from anyone since he and Sharon were together.

He opened his computer, searched 'baetyl', and read about Zeus's eagles flying from opposite poles and simultaneously locating the navel of the world – the omphalos. He read about the hollowed, carved stone at the temple of Delphi; about the high iron content of meteorites, and the black stone of the Ka'aba.

133

Then he looked up *tertön*, which made no sense since he was not, nor ever had been, nor ever intended to be a Buddhist, moreover it seemed like a *tertön* generally sought hidden texts, whereas he was apparently looking for a meteorite. In any case, Rune was no doubt speaking figuratively, making an analogy. He did, however, come across an intriguing reference to *dakini*:

> These tantric deities, acting as consorts, are thought to be very important to tertöns. The practice of sexual yoga is used to accelerate and enhance their capacity for realization.

This excited Brendon a great deal, his stomach tightened in anticipation of undreamed of sexual abandon with a woman of tremendous expertise and 'enhanced capacity for realization'. How it would ever occur, seeing as he was in one world and she in another, and the world she was in did not, apparently, insist upon physical bodies, was, as yet, a mystery to him, but he had been assured that all would be made clear in time. He laughed at the stupidity of it, the arrogance of it, but he could still feel the lingering *energy* or whatever it was which she had given him. He knew it had not come from himself, it had come through Rune. He even liked Rune more now, but he was quite certain that Rune and Skydancer were separate beings, and that one of them loved him in a way the other did not.

* * *

"Dead Man's Pass? Seriously?" This designation was torched into a piece of steel plate, and gave the same sort of impression as if Yosemite Sam had delineated it right in front of them with bullet holes.

"Yeah," Dennis chuckled, "Supposed to have been an Indian grave around here somewhere. I'm thinking maybe that print is showing a view from Mescal Mountain, over there on the right. The trail gets pretty steep, and to get all the way to the top is going to be rough, but the view is worth it, even if it's not the one you're looking for. I was up there once a long time ago."

"Sounds good."

As they started off, moving briskly in the early light, a shiny white van entered the parking lot.

"Did you bring your camera?"

"No. Well, I've got my phone."

"You'll want to get a picture to compare, no?"

"Sure. Yeah, I have a shot of the print on my phone that we can use. I'm supposed to be looking for a rock, too."

"A rock? There are plenty of rocks out here..."

"I mean like a special stone, like a sacred marker or something. Maybe there are some petroglyphs up there?"

"Uh... I don't think so. I've never heard of there being any up there anyway. This area is pretty well covered on a regular basis."

Dennis looked back and frowned. Brendon followed his gaze. There were two men on the trail behind them, wearing matching white button-down shirts, black pants, black ties and reflective sunglasses. They looked harmless enough, despite their odd hiking attire.

"So this artist in Ojai told you to look for petroglyphs?" Dennis asked, quickening his pace.

"No. No, it was Rune. He gave me a healing and reading couple nights ago."

"Oh Christ."

"Well. Whatever. He said there's a stone which only I can find, which will be revealed to me, and which will reveal."

Dennis laughed. Brendon did not mention the *dakini*.

"He's messing with your head, Pearce. Don't let him get you all weirded out with his metaphysics game. The stone is a metaphor for your higher self, your soul. They want you to get in touch with your soul."

"Who does?"

"All of them. Crystal. Rune, Harmony. Even Michael."

"But not you," Brendon laughed, "You just want me to spend forty nights in the desert facing my demons and having catharses."

"Well, sure, I think it'll free you up. But I'm not gonna bullshit you about it. We all want to be in touch with something bigger or better than ourselves; at least I'm honest with you. I mean, here's the thing, there's no difference between my soul and your soul. If you get in touch with it."

Again, Dennis turned slightly to look behind. The two men were still there, and seemed to be gaining on them.

"What are they, Mormons?" Brendon chuckled.

"Maybe they're looking to proselytize the cypress," Dennis suggested with a smile.

"They want to get in touch with your soul."

"That must be it."

"Lucky for you this is all part of a mind event, right? The soul is just another character in your dream."

"Not exactly. But you're not going to find it in a rock, no matter how many petroglyphs are on it. Well, I mean you *could*. But not the way Rune means. Besides, you'd have to go way out to discover anything. Like I said, these mesas have been pretty well scoured."

"Yeah. You're right. I fell for it. The little shit."

"Don't be too hard on him. He's only trying to help."

"I guess."

"He's pretty far gone, really. I don't doubt he believes what he tells people. It's just kind of a dangerous game."

"Unlike telling people their whole life is a dream," Brendon quipped.

"Touché."

After a few more minutes, the two younger, faster men passed them by. Greetings were exchanged, nothing more. Brendon and Dennis smirked at each other, and tried not to laugh until the Mormons in Black were out of earshot.

"Who *does* that? Wears a tie when hiking?"

"Come on, don't lose them," Dennis urged, moving faster.

"What? Why?"

"They'll lead us right to the petroglyphs," he suggested, winking.

"Yeah, right."

Dennis chuckled, but didn't slow down. He was intent on following them. Brendon began to fall behind. Before long, the other men were out of sight. He wondered how close they were to the legendary resort/underground installation, and if Dennis might really be some sort of operative.

"Wait up," he called, the necessity of which made him feel like child. LeRose looked over his shoulder and waved him forward, as if that gesture alone would pull his body up the slope, but he did not wait, so Brendon gave up, and slackened his gait to a more tolerable speed. Dennis disappeared over the rise.

It was a full half hour before he saw his friend again. He was sitting in the shade of a gnarled juniper on top of a ridge in the terrain, looking dejected.

"I lost 'em," he said.

Brendon said nothing, but stood looking down in the canyon below, catching his breath. There was not a white shirt to be seen anywhere.

"They must have slipped off the trail somewhere," Dennis asserted.

"Are you sure they didn't go up higher?"

"We would be able to see them from here if they had," he pointed out. "There's no way they could have climbed out of sight, I wasn't that far behind."

"Maybe they were dreaming being here, and they woke up."

"Screw you," he chuckled.

"Well if they didn't go up, they must have gone down," Brendon suggested, "there must be an entrance around here someplace, to their secret underground barracks."

"Why do you think I was following them?" Dennis retorted, laughing, but not quite as sincerely as usual.

"Maybe they were beamed up," Brendon offered, sitting down and pulling a protein bar out of his pocket.

"Maybe I'm just getting older than I thought."

"You left me in the dust."

"Sorry about that."

"So now what, is this the view you were thinking of, or do we need to go higher? Cause this doesn't really look anything like the print." To prove it, Brendon took out his phone and brought up the picture he had taken of it.

"You're right, this can't be it. The view from the summit is essentially the same, only higher. But maybe your rock is up there."

"Yeah, or your superhuman Mormon friends."

"We could check it out, if you're up to it."

"Just give me a minute to recoup my losses."

* * *

Brendon turned off the road and followed the signs for parking past the complex, into the hollow. He parked and climbed a dozen steps up to a different lot. His legs were sore from the hike that day with Dennis. It had been enjoyable enough, a beautiful day, but fruitless as far as locating the sought for view, or finding any carved, marked, or otherwise unusual stones. Dennis never did stop moaning about the guys who out-hiked him.

Two more stairways brought him to the base of a wide coiling ramp that led to the main building. The Creative Life Center's rounded brown stucco walls rose organically from the hillside like the crown of some living god of the earth. Old growth trees had been left in place in the various courtyards, shading them from the relentless desert sun. Accompanying the ramp was a narrow channel of water flowing down from an upper fount he could not immediately locate. He followed the signs for the heart-opening workshop, thinking all the while what a crazy, beautiful place Sedona was.

There were about twenty people there. Brendon recognized the southern gentleman with the droopy mustache and his gracious wife. They nodded in greeting. The awkward guy with the thick glasses was there too. The host of the workshop was not impressive; he was quite overweight, bumbling about with an outdated microphone and audio cassette player, talking to someone in the front row about why he was late, and his testy marriage.

"Good evening," he said, projecting his voice now, "my name is Dexter, and tonight we're going to be talking about opening the heart."

People settled in their seats and became quiet.

"Now I'm not talking about surgery, or lowering your cholesterol, although it is all related."

There were a few chuckles. Brendon felt sleepy, and stifled a yawn.

"I'm talking about the subtle bodies, and opening the heart chakra. I'm going to presume that since you're here, you have some idea what I'm referring to."

Several people smiled or nodded, but one woman in the back raised her hand.

"Yes?"

"Um, yes, I know about chakras, but the other thing you said..."

"The subtle bodies."

"What do you mean by that?" She had a tremulous, halting voice which Brendon found annoying. Her straggly gray hair and flaccid face seemed full of pain. He reprimanded himself for not being more sympathetic.

"Okay, you know how people see auras? Do any of you here tonight see auras?" A few people nodded. "And you've seen the signs around town for aura photographs, I'm sure. The aura is a body of energy, interpenetrating and in most cases extending out from the dense physical body. It is part of your being which is vibrating at a different frequency, a frequency that is not detectable by the eyes, just as there are frequencies of light, for instance infrared, which are not detectable by the eye, but can be recorded by special cameras. People who see auras are seeing them with a different part of the brain. Because they are normally invisible, we refer to them as the *subtle* bodies, but they are just as real, and just as much a part of you as the frequencies of energy that your senses *do* have the ability to detect. Everybody with me so far?"

Most mumbled assent.

"Good. Now those of you who have seen auras know that some people's auras are larger than others, or that someone's aura might be wider one day than the next, depending on how they feel, because the subtle bodies have much to do with our emotions and our thoughts and our spiritual development. I've seen auras extending as much as ten, twelve feet from the body. The bodies of a guru or a saint are said to extend further. And we all feel this, whether we can 'see' the aura or not, we recognize the energy emanating from others. Someone gives us a bad vibe, gives us the creeps, or someone else we say is charismatic, that kind of feeling you get from someone is your energy body picking up signals from their energy body, so in a sense everyone sees everyone else's aura, it's just a matter of training the mind to stop ignoring those signals, to recognize what it is sensing, and to translate these other frequencies of energy into images.

"But what we want to talk about tonight specifically is the heart. We want to learn to expand it as wide as possible, we want to increase our capacity, not just to put our energy out there, but to connect with one another on the heart level. That's what the shift is all about," Dexter asserted. He held his hands out in front of his chest, cupping his palms around a grapefruit sized pocket of air.

"The heart chakra expands and contracts, all the time. From day to day, month to month, year to year, depending on the stability of your emotional body, and what's happening in your life." He kept moving his hands in and out, illustrating how the pumping of the heart chakra might be similar to the way the heart pumps blood. "You all know if it's open or if it's closed, you can tell by the way you feel; joy is expansion, grief is contraction. We are rarely in a state of complete joy or complete grief, so your heart chakra is not normally going to be much wider than what you see now, between my hands. But what I want to teach you today is that you can learn to control it, to expand it by use of the will, by making the choice for love, for connection. When you make that decision to open your heart to others, they will feel it. The energy moves freely between you, and compounds; joy feeds joy. If you've ever been in love or had a close friend, you know what I'm talking about, you've felt that heart connection, and it's not because that person was so much more awesome than anyone else. You felt the energy between you because your mind *decided* that they were awesome, and with that decision you made the *choice* to open your heart to them. Is this making any sense to you?"

Several people said 'oh yes' or 'definitely'. Brendon thought he understood but wasn't sure the concept was helpful.

"Many people have had a bad experience from opening their heart to someone, not necessarily romantically, but at some point we have all been rejected or judged in some way. Or perhaps someone has been taken from you, or left you after many years. Heartbreak is a real phenomenon, which can happen to the heart chakra. It isn't really broken, but it shrinks and shuts off for a time. You know, it's an autonomic response, a knee-jerk reaction, like those deep sea marine worms that slip back into their sheath when threatened, or a turtle pulling it's head into it's shell. Only the bigger the heart is, the more expanded with joy when the heartbreak comes, the tighter it will contract. Those with a greater capacity for love are at greater risk. It's like a black hole, collapsing in on itself, and it can be very difficult to overcome.

"But what people don't realize is that a crisis can be something to celebrate, sometimes it takes a crisis to open your heart. People come back from a near death experience more open, softer, more appreciative of life, because they have learned that being open is a better defense than being closed. In the old days if your city was under attack, you would close the gates, but by closing the gates you would cut your own supply lines.

A closed off heart gets no input. It will become encrusted. You need to exercise it, keep it moving. If your aura is full of energy, others' energy cannot impinge on you, if you withdraw your energy tightly into yourself, the energy of others will be sucked into the vacuum, into your space, and if their energy is negative, you want to recoil even further. What I would wish for all of you is to learn to open your heart at will. Yes?"

The same woman in the back, with the straggly hair, had another question.

"I've read descriptions, and seen diagrams of the heart chakra, and they always say it has twelve petals. Why is that, and what do the petals mean?"

"The petals represent lines of transmission, places from which the waves of energy emanate. You might hear people talking about the silver thread, for instance. This is not really a thread, it's a vortex of energy connecting two entities, perhaps you to your soul, perhaps my heart to your heart. The heart chakra is where heaven and earth meet, or spirit and matter, or male and female. There are three chakras above, and three below. This meeting is usually depicted by the intersection of two triangles, one pointing up, and one pointing down. Their intersection creates a six-pointed star, which of course has twelve sides, two for each point. I think this is why it is traditionally assigned twelve petals. But in the Tibetan system, the heart chakra only has eight petals, all pointing downward. You know, I've seen diagrams where they make the chakras look like flowers, or funnels..."

"I read somewhere that they were in the geometrical shape of a tube torus, where the energy vortex is the hole of the doughnut," Greg, the guy with the thick glasses, interjected.

"Yes, and some people say inside every chakra is one of the Platonic solids. And all these things are probably true at one time or another; the chakras are not static, they're always changing. The word chakra means 'turning', or 'wheel'. When I see them, especially when they are really fired up, they look like wheels within wheels within wheels. They move, ebb and flow as the energy flows, they span more than three dimensions, and they contain different layers of energy vibrating at different frequencies simultaneously. A Master of the Wisdom might well open a thousand petals on her heart chakra, or create an entirely new chakra where it is needed. But most people have only a few petals open to their heart, only a few connections. And that is what we're here to learn, to open more connections. When you look at a rose, do you count the petals?"

"No," the gracious gentlewoman replied.

"No. Nor does the rose. The rose does not need to know it's own workings to open. Open your heart, make the decision to love, and the energy will flow."

"So how do you open it?"

"Practice. The heart is a muscle, so is the heart chakra. Essentially, to open the heart is a choice; it's an act of inclusion, the acceptance of someone or something *as it is*. It is an act of love."

"But you can't *choose* to love someone," the straggle haired woman objected.

"You can't choose to be infatuated, you can't choose to be attracted, you can't control an autonomic response to pheromone stimuli, but you *can* choose to love, to accept who or what someone or something is, and be grateful that they are, to recognize that the universal spirit resides in them as well as in yourself. That is love. That is wisdom. Now let's try an exercise together."

He sat facing them, and with his hands on his knees he rocked back and forth, spreading his legs wider, adjusting his pants, looking a little like a sumo wrestler performing the preparatory *shiko*.

"Breathing is key," he noted, taking a deep breath. "Everyone take a deep breath, and hold it for a second, then release it slowly. Breathe from the belly," he added, taking another breath. He's certainly got the belly for it, Brendon thought.

"So imagine the chakra however you want to see it," he instructed, holding his hands up in front of his chest again, "like a flower if you want, or a funnel, or a ball of light, an orb. See if you can feel it between your hands." Everyone held their hands up also, around their invisible hearts.

"Now just expand that, breathe in and expand. Feel your belly and your chest expand, and feel the heart expand. It's subtle, but you *can* feel it."

Brendon moved his hands and felt for the energy, but try as he might, he found nothing save a little heat coming from his palms. He wondered if anyone else could feel what they were supposed to be feeling, these mysterious expansions and connections.

"So I'm going to work with each one of you individually now, so that you can feel what we've been talking about. Once you can identify the feeling, you can work with that energy on your own. I'm going to start over here," he said, pointing to the opposite side of the room from Brendon, "but if you keep your eyes on me, any one of you might see some unusual things as I expand my heart and my aura. On the other hand, if you need to take a break, use the restroom or anything, this might be a good time because it'll take a while for me to work around the room."

One person left, the others shifted in their chairs to watch him.

"I want you to focus on me, right at my eyes, and try not to blink." He was addressing a young Japanese woman, who immediately giggled.

"You may find that what you see changes. You may see me differently. Don't worry about that, focus on the feeling in your chest." Again the girl tittered. Now the facilitator smiled broadly.

"There, you feel that rising, don't you. Now let it expand. Take a deep breath and let it grow. Bigger. I see a lotus in your hands. Don't be afraid to open it. It is your gift to the world." She stopped laughing and blushed.

"There is nothing to be embarrassed about when you connect heart to heart," he said. "All beings can connect on this level. All beings *should* connect on this level, if we want to save the planet. You will never forget this feeling and you will be able to recall it at will. There are more than twelve petals on the lotus, far more, you are already well connected. So I want you to teach this to all of your friends. Keep those connections, grow those connections. You know you are a lightworker."

"Yes," the woman nodded. There were now tears at the corners of her eyes.

And so he went around the room, locking eyes with everyone, touching hearts, pulling images out of the air that seemed to affect each person deeply. In one person's heart he said he saw a chalice, filled with light; another was a tree with its roots in the heavens and its leaves on the Earth. After about twenty minutes of waiting and watching it was Brendon's turn. He was a little wary – of what, he wasn't sure. The seer shifted his belly and his legs to face him more directly. Brendon stared at his face, into his eyes as well as he could from twelve feet away. After a minute or so, he realized that the room around them had faded, blended, and blurred. It looked like a fog was surrounding Dexter's face. Was it just because he wasn't blinking, an optical illusion caused by the dim, even space, the bland color of the walls and carpeting, or was he seeing with a previously unused sense?

"Try and think of some moment in which you were relaxed, in which you felt joy," Dexter instructed.

Brendon found it difficult to come up with something on the spot. Memories of Sharon were all tinged with sorrow. He thought of Cass, but there was always tension. He tried a puppy.

"That's it, now let it grow," he said. "You have a lot of trouble with the back of your neck. It's very tight, even now."

"Yes," Brendon admitted. Dexter's pudgy face had morphed, turned ancient, almost gaunt, those eyes seemed to recede into his head. Was it merely hypnotic suggestion, Brendon wondered?

"Your higher self has been trying to enter for about three years," he said. Brendon wasn't sure what this meant, but tried to think back three years. Right about the time he and Sharon had parted. Right about the time he had found himself in 'that midlife thing' as Cass referred to it.

"There is a woman working with you."

"Uh... I'm not actually working at all right now," Brendon protested. Dexter chuckled.

"I'm talking about real work. Spiritual work."

"No, I'm not working with anyone," he insisted, pretending he didn't know who he was referring to, wanting to keep her a secret, to himself, yet grateful for another verification, another reassurance that she was truly there.

"I'm looking at her right now," he avowed. "She's standing behind you, with her hands on your shoulders. She wants you to stop resisting, *she* wants you to open your heart." Now the speaker morphed again, the face smoothed, turned gentle, youthful, feminine; the eyes softened with unswerving kindness, she seemed to glow with an inner radiance. Brendon felt a concentration in his chest, a pushing, as if something were trying to emerge, as if a longing were seeking to escape.

"And she is working with you at night, to clear your etheric body. Have you been having trouble sleeping?"

"No, not really. Sometimes."

"Well, from now on take note of any unusual sensations. Write down your dreams. She wants you to work with her. Okay?"

"Okay."

"Are you an artist?"

"In a manner of speaking."

"She's been helping you paint."

"Oh," Brendon muttered, "Well that explains a lot," he confirmed.

"You are truly blessed to have such a one guiding you through this shift," Dexter continued, his face returning to normal, "This initiation."

"What if I don't *want* to be shifted? Inducted or whatever."

"I'm afraid you don't understand; your soul has made this decision. You have agreed to it. You are already hard at work building the *antahkarana*, the Path to awakening. The shining one is with you all the time, whether you are sensing her or not. She's part of your family now. She's one of the seven. She wants you to know that she has your back. She asks nothing but that you embrace her, and allow her to embrace you."

Brendon nodded, Dexter moved on to the next participant. Despite his determination not to, Brendon, like so many of the others, teared up and was left speechless.

CHAPTER TEN

NEARBY, scruffy desert trees twisted and writhed out of the parched earth. How thirsty they looked, he thought, reaching for his water bottle, how sorrowful they felt. He had painted a cypress the day before, and for some reason had included a swirl of color around its trunk like a gauzy scarf. He remembered Michael talking to the houseplants, treating them like individuals, like *conscious* beings who craved not only water and light, but interaction. Did these individuals, these junipers, cypress and manzanitas clinging to crags of rock, interact with one another? Were they aware of him? Suddenly he was struck with a vision of how much *more* desolate the landscape would have been without them, without their roots to stem the erosion which had already scoured the area, without their willingness to host the vast numbers of other beings which depended on them for shelter, food, even moisture, and how uninhabitable the whole world would be without their constant production of oxygen. It made him feel shiftless, selfish, and ungrateful to think of the decades they had spent patiently supporting the lives of others. What kind of consciousness could withstand such sacrifice? Surely they were not aware of the passage of time. Or perhaps... perhaps their consciousness existed in another dimension entirely, perhaps what he saw straining to survive under the desert sun was but the rudest indication, the merest shadow of their true form, which lived where time was not linear or recurring, but synchronous.

Carol was set up about fifty feet away; her back was to him. She held her palette in one hand as she painted, in the traditional manner. Brendon's easel came equipped with a little platform on which he let his rest. She stood, he preferred to sit. He had finally purchased a broad brimmed hat to ward off the sun. They were quite a distance from the road, and had spent a half hour making two trips from the car with their gear. Carol had assured him it was worth it, and the view was, but Brendon doubted his painting would be. The rocks were so complex – the way one layer of color merged into the next, the way spires and buttes twisted and curved, the way one range towered above another – and his effort after two hours of dabbling was flat, dimensionless, and as uninspired as the actual view was inspiring.

"I thought you were helping me paint," he muttered reproachfully, and added, silently, 'you who are always with me, part of my family now.' He put the brush down, rubbed his eyes, took a drink, and looked over at Carol. She showed no signs of slowing. He watched a hawk circling over his chosen segment of Sedona's ruddy arms.

It was quiet, quiet enough that the tinnitus could not escape his attention. Or was it a fly? The top of his head tingled. He swatted at his hair, but there was no fly, he decided, just the sibilance of a soft breeze brushing along the desert floor. The tingling continued.

More umber. He took up his brush again, pushed the color into the picture – here, he thought, and here, shadow, shadow, shadow. Some internal sense, an interoceptive equilibrium, was tasked; it registered a subtle disturbance, as if perfused with an unexpected weight or volume. His head tilted involuntarily, not to balance his body in the world, but his self in the body. His arm moved again, to the palette, to the canvas, to the palette; mixing shades, drawing shadows. A part of him watched it moving, while the part moving it watched the world it sought to echo with a multiple, a harmonic of that world. We are painting an overtone, he thought, and observed how he was thinking about painting while he painted, rather than thinking about the paint and the color and the tone of stone and sky, and now he was thinking about thinking about painting while someone painted and moved his arm, as if his involvement was not only unnecessary, but a hindrance, and he stopped looking and thinking, and thinking of thinking altogether, and observed and listened only.

There was a quietly rhythmic sound, almost like breathing, like the sough of surf in a tropical dream. The sun crackled and sizzled and kissed the ground. The flight of the hawk spoke a spiral in the air. A voice was singing a tingling across his chest and down his arm.

"Marry me," she sweetly said.

Brendon shuddered, turned and looked at Carol, but she was facing away, intent on her work. She had not spoken, nor would she have been heard from that distance without shouting, and the voice had not shouted, it had been soft, intimate, in his ear: *Marry me.* He stood and looked all around him.

"Hello?" he called out, searching for the source.

It was impossible, but no one was there. His heart was pounding. He felt all pink and green. Had he fallen asleep? He tried to remember a dream, but there had been none, just the painting and the thinking about painting and the observance of the thinking. Yet the sound had been so *real*. Carol now turned toward him, in response to his call of 'hello'.

"How's it going?" she asked. Her voice did sound loud, projected, as it had to from way over there, utterly opposite of the irresistible, loving tone that lingered in his body, a tone which had not so much come *at* him as tugged him away in invitation.

151

"Uh... okay. I guess I'm getting a little wiggy out here though," he answered as he worked his way across the rock to Carol's easel. "It's awful hot."

"I'm almost done," she assured him. "What do you think?"

"That's great," Brendon said, "Way better than mine, that's for sure. How do you get the patterns in the rock to look so real without painting every single ridge? I've had a terrible time with that."

"Well I lay in the shadow first, then I go over it with a palette knife for the highlights. You kind of scrape it on so it doesn't all stick. I'll show you." She gathered some paint on her knife and pulled it across the canvas, leaving bits of color behind.

"Oh my God, why didn't I try that? I've been so frustrated with those rocks all day."

"There are lot's of little tricks. You should take a class at the art center."

"I guess so."

"I just want to get in some of this foreground, then I'll be done."

"No hurry." Brendon went back to his own work, wondering if it was too late to try the palette knife thing. When he got to his easel, he hardly recognized the painting. In front of the butte, which had been the main subject, was a whirling cloud of red earth, shaped like an upside down funnel, spiraling upward. Pointing down from the top of the canvas was a matching vortex of pale gray clouds covering the blue he remembered painting. These two whirlwinds met in the center, atop the butte. Little scrawls and flashes of bright yellows and greens added to the sense of movement. He was astounded; it was all he could do not to shout his astonishment, but this feeling of elation was quickly followed by embarrassment and confusion. What in the world is happening to me, he wondered, and answered himself – I'm going crazy. He put away his paints and folded his easel. Carol joined him and saw his painting.

"Ah, heaven and earth, wonderful!" Carol exclaimed. "They certainly do seem to come together here in Sedona."

"Oh. Right. I, uh... wasn't really aware of what I was doing. The same thing happened to me the other day, actually," he revealed, but Carol wasn't listening, she was studying the picture.

"From above it's gyrating clockwise, from below counterclockwise, you see? That's always the way inside the torus." She drew her finger around his canvas, as if indicating a large circle. "And here is the stream, just beginning," she added, pointing to a tentative stroke of white which moved from top to bottom, through both vortices and into the valley floor. Despite the thinness of its application, it managed to suggest cylindrical solidity, continuity, and power. "The Rod of Initiation," Carol said, smiling with the air of someone who was stating the obvious. "This is marvelous, you must show Crystal."

"You know I don't even remember putting that in, the uh... storm."

"No? So much the better. That just goes to show the clarity of your connection to spirit."

"Oh yeah? All I remember is the sound of the hawk flying." How could I have *heard* a hawk flying, he thought, looking up, and wondered if there was something other than a hawk in the sky. "And I kept feeling a tingling on the top of my head." And someone asked me to marry her, he thought, but kept that to himself.

"*Afflatus divinus* they used to call that. Divine wind. Spirit breathing into you, divine inspiration. People forget that it is a physical, as well as a metaphysical experience."

"Does that happen to you? Out here?"

"The prickly sensations? I don't usually notice it."

153

"But the not remembering what you painted? I mean, I'm a little freaked out right now."

"The first time I painted something I had not planned on, many years ago, I didn't remember. I finished a painting and then saw the entity in the clouds I had painted. Because I had blocked it out, you know. Many of us who have an awakening don't know what to do with it, so we block it out. We go back to sleep. It eventually resurfaces. I began to remember, and then I was able to... to be present, yet not get in the way when the information comes through. You're still afraid, dear, these truths are unsettling at first, but that will pass."

"But what 'truths' are we talking about? There's not a cloud in the sky," he protested, looking again at the whirling storms he had painted.

"Senses are ticklish things, they are easily fooled, and easily ignored. They only work in conjunction with awareness. Moreover, your mind will cross reference different senses. The ear may not be able to hear below 20hz, but the body can feel vibrations below this range. You think you know what basil tastes like, when what you know is how it smells in your mouth. We must remain open to the possibility that our senses are evolving, and that everything you see does not have to come through your eyes. If you witness a thing through one of your senses, and it does not relate to anything you have experienced in the past, your awareness may well dismiss it, as 'not really there', or your sensory system itself may dismiss it unconsciously so that there is in essence, no observation. It's called perceptual blindness. Then again, if not dismissed altogether, your sensory system may project a partial 'match' onto the incoming data, labeling an unusual cloud pattern as an angel, or a levitating vehicle of some kind."

"Or vice versa."

"Or vice versa. Or it might interpret a wave of energy not manifested into particle form as a dust devil or funnel cloud."

"So you think I've painted one of these vortexes everyone's always talking about."

"Of course you have, dear. Now you must stop pretending you don't belong here and get on with the work."

He smiled, nodded and began carrying things back to the car. He helped her load up her easel too, and they started driving back to the house.

"Carol, what is this... initiation," he asked, "or shift, or induction people keep hinting at? Is that why I don't remember what I'm painting?"

"Perhaps. You can't remember because you are stepping aside to allow the image to present itself. And you are stepping aside, perhaps, to aid in the shift of your awareness."

"But... what *exactly* is happening to me?"

"Well, the most succinct definition I have come across is: *Initiation is a process of developing inclusiveness*. It comes from one of the blue books in Crystal's office."

"Am I being included in something, or am I including something?"

"Both. Or rather, you are becoming *conscious* of what you include and are included in. But I think induction and initiation are really two different things. The induction brings about initiation."

"Okay. But becoming conscious seems like the opposite of what's happening, it's like I'm *losing* consciousness, I'm losing time, I've never been *less* aware of... of what the hell's going on," he chuckled.

"Don't forget, in order to move into the unknown, you must first let go of the known. This is all preliminary, Brendon. When the shift comes, you will know it, and there is no returning. It is like a quantum leap."

"And what exactly is that again?"

"At the quantum level, electrons can only be *here* or *there* – they must follow specific orbits around a nucleus. New energy introduced into the system may appear to have little or no effect, up to a certain point. When they get enough additional energy, the electrons jump to a new orbit, *without crossing* through the interim."

"Ah, that's why they call it a leap. Makes sense."

"Yes. It's the same in spirit as it is on the quantum level; a specific amount of energy builds, or is *induced*, then a leap is made – a leap in awareness, a leap in vibration – similar to shifting from one orbit to another, one octave to another, one plane of existence to another."

"So initiation is like a new understanding."

"No, new understanding is both a prerequisite and a result, but it is not the crux of the event. Initiation is the establishment of a new baseline frequency, a new fundamental. Once the median frequency has crossed the waveguide (the egoic bubble) identity will also cross and a higher harmonic is achieved, a further occurrence of self is comprehended and compassed by a membrane of greater magnitude. Eventually each of us will reach that initiation, that phase transition which will free us from this particular brane of the eleven-dimensional multiverse, and allow us to fully experience those states, locales, or periods which we know are there just beyond our grasp, those planes or orbits or clear frequencies that we cannot reach as we would by walking across a room, but which can only be attained by a leap of faith, and assistance from that which we would attain."

"Assistance?"

"Of course. Just as you have painted it. The *antahkarana* is constructed from both ends and traversed in both directions.

Those above reach toward you as much as you reach toward them. Did you think you were alone?"

* * *

Brendon stirred and turned over on his back, trying to alleviate the familiar knot in his neck, the ringing and pulsing in his ears. He was *so* tired, he felt drugged and wanted just to go back to sleep. Something was different; a part of his sleeping brain sluggishly detected excess warmth in his torso, almost as if he had eaten too much, which he had not. Along with this warmth was an electrical sensation, a subtle but undeniable vibration humming through his diaphragm, similar to the vibrations he had felt with Harmony when she used the sounding bowls, but there was no sound he could hear. He registered a directive to remain immobile, and an alarm that he was not alone, that someone was applying some type of force. There was a moment of panic as the word *abduction* presented itself for consideration. Did he dare to open his eyes? How large might the eyes looking back be?

This moment quickly passed, for in his heart he knew it was her, the shining one who was there for *him,* and whether she was an angel or a Grey did not matter; he sensed her unflagging kindness, and her loving intent. He recalled Dexter's words: 'she wants you to work with her', and also, 'to open the heart is a choice, it's an act of inclusion, of acceptance of something *as it is.*' So rather than fear, he chose to realize gratitude, and his body relaxed into receptivity. At first this force, this touch, washed into him just above the navel, but as he became alert and aware of it, aware of *her*, as he imagined her, shining and beautiful and giving, the stream of energy began to move downward, and he became powerfully aroused. Almost immediately it began to recede, as if she were leaving, as if he had offended her, and certain phrases crossed his awareness; *divert desires to a higher cause, step it up an octave, raise your vibration, energy flows where attention goes, you're making a mistake.*

He formed an apology in his mind, and a question: is it wrong? The answer came to him in Rune's voice, 'there is nothing wrong with any vibration', 'she is with you to assist', and 'I've got your back'. He did not hear a new voice, or new words, yet it was like having a conversation with someone new, someone who was pulling what they wanted from the files of his mind, holding phrases like flashcards in a purposeful sequence; it was quite unlike the normal flow of his thoughts. He felt incredibly grateful to her, and honored that some entity with these capabilities thought him worthy of their application.

The waves of energy resumed and he or she or they moved them through the chakras toward his throat, he could feel it surging up and meeting resistance and he knew he was the resistance and the wave both, and he was given to understand that higher frequencies cannot be reached if the focus is below, like trying to spin but holding old baggage, things which do not translate to the new realm. He saw them as clusters of magnetized trash and burned out fibers, used bits and pieces, habitual thought forms and fantasies, pinning him to the dense physical world, doggedly reconstituting themselves, entangling the instrument of his soul.

His brow was seething now, pulsing as the cycles of light and love came through him, clearing him and impressing in his mind that the clumping and clotting remnants of yesterday's joys were not clinging to him, it was he that clung to them. The solution was so simple: release and be new. In order to make the shift, escape the ring-pass-not, dispel the waveguide, he had only to change his thoughts. Let go of one old idea and rotational speed would increase, which would make the next easier to drop, and soon they would be flying away from center like water from a spinning wheel.

He kept his body immobile, so as not to disturb the process or to halt in any way the sensations, the flow of energy. It was a revelation to understand the ponderous limitations of chronic longing and lust, but he strove to make his mind quiescent, and focused upward. He knew it was important to remain in a somnolescent state, that adrenaline or movement, or arousal would overpower the subtler sensations she intended to impart. Eventually the flow ebbed, and Brendon succumbed to sleep once more.

In the morning he woke with a sense of excitement that something definitive had occurred, that he had truly made contact with another kind of intelligence, or another plane of existence, but more than that, he had come away with a new and concrete understanding that remained even as the sensations, the vitalizing effect of that contact, began to fade. He opened the blinds; there was no one on the patio or in the pool, it was too early. After a quick shower he went down the hall, hardly realizing his intention, which was to tell Harmony about it, about the visitation in the night, about the waves of energy. He wanted to share his astonishment that he had been able to sense them at all, that he had been able to keep himself open to it, that it had gone on for so long – at least several minutes – and that he finally understood what she had tried to explain during the sound therapy, about raising the energy, about choosing love over longing. Turning in to the kitchen he found only Rune there, putting dishes away.

"Good morning," the psychic said.

"Morning," Brendon replied, and looked aimlessly in the refrigerator for a minute. Invigorated as he was, he wasn't comfortable enough with Rune to discuss it; it was too personal. He left the kitchen and headed back down the corridor. As he came into view of Harmony's door, it opened, and Dennis emerged, very carefully slipping out and quietly closing it again. When he turned and saw that Brendon had seen him, a leer crept across his face, he nodded once, that familiar upward nod, bouncing his thick hair at him, then winked before slinking back into his own room.

* * *

There was hugging. He enjoyed that, much to his surprise, even with Rune. Dennis did a shake and slide – a handshake, then the other arm quickly around the shoulder and sliding off all in one motion. Michael put some muscle into it; it made him smile. Crystal gripped his shoulders and pecked his cheek. Harmony did not hold back. Carol would not readily let go.

Crystal lit the three wicks of the big candle as the sun disappeared below the horizon. Someone turned off the lamps, leaving them, Buddha, Guanyin, and St. Francis in flickering shadows. Everyone got comfortable on the circular couch. Harmony sounded a didge for a few minutes, moving its bell end over their heads. The earthy vibration rose up through his feet and rumbled his chest, not unlike the drumming he had heard on his walk, except here it calmed him and chased doubts away. The phrase *you are in exactly the right place* replayed in his head, bringing with it that puckish woman's smile over the counter at the bookshop. He could hardly believe that it had only been a few weeks since he had come to Sedona, since he had met these people who welcomed him in their arms. He knew next to nothing about them, but knew their affection, their goodwill, to be sincere.

"Take a deep breath... let go... relax the muscles in your feet, in your legs..." Crystal said. He followed her little directives, breathing, feeling the tension fade as she worked her way up to the jaw and the eyes. He focused on the sensations; her words faded to the background. His breathing slowed. Thoughts paraded by, words remembered, resurfacing in an unbroken chain of undisclosed significance like a trail of bread crumbs, or a thread followed through a labyrinth: *mind event... wake up... forward progression of events... involutionary arc...*

"If worries or memories trouble you," Crystal continued, "take a step back, out of your mind, and become the observer. See the ideas going by... don't try to repress them, notice them... but let them go. Focus your attention in the heart."

He kept following the thread: *...open your heart... vortex... wheels upon wheels...*

"Send a line of light from the heart center to every other person in the room so that we are all connected at the heart."

This directive was easy for Brendon, because the feeling from the hugs lingered, his arms and chest remembered the contact, he saw a light passing from chest to chest in a circle around the group, spinning round and round, with a rhythm at first almost imperceptible, a pulsing vibration as it passed through him and on to the others, and a thought came up that maybe the pulse was only his own heartbeat, but he let that go and focused on the sensation, the subtle yet intense force moving from and to and through them. Yes, if he *chose,* he could dismiss it, he could rise from the couch and walk away, he could reject it all as mumbo jumbo woo woo, but he knew it was there moving through the circle, he knew if he had been sitting alone he would not have felt it spinning and spinning... *everything is spinning... poloidal spin ratio... egoic bubble torus... seven equal regions each in contact with the other six... group endeavor... big ol' gopher nest... nested standing waves... induced wave pattern...*

"Now see the light of the heart lifted up, it is coming together as one, it is raised above our heads," Crystal continued, her voice quietly hypnotic. And the thread of thought filled her pauses:

...raise your vibration... very high energy... we meet in the margins...

"And from the light of the soul," she intoned, "see a line of Light descend into your head and into the heads of everyone in the group, directly into the center of the brain."

Brendon drew the Light descending in his mind's eye, and felt that tingling on the top of his head, a connection made. By himself, without Crystal's direction, he would have rationalized the feeling as a breeze bending his hair or a bug crawling on his scalp, but because the sensation was synchronized with the words, with the visualizing, it was not dismissible, it was memorable.

"Now look for a little blue spark there in the cave, as we induce the head center, see the stream of light descending and kindling..."

And he saw the lambent flame filling the cave, the bluish, whitish glow flickering and flowing like an aurora, a plasmic fire awakening and dancing, immolating the debris of life's disappointments and broken schemes. His vision brightened with golden light, as if someone had flipped the switch on the wall or the sun had suddenly risen and suffused the great room with its brightness, and still he observed the chain of thoughts:

...shining like the sun... tantric deity... what is she doing in my dream... I like Ike... Marry me... the body is not a principle... conquer lower three worlds...

His head and shoulders began bobbing slightly in response to the pulse of energy circuiting the group. There was a rising of his mind, his eyes moved upward, his scalp tightened backward, his face formed an odd, joyful grimace and a few tears rolled down his cheeks as he experienced a blessed release of weight and refuse he had been unaware of clutching.

"We see the perfected form..." Crystal directed.

...perfectly resonating multiples, Brendon remembered, *...it will be revealed, and it will reveal... I've got your back...*

"...and allow it to descend into the cave."

...Spirit into Matter... omphalos... Rod of Initiation... know that God is fire...

A jolt of energy came, which might have frightened him, but it was brought to his mind that *...being open is a better defense than being closed.* He resisted that impulse to recoil, retract back into his sheath, and instead chose the thoughtform *I allow only beings of Light...* and *...allow her to embrace you...*

Crystal continued, "Hold the perfected form in the Light of Love, allow it to impress upon your being all that is required to bring it into manifestation."

Unaccountably, though the name of Skydancer was on his lips, though his heart had opened to her love, though his entire being longed for contact with her, Brendon saw in the cave of his imagination, not a shining angelic woman, but the Earth, bathed in electric auras of auroral fire that played through a scintillant reticular structure, a matrix which he *knew* was not manufactured, grown, or otherwise created, but *entered into.* He watched it rotate, the big blue marble, and each of its colored globes of energy, its interpenetrating subtle bodies, moved independently as wheels within wheels, but all perfectly centered, stable, and *awake.* Here was a vision of the planet as not merely alive and aware, but sacred. The clarity of this idea, the scope of it, and the certainty that he had never before considered anything of the sort, shocked Brendon. It was not a recollection or a reconstruction of something that had come into his mind previously and escaped his notice, he had not simply rearranged previous knowledge to form a new conclusion, he had most certainly been *given* something, and this was what really grabbed him. This in itself was an intriguing, fanciful idea, but where had this picture of the world come from, *who* had given it, he wondered, Crystal? Skydancer? The group mind?

"Slowly return your awareness to the body," Crystal now instructed. "We are thankful for this time together," she continued, "and for the vision Spirit has impressed upon us this evening. We take a moment to radiate that energy to the Sedona area, humanity, and the world."

Brendon shifted his legs and wiped the tears from his eyes.

"And we will close with the Great Invocation. From the point of Light..." she began. Other voices in the room joined her; the sound startled him. They were attempting to speak in unison, but the cadence of the phrases varied form person to person.

"...let Light stream forth into the minds of men... let Light descend on Earth."

What the hell, Brendon thought. The comfort he had felt at the beginning of the exercise vanished. A creepy, frightened feeling took him over as they continued their cultish chanting; it smacked of religiosity, or witchcraft. He looked around the circle; the others still had theirs eyes closed. The candlelight colored them all in the same tones of dull gold. Harmony sat cross-legged beside him, her left knee almost touching his thigh, her posture impeccable. He turned his head toward her and inhaled her earthy scent, allowing it to calm him again, trusting that if she was okay with it, it must be harmless enough.

"From the center which *we* call the race of men..." they continued, stressing the word 'we', "...let the Plan of Love and Light work out..."

He was struck by that odd emphasis on *we*; was there someone else calling it something else? The center of what? Whose plan?

Presently they finished their prayer or incantation and began going about their business. Someone turned on the lights.

"How was it for you?" Harmony asked, placing a hand on his shoulder.

"Uh... good, I guess," he said, turning to face her, resisting the urge to embrace her, trying to ignore the enticing touch of her slender fingers. "I couldn't stop thinking. But I felt like, energy I guess," he laughed.

"It's okay if you don't want to talk about it," she assured him, standing. He rose too, leaning closer, giving in to the pull of her kindness. There was a vitality about Harmony, a radiant warmth that he found irresistible, despite the knowledge that she didn't want him.

"No, I just don't know what I'm trying to say. I mean... I felt *something* going on." He found he still trusted her; after all, he hadn't actually *seen* them together, Dennis could have been in her room entirely without her knowledge, he wouldn't put it past him for a second.

"Well great! A lot of what happens or what we see or feel doesn't really translate. And that's okay. You're making great progress."

"Yeah," he agreed, "I think I am."

"Brandon, I hear there are paintings," Crystal noted, stepping towards him. Harmony smiled and turned away. It was necessary for him to make a conscious decision not to follow her, to stay and address Crystal.

"Yes, a few." Had Carol told her, he wondered, or someone with a less substantial form?

"I would love to see them," she said with enthusiasm.

"Now?"

"If you don't mind."

"They're not... I haven't really painted in a while," he warned as she led the way to the studio, her scarf rippling gently behind her.

"Never apologize for your work," she ordered, "it is disrespectful to Spirit, and yourself. And in case you're not clear on that point, they are one and the same."

She opened the door and flipped on the lights then turned to him expectantly. He had left the paintings hiding on a shelf from which he now retrieved them; the one of the thundercloud with sheets of rain falling up as well as down, the one of the ancient cypress tree, and the one with the vortex clouds meeting in the center.

"Oh, isn't he magnificent, with his pink cloak," she said of the tree"Yeah, I'm not sure why I did that, it just kind of showed up there."

"To honor him, as he honors the earth. That is his love, his work. He is a Master, Brandon, he is a perfect conduit, ushering spirit into matter, guiding the Light into the planet. And this is just how he does it, with the twisting of his body. Everyone gets it wrong, you know, the energy does not twist the trees, *they* twist to assist the energy. They become the Path."

"Hmm. I never thought of it that way," he admitted. The truth was, he had never thought of it at all, and wasn't quite sure what she meant.

"And this one..." she continued, taking in the thundercloud, "...preparation, I think. Sort of a back-washing. Clearing the field before the influx. Which brings us to the portal," she said, picking up the last of the three. "This is a very powerful painting, Brandon."

"Actually, it's Brendon," he finally said.

"I'm sorry, dear. Come, let me show you," she said, turning elegantly, chin held high, vacating the studio with the painting in hand. They went back through the great room, and down the opposite hall to Crystal's office. She held it up to the wall, below the diagram of the torus.

"It's a pass-through, you see?" Her bright smile defied any other interpretation. "This center has long been activated. It's one of the three receivers of prana. The energy is so strong here because it is accepted. It is allowed, it is welcomed, the upward reaching vortex meets that which is descending, here," she explained, pointing at the place in the painting where the two vortices met. "You have rendered it beautifully! The omphalos. The origin of distribution. The wormhole. The Sipapuni."

"I... to be honest, I didn't even realize I was painting it," he confessed.

"Ah, a direct expression, then. A gift. May I keep it here?" she asked, rhetorically, leaning it up against the wall without waiting for his response.

"Sure."

"You see? It's all coming together," she asserted with a blissful sigh, gesturing broadly at her chaotic wall of images and charts.

CHAPTER ELEVEN

BRENDON had avoided Dennis for two weeks. Interaction might have lead to confirmation about that morning when he had witnessed the writer coming out of Harmony's room. He had not seen them together since, but had not really seen either one more than a couple times, because he had been out of the house so much. He had no right to question either of them about it, he had no right to assume anything had happened between them, he couldn't blame Dennis for going after what he himself had wanted, nor could he blame him for succeeding where he himself had failed, but he certainly didn't want to hear about it. Besides, he knew Dennis was just as likely to have been in the room without Harmony's knowledge as he was to have 'been' with her. Either way, it was none of his business, so for those two weeks he had tried to stay out of their way, to keep his heart open to both of them, and to let the whole thing go.

All this time he told those who asked that he was going out to paint. He painted nothing. In the mornings he searched for the view in the print, hiking every trail he could find, venturing off them now and then to get a higher vantage point, with no success. He knew it was useless, there was too much ground to cover and he was too timid. Without a doubt, if the view did in fact exist, it was not close to any known trail, and he didn't have the outdoor skills to wander through the desert or climb the steep precipices that promised the best hope of providing the scene depicted in the print. Nevertheless, he tried, mindful that it was all about willingness.

In the afternoons he did what he could to keep cool. He sat with his feet in Oak Creek, he went to the movies, he went to Cottonwood and wandered through Walmart and Home Depot, anything to stay away from the house. When Dennis finally cornered him it was to inform him that he and his Hopi friend Ben would be spending the following night at an unnamed but carefully selected isolated locale far from city lights, and that he should join them to look at the stars and 'expand his mind'. Although this invitation was proffered with Dennis's typical hair bobbing charm, it seemed like a challenge of sorts; the decision whether to accept or decline was itself a test of courage or intelligence, Brendon couldn't tell which. In the end, out of boredom, he decided to go along.

"Let's make a labyrinth," Dennis suggested.

"Go play with yourself," Ben replied blandly. They were indeed far from Sedona's lights, but there were a few hours of daylight left. They were sitting beneath the one tree in the area that provided adequate shade. Buttes rose in front of them, at their backs the desert stretched to the horizon.

"Come on, this is a perfect spot for it. Just think, it'll be here for eons, we'll be making our mark. It'll be a work of art. Brendon, you believe in art, right?"

"Are you serious?" Brendon asked, because he honestly couldn't tell. He rarely could read the true intent behind any of the writer's statements, including his claim to be a writer.

"Yeah," Dennis assured them, but there was laughter in his voice and that twinkle in his eye.

"No damn way," Ben reiterated. "You didn't say anything about working, Denise. You said," and here Ben raised his voice to the pitch of a whiny little girl, "spend the night in the desert with me, I'm too scared to do it alone."

"I never said that," he protested.

"Yeah, you kinda did," Brendon reminded him, "you said you wanted to face your fears, as I recall. Something about snakes and tigers and old clothes."

"What?" Ben grunted. Dennis laughed.

"I was just..."

"Just trying to get us out here to make your mark for you?"

"You were just being full of shit, as usual," Ben scolded.

"No, I'm just exploring options, mind options."

"Trying to find a way to burst your water balloon consciousness again?" Brendon suggested.

"Yeah. Isolate the mind from normalcy, and it has a chance to see things differently."

"Then what did you drag us along for if you want to be isolated?"

"I'm just trying to offer you guys the same opportunity for growth," he claimed, chuckling.

"You're chicken shit, that's what."

"So when you say a labyrinth, what are we talking about, just laying out some stones?" Brendon asked.

"Yeah, basically. Then you walk the labyrinth and it takes you to an altered state."

"How are you gonna draw it out, how're you gonna find true north, you gotta prepare for these things, you can't just scatter some rocks around," protested Ben.

Dennis grinned and pulled a package of cord and some spikes out of his backpack.

"You dipshit," the other sneered.

"How 'bout it, Brenda, are you in?"

Brendon liked Dennis, he couldn't help it. He was glad the man had showed up in his dream with his repetitious insistence on detaching oneself from mundane realities, on seeking a different mind event. He wanted to cooperate, and except for the heat, constructing a labyrinth seemed more interesting than waiting for day to turn to dusk to turn to dawn.

"Yeah, why not, but only for you, Denise. I have no idea how to go about it, though."

"That's okay, Ben knows."

"I know you're a pain in the ass, that's what I know. You think because I'm Hopi I know how to make a labyrinth? That shit's for tourists, man."

"But you make all that jewelry, like these belt buckles with the maze," Dennis objected, pulling on the large silver buckle he was wearing.

"Like I said, for tourists," Ben grinned, "the Man in the Maze isn't even really Hopi, that's a thing with the Pimas. Don't tell anyone I said that though, or I'll scalp you."

"You fraud!" Dennis laughed. "Just for that you have to help us plot it out."

"It's not that easy. I've never done it bigger than a few inches around. Why don't you do a medicine wheel instead?"

"That's a possibility," he conceded, "but you can't walk a medicine wheel. It doesn't take you anywhere, right?"

"There's nowhere to go, man. This is it."

"How 'bout we just make a spiral?" Brendon offered.

"There you go," Ben agreed, "That should be simple enough. You guys do that. Now where's the beer?"

"No beer, we want our minds clear," Dennis observed.

"I thought you wanted to come out here to do peyote," Brendon reminded him.

"Alcohol is a depressant, dulls the senses. Peyote heightens them. But I wasn't able to get hold of any."

"But I thought..."

"So did I, but Benny didn't come through."

"Hey, peyote is not Hopi medicine. I'm not gonna score your shit for you, just cause you bought a couple pieces of jewelry," Ben laughed, pulling a flask from his hip pocket and taking a swig. "And I'm not going to carry rocks for you in this heat. I'm just here to hold your hand when it gets dark."

"Alright, okay," Dennis chuckled, and threw Brendon a wink. "Brenda and I can do it without you." Then he took his belt off so he could scrutinize the maze design.

"Sure thing, Denise, but only if you keep your pants on."

Dennis handed the belt buckle to Brendon to look at. It was a familiar design, one he had seen large on the wall of Crystal's office. There was something three dimensional about it; a little figure at the top looked like it was about to embark on a journey not just through a maze, but down inside a crater or funnel to a hole in the center.

"Here, grab that cord."

Brendon took one end of the nylon cord; Dennis took the bulk of it and walked out into the sun, looking over the ground for a starting point, unwinding the cord as he went. He made a decision, picked up a rock, and began pounding a spike into the earth. "There. That's the eye," he shouted back, "or is it the navel?"

"It's neither of those, you jackass," Ben shouted back, "It's the sipapu." Dennis tied the cord to the stake.

"Now tie your end to the other spike," Dennis directed Brendon, "and scratch a circle around me."

"Wait," Ben interjected, pushing himself to his feet, "Wait, wait, you gotta find north. And how are you going to shorten the rope? Are you doing a spiral, or what?"

"You tell me."

"What's a sipapu?" Brendon asked, as Ben passed by him, looking at the sky.

"It's like a doorway. The world is layered. The Spider Woman guided the people from the third world into this, the fourth world, through the sipapuni. Every kiva has a sipapu, a little hole in the ground to remind us that soon we will be leaving the fourth world for the fifth world. Through the open door on the top of the head of the earth."

"But that's just for the tourists, right?" Dennis chided.

"Hey, what do want from me, do you really believe Christ climbed out of his tomb on the third day?"

"So what *really* goes on in the kiva? Poker games?"

"If he told you, he'd have to kill you," Brendon suggested.

"That's my line."

"Yeah, we're not looking for converts. There's not enough room in my heaven for your kind," Ben teased, now looking at the shadow of the tree they had just been resting beneath.

"And what kind is that?" Dennis prodded.

"Posers. You go around tasting a little from every pot, instead of having respect for your ancestors."

"Well that's true enough I guess. But you're not going to hold that against me, I hope?"

"No. We are not a cruel people. This is north," he declared, thrusting his arm towards the nearest buttes.

"Okay. What does that mean?"

"You want the opening to the north. So start here," he said to Brendon, guiding him to a spot about fifteen feet counter-clockwise from his original position. "Now Denise, you have to wind the cord around something bigger than that pin, or the circle won't get much smaller. You want the second pass to be a couple feet inside the first one, and so on, right? Then you have a spiral you can walk in and out of."

"We're not doing the maze?"

"No. Too hard, man. Besides, you'll be lucky if you get one ring of stones laid out before dark."

"So we need like four stones here in the center for the rope to wrap around?"

"At least, if you want it to be round."

"With a circumference of about three feet."

"Yeah."

Dennis gathered some rocks into a circle and tied the cord to one of them.

"Now you go that way," Ben ordered Brendon. He walked along, bent over and scratching the ground with his spike. Dennis made sure the rope wound around the cluster of rocks, drawing in the length as Brendon walked. In this way, he inscribed a spiral about thirty feet in diameter.

"Awesome!" Dennis exclaimed, more than once as the work proceeded. He was almost giddy when they had finished.

"That's the easy part, Denise," Ben reminded him.

"Yeah, but now all we have to do is place the stones along the lines."

"Have fun with that," Ben said, returning to sit in the shade. Brendon sighed and coiled up the rope.

"Did you bring any gloves?" he asked.

"Yeah," Dennis said, reaching into his backpack.

"How long have you had this planned?" Brendon demanded, catching the work gloves Dennis tossed at him.

"I just thought of it yesterday."

"Bullshit."

"No, really. Picked up this stuff this morning."

"Ben, what are the chances we're going to find rattlesnakes underneath the rocks out here?" Brendon asked.

"I'd say there's about a hundred percent chance one of us will be dead by morning."

"Quit scaring him," Dennis protested.

"Well, just don't move the big rocks by yourself. One person tip a rock while the other looks underneath for snakes, you'll be okay. Or better yet, use small rocks and pile them up. Or even better still, come back in the winter when it's not so damned hot and the snakes are asleep. It's really the scorpions you have to watch our for anyway."

"Quit scaring *me*," the writer laughed.

"Well they can't get you through the gloves," he added sounding a little more sympathetic. "Just be careful. Look, if you're going to do this," he went on, his voice now taking on a serious tone, "it should be done with reverence. You want to do something the Hopi way? That is what you need to do. You know in the Hopi language, God is not a noun. Spirit is a process, a way of being. It's not some thing you interact with; it is the *way* to interact with each other. If you are going to disturb the stones for your monument, you should hold in your mind what it is for. Like, you should be praying while you do this, not joking around."

"You're the one screwing around," Dennis pointed out.

"I know, I know. I'm just saying. The earth gives itself to you every day. This wheel is good; it's a good way to give to the earth. But only if done in the right frame of mind. So there is no mistake. And if you are moving the home of your brother the snake or your brother the scorpion, you must thank them for their home. If you act in reverence, you have nothing to fear. They will gladly move house for their brother, but not for their enemy. You decide what you are to everything you encounter. The Hopi way is to be brothers."

"Thank you," Dennis said, very sincerely, "for reminding us that we're all connected."

"Yeah," Brendon echoed, "That puts it in perspective."

"Well. It's not just words."

"No, no, I get it. Now I know this is going to be powerful."

Dennis and Brendon set to work seeking out and carrying stones from the surrounding area to the spiral they had inscribed. Ben soon joined them. Brendon was gingerly tipping rocks over with his booted foot, checking for scorpions and snakes.

"I didn't mean to scare you," Ben chuckled.

"Well, it's good to be cautious."

"Except now you're defensive. Closed off. It's my fault, I said that all wrong, that worrying about the scorpions. You don't have to look out for scorpions; you have to look out for yourself. You have to watch that you don't close your heart to the earth. The scorpion is your brother."

"Like the rattlesnake can smell my fear, so if it bites me it's my own fault?" Dennis proposed as he passed them with a watermelon-sized stone in his arms.

"People say animals smell fear," Ben agreed, "but what is fear except your sense of separation from the animal? You know, when you lift the rock, the goal is not to see the scorpion first and say, ahhah! Scorpion! Saw you first, you can't get me!" he laughed, "Your job is to see the scorpion and say, brother scorpion, may I take this rock?"

"Okay," the other chuckled, "I'll try that."

"But seriously. This is the way of the heart. The way of the ancestors. The snake is not going to strike a rock, or a cactus, not just because it isn't moving, but because it perceives no separation from them. That sense of separation comes from the mouse or the bird, that comes from you. You must remain open to all the Earth and its creatures. If you feel no separation, neither can the snake. If you open your heart to the wolf, the wolf will not bite, because it cannot eat itself."

"Wow," Brendon said, "That's beautiful."

"The old ones were more connected to the earth than we are today. The old ones could lift the rock, and see only themselves, not 'scorpion'. They would say, 'look, there I am under the rock, and even, see here, I am the rock."

"They lived in a place where words and labels are inapplicable," Dennis observed.

They went back to work, gathering dozens of red rocks, laying them carefully along the arcs, spacing them evenly, stacking smaller stones to the height of the largest they managed to place, growing the spiral up out of the ground. No snakes were disturbed, that any of them noticed. Brendon encountered nothing more challenging than a great many ants and a few dozen beetles. Ben's words worked on him as he worked on the labyrinth. He made a conscious effort to feel reverence and love for the stones and anyone who might live beneath them as he moved them. He did not speak aloud, but he did repeat in his mind 'may I take this rock?'

Later, the three of them were working together to pry a particularly large participant from its resting place.

"This will be great for the center," said Dennis.

"Yeah."

"You're going have to roll this one," Ben noted.

The ground finally loosened and gave it up; they turned it once and stopped to rest. The impression it had left was marked with termite trails and channels; a metropolis in miniature. Brendon silently thanked the insects for their sacrifice. Ben did so aloud.

"Forgive us, brothers," he said, pushing a little dirt over the top so they were not so exposed. "We are grateful to you for giving up your roof."

Brendon asked, "Is that Loy Butte over there?" He pointed to the west. It looked familiar to him and he thought he had hiked around it.

"No," Ben corrected, "You're all turned around, Loy is in the other direction. That's Black Mountain."

"Oh. Black Mountain."

"Or do you mean Black Ops Mountain?" Dennis joked. Ben chuckled amiably.

"I don't think I've ever heard any stories about paramilitaries being seen over that way. It's mostly Secret Mountain, and Secret Canyon, which are that way," he said, pointing, "But you can't see them from here." Brendon scanned the horizon in the direction he had pointed.

"Watch your feet."

They rolled it about twenty feet and paused to straighten their backs.

"Have you ever seen any black ops guys, or UFOs or anything?" Brendon inquired.

"I've seen a few odd looking motorcades heading up the canyon. Saw a couple guys in black suits with earpieces at a hardware store once. As far as UFOs... I've seen a lot of things I couldn't identify in the sky over the years. But identification is overrated. To me, it doesn't matter whether they come from space or out of the ground, whether they *look* like lizards or are lizards, whether they're aliens from Mexico or aliens from Mars; all beings are our brothers, and we should treat them with respect. We don't own the sky any more than we own the land. It is not for us to say who can come and go. If there are unknown beings around me, I would approach them with goodwill, and

179

look to see them in the light of love, and that way they would not remain unknown."

Brendon smiled and nodded. He liked Ben a lot.

For two hours they worked, but when the sun had set and it was too dark to continue, they had only completed two revolutions of the design, with just a smattering of stones on the inner turns to indicate their positions. They returned to their staging ground where they had left their packs.

"Now I wish I had that beer," Dennis admitted, reaching for a water bottle.

"I'm too old to be playing with you boys," Ben groaned, folding himself to the ground.

"Thanks for helping," said Brendon, "Maybe we can finish it in the morning."

"You two can manage it alone. I'm going home at first light, when Denise takes the pacifier out of her mouth."

Dennis laughed. "Very funny. You're enjoying yourself though, don't deny it."

"Well somebody's got to keep you from falling into the nearest wash and filling your lungs with sand."

Dennis claimed fasting was paramount to the alternate reality they sought, but after carrying rocks, Brendon felt depleted, so he discretely munched on an energy bar. The day, the week, and the summer circulated in his head. Ben's words, falling in line with those of so many others who had appeared in his dream that summer, made him acutely aware of the discrepancy between his nominal beliefs and his actual behavior; between his stated desires and his active intention. He hardly ever treated anyone like a brother, let alone snakes or scorpions. Even Cass, he had been unkind to on a regular basis.

Putting his hands in the dirt, moving and arranging the stones, had left him feeling that he had done something for posterity, and the Earth, it had felt good. But now that the activity was over, he was left alone with knowledge of himself, of the many years spent doing little to nothing for anyone or anything. He had wasted his life; there was no way around it. Being there in the uninhabited desert, away from the electronic world which continually confirmed his importance by needing him to turn on and off and click and send vagaries and ephemera to others so they could confirm their importance by clicking and reading and looking; being this long cut off, and spending a few hours with his hands and knees grounded to the magnitude of the planet, he suddenly knew how utterly insignificant he was, had been, and always would be, and he was overcome with a desire to be other than what he was, to end his self so that another, better self could exist in his place. This decision was definite, yet he was a step removed from it, observing it, and recognized it as a recapitulation of what he had passed through during the last several years of disaffected loitering. It was an aftershock, a reflection of disturbances experienced on a previous circuit of the cycle, a reminder of what he had struggled with and already released. It did not reduce him to despair; rather he welcomed the reinforcement of hard won gains.

Ben and Dennis continued their banter, how long, Brendon could not have said. He fell asleep with the protein bar wrapper still in his hands.

There was movement; Brendon was certain he had seen it, through blurry, sleep-encrusted lashes. Dennis scuffed his feet; he had seen it too. He probably had not slept yet, being too busy facing his mind events. Again, something passed through Brendon's field of view, moving fluidly over the desert floor, a grayness reflecting the dim moonlight. Dennis picked up a flashlight, pointed it, and clicked it on. Dark, glassy orbs returned the beam, blinked, disappeared. Dennis jerked the light right and left, then scanned the area systematically, but could not relocate the subject of his search.

"Did you see that?" Dennis whispered.

"What the hell was it?"

"Brother coyote, inspecting our work," Ben grunted with irritation. "Now go back to sleep."

"No way was that a coyote," Dennis averred, "Did you see the size of those eyes?"

"It was really... gray," Brendon added. A cool breeze had picked up.

"Then it was one of the space brothers inspecting our work. Now go back to sleep."

"I haven't *been* to sleep," Dennis chuckled. "How can you sleep? You're missing this transformative opportunity."

"Do you really think it was an alien?" Brendon asked.

"It sure as hell was *something*," Dennis said.

"I really think it doesn't matter," growled Ben, "it's gone now, isn't it? Do I have to hold your hand? Go back to sleep."

A moment of silence followed. Brendon looked through the swaying branches at the stars, scanning the sky for movement. He felt a prickly sensation at the top of his scalp. An idea was dropped into his mind.

"No, no," he said suddenly, rising. "Get up. This is the time, this is when we should walk the labyrinth."

"Oh, for pity's sake," Ben moaned.

"Come on, it's perfect. Walk it by moonlight."

"I don't know, man, something's out there," Dennis reminded him.

"What if there is? It's all a mind event anyway."

"He's got you there, Denise," Ben agreed, "using your own words against you. And if there is a Grey out there, I'm sure he'd be happy to put you in an altered state. Isn't that what you wanted to get out of this?"

Brendon didn't hesitate, he had slipped his boots on and strode out from under the tree towards the opening of the spiral; Dennis chuckled nervously and mumbled something, which was lost in the crescive siffle of the night wind swirling through the twisted junipers. They would follow him, he knew. The moonlight had leeched the rocks of their more sanguine daytime appearance; the circuit had a ghostly appearance. He paused at the entrance; spread his arms wide, and looked to the zenith. It was a spontaneous gesture, the sort of thing he was normally too self-conscious to permit, and he smiled at the silliness of such a dramatic pose. The chill of the breeze invigorated him, though it whipped sand in his face. Blinking and ducking his head down again, and folding his hands across his abdomen in a meditative pose he must have seen somewhere, he proceeded to walk slowly between the arcs of stones. With each step, Brendon set intention, as a farmer sows seed. He made the conscious decision to open his heart – to wolf, coyote, snake, or scorpion, and even to the Grey space brothers – knowing he could do no more than reveal his heart to himself – acknowledging, when it at last creaked open to the exuberant sky, that what emerged was a sincere desire to be changed, repatterned, and restructured.

When he reached the bottom of the spiral, he saw that Dennis, looking legless in his dark jeans, had just entered the separated space, the *temenos*, and had adopted the same slow pace. He smiled at his friend. It was all well and good to play at having seen something in the dark, now was his chance to learn what he had invited into his dream; a god, a monster, or a pile of clothes. Soon Ben too, approached the whorl, looked to the zenith, and opened his arms to Spirit.

It was not raining, there were no clouds, yet there in the Arizonan aridity a light fog seemed to be forming, an aureate particulation of the atmosphere. The breeze, which had been coming steadily from the south, was now following them, or urging them, around the spiral, and another sound could be heard, marrying the rush of the wind, which he could not quite designate as cicadas, for it seemed more of a whispered whirring from some rotational force. Little eddies of dust churned along the ground. Glimmers flashed above them. He resisted the notion that these transient luminous events were other than stray mutations of heat lightening, or random occurrences of moonlight reflecting chance agglomerations of the wind's gathering debris. He hesitated to acknowledge that something other than a summer storm was occurring, because his subconscious was afraid of the ramifications, that since it was impossible, accepting it would be crazy. That would go too far, that would change him beyond recognition, take him to a place past reverting, into a new paradigm. Yet he had set the intention to keep his heart and mind open, it was embedded in the soil all around him, hence, gently, calmly, his resistance was overwhelmed, and he succumbed to the certain knowledge that they were not alone, that minds deeper than his own, that hearts greater than his own were present.

New, focused lights could be seen against the stippled vault of the cosmos, descending, emerging, *precipitating* from some unperceived realm, some other theater of form. His body sensed an electro-magnetic potential, but there was no thunder, these lights were not lightening; they were not volatile, they were not candent and consuming, they were abiding, conferring, and pulsing with benign luminosity. There were three of these orbs, and they situated themselves above the three men, leading them, and rotating as they followed the revolutions of stone, becoming ever more substantial. Their makeup, as they came closer, appeared as wheels upon wheels, a complex but consistent convolving of fluid phosphorescence, taking the basic shape of a sphere, but composed of multiple flames or currents twirling in concentric, perpendicular, interpenetrating orbits.

Brendon loved them, was grateful for their presence, and greeted them as a call from home.

As he watched them, a cord or beam of light reached out from one to the next, to the next so that a radiant triangle was inscribed in the air above their heads. Through the center of this triangle, a new beam materialized, broader, brighter, more directed. It stretched down toward the ground and entered Ben, who stood with his arms outstretched. From his right arm the light moved to Dennis, then simultaneously from Dennis and Ben, this light streamed toward Brendon's head.

He rose to meet it, and heard himself, without resounding timbre or urgency, speak these unfamiliar words, "*Kýrie, eléison.*"

Briefly, as he withdrew into the motive light, he saw that he had finished the walk, that he had been standing at the center of the spiral, and that his body, and those of his two friends, had collapsed to the ground.

CHAPTER TWELVE

LEAFLESS branches rattling, the smell of gun oil and leather, the smoothness of bullets, the gravel of his father's voice: *wait... wait...* A rustle, then the crush of the copse, a flash of white bobbing away, the pat on the back forgiving his hesitation.

Exactly 1,872 drops of muddy water flying off of Barney the Springer Spaniel's curly brown fur; 38 of them landing on his face the day he learned a dog could smile.

Coral and robin's egg blue, cream to tangerine shafts streaming through the oak leaves, announcing the return of summer day; brown rope creaking and twisting above the tire swing as he waited for the world to wake.

The sugary perfume of pink rosettes with chocolate petals, velvet frosting speaking his name as he handed the last piece of birthday cake to Cass, her brown curls draped on the new pink sweater. Disbelief and confusion, seeing her cut it in half and hand him back the smaller piece.

Yelling 'Get out of my room, you fat pig!' and scrambling to cover himself while Cass worked to mask her smirk.

Lying in bed watching yet another blizzard, cold feet, heavy blankets, struggling through each breath due to cracked ribs, pondering the legitimacy of snow, wondering how anyone could pretend there was a god.

Feeling against his fingers the torsion in the small of Linda's back. The color of her hair melding with the tan sheets, her tumid lips parted in anticipation.

The proboscis of the injured wasp dipping into the bottlecap full of golden honey he had set there on the windowsill for it, beside the African violet which would not bloom.

Linda-who-never-cried's tear as she turned and walked away from him for the last time; her shoulders set firmly, her head not flinching when he called her name – Lindyhop.

Wondering if there was any cashew chicken left in the fridge, and how he could be starving, and if the people working at Wok 'n' Roll knew their phone number was a palindrome; while buxom Sharon, smelling of strawberries and soap, held him close, to comfort him after saying she was moving out because of his failure to be present.

Wiping dust off the lid of a mason jar of applesauce in the basement in Baraboo, when the power went out, with a deceptively muted click.

Sitting high in the white pine when his father came home, noticing how his bald spot glared in the sun, the rusty red patch on the roof of the car, and how small they both seemed from up there.

Ishtar, Venus, Mary Mother of God, all present through the innocent face, a perfect complementary reflection of his own six year old divinity, the capacity to enthrall already hers, unrelenting longing already his. He reached out in the only method available to him, assimilated from his peers, the taunt.

'That dress is stupid, Krista.' It was pink, flared, fluffy. She, the beloved, did not respond in a playful manner; the hoped for physical contact – a shove, a punch – did not occur. Instead, as she removed her beatific presence she cried, 'I hate you Brendon Pearce.'

These and a million moments more he relived in an instant as he moved toward the light, as if they were all stored in a subtle cinema above his skull, an atom of truth that had collected all he had experienced. Along the tunnel, forms of many he had known and many he had forgotten greeted him as he passed, their love coming to him in warm waves. He turned as he rose, rotating counter-clockwise towards a brighter and brighter light, while through gnosis unsought the nature of this passage was revealed to him; that his consciousness was exiting the vehicle, not only the physical body, but the subtle bodies, the bubble of awareness that had constrained him to the fourth world. He was passing through the wormhole, the vortex of the torus, the silver thread, the omphalos, the sipapuni.

Then all was white, he was in the Light, bathed in flowing radiance of such glory that for a time (which may have been eons or may have been moments, for time was suddenly meaningless) he could discern nothing else. The data was overwhelming. He was free to be anything, everything, everywhere, expanding until eubstance eluded him.

* * *

There was a lacuna, a gap, as if he had passed out and knew only that he had been absent. A suspicion registered, of worlds slipping away, as when one wakes from an evanescent dream.

Sensations began to return, but the senses themselves seemed altered to fit the new scene. It was intensely bright; his sight slowly adjusted. Some contrast developed, colors differentiated. Sky, pale green and white, forms of light and shadow, some undulating, some static, were discernible. The familiarity of above and below was calming. He felt weightless, yet securely anchored. One wavy nebula drew closer, coming into focus as it neared, as if crystallizing merely for his benefit, or as if the specific distances at which his senses functioned had been modified. The fluxing amber energies and swarming golden scintillas slowly composed themselves into the figure of a man. It was Dennis, smiling that familiar sly smile.

"Hey," he said, his head bobbing upwards in acknowledgment. Brendon felt great relief at seeing him.

"Are we dead?" he asked.

"There is no death, agent Pearce," he replied.

"What just happened?"

Dennis chuckled. "Well, Crystal would call it *The Application of the Rod*. Others might call it *shaktipat*, or the lifting of the veil, baptism, kundalini awakening. I like to think of it as a friendly nudge." He fluctuated while he spoke, as if all the parts of him were still coming into coherence.

"Were we struck by lightening?" Brendon still felt woozy, and seemed to have forgotten more than he ever knew.

"Not exactly. Often a little extra stimulus is required to bring on the liminal moment, to draw you across a perceptual threshold. It's not usually that dramatic."

Brendon did not understand this explanation and so ignored it. Dennis's face would not be still; it came and went, degrading into pointillized contours devoid of color, his eyes shifting into dark ovoids.

"Why are you flickering?"

"It's not me, it's you," he laughed, "You're no longer sure of what you *should* be seeing."

Brendon looked around. Figures continued to register in his sight, whether mineral or vegetable, human, animal or spectral, he could only begin to determine. There was a noticeable low drone, but again, whether it was inherent in the place, due to some force applied, or merely a fault of his faculties, he had no way of knowing. The ground beneath them was similar to Sedona's red rocks, only more continuous as though a single flow of stone had frozen in whorls of smooth ridges on which erosive forces had no effect. It had its own luminescence, from concentrated coppery streaks and flecks that drifted according to their own peculiar tides.

"Come on, there's someone you came to meet," Dennis said, moving away. Brendon followed. Here and there shapes rose up from the glistening surface like stalagmites. Apparently they were marking or guarding a way, because Dennis led him between them. Although it led off into the distance, it reminded Brendon immediately of the spiral labyrinth they and Ben had been working on before the lights appeared.

"Where's Ben?" he asked.

"He's not on this mission," Dennis answered, winking a fulgurating eye.

"Mission?"

"Yes. Sorry I couldn't be upfront with you from the start. Not in the directive. You're on a strict ability-to-know basis."

"You really are with the CIA?"

"No," he chuckled dismissively, "I'm with the Hierarchy."

"The hierarchy?"

"The Masters of the Wisdom. The Body of Aeons. The Heavenly Host? Call it what you will, I serve humanity through them, and they through me. Now you do too. Everyone does in the end."

"I don't *serve* anyone. I've never heard of... what the hell are you talking about?"

"I know it's confusing right now, but don't worry. All part of the Plan."

"What plan? Whose plan?" he scoffed.

"The Plan for the evolution of consciousness. The Plan for peace. The Plan for the embodiment of the most high within the most low. The Plan you came to execute."

"I don't know anything about any of this. You can't *make* me do anything. Why should I cooperate with this supposed *plan*?"

"Because you are essential."

"Horseshit. I'm not essential to anything."

Before he could blink, Dennis had Brendon in a headlock, twisting his neck uncomfortably.

"If this tiny little nerve, here," he argued flatly, pinching his cheek, "this nonessential part of your nonessential body gets pinched, or say, cut out, what happens?"

"Geck... ack..."

"Exactly. Your tongue goes numb, maybe your jaw too. You can't feel what's in your mouth. If one little nerve cell refuses to cooperate, those around it are disconnected, see, they have no chance to cooperate even if they want to. Now is that fair?"

"Igg... dahrr..."

"Sure, they will eventually find a way to work around the... uncooperative part, but time is of the essence when your tongue is numb, don't you agree?"

"Uhnng... guh..."

"Now another way to look at it is," LeRose continued, releasing his grip, "the more parts that cooperate, pass along their little piece of the puzzle, the more likely it is that those around them will thrive, and so the whole face feels better, doesn't it?"

"Yeah," Brendon nodded nervously.

"Everyone is essential to the Plan. If they weren't, they wouldn't *be*. Capisce?"

Brendon started to laugh, because Dennis had put on a Mafioso voice and was grinning at him, because his neck didn't really hurt, because it was all a dream.

Ahead, the mesa began to slope away. They reached the crest of a rise, and Brendon saw a gathering of houses below. They were smooth and seemed to extrude from the ground, adjoining one another like a pueblo – there were even ladders leading to the upper stories. These dwellings rambled around the valley in a rough circle, surrounding a tall round building in the center. It was slightly flared at the top and looked like a nuclear power plant, or a massive pot thrown on a potter's wheel. The place was hauntingly familiar, and the chatoyant material from which it was made lent it supernal power. He felt he knew the paths, knew what lay behind each doorway, yet he was anxious about progressing any further. Tiny figures were milling about the village; people or phantoms or sprites, some were shadows and some luminaries.

"This is just a mind event," he reminded himself aloud, "I'm dreaming."

"Different dream, Brenda. Different mind."

An older man was moving toward them, working his way up the trail. He had a deeply lined, elongated face and was adorned in fringed buckskin, breechcloth, leggings, and an elaborate feather headdress. He was laughing, and paused occasionally to look up at the celadon sky.

"Grandfather," said Dennis, nodding in acknowledgment as they reached him.

"Brother Rose."

Grandfather eyed Brendon up and down, chuckling contagiously. "Welcome, Brother Pearce. You are most fortunate."

"Thank you," Brendon replied, grinning, about what he couldn't fathom.

The wizened face turned toward the horizon and pointed. "The *merkaba* approaches," he rumbled cryptically.

Dennis nodded again; the man continued on his way. Brendon turned to gawk at the full regalia, that feathered crown trailing down his back, but it dissolved in a shower of coruscations, like a sparkler, leaving Grandfather luminously naked.

"Where *are* we?" Brendon inquired incredulously.

"Palatkwapi."

"Palawhat?"

"Palatkwapi. It's a very important hub. One of the primary distribution centers of planetary prana." An image of his last painting came to mind, and something Crystal had said about prana.

"But we're not... I mean did you see that?"

"You have a feeling we're not in Arizona anymore?" Dennis chuckled. "Well... yes and no. We're not as far from Sedona as you might think. This is the third globe, Pearce. Or the fifth world as Grandfather would say. The count differs according to the arc. As far as what you *saw*, mindfulness will bring your sensatory capacity online, but you have to remember that many of those present are fluent in form."

Dennis scanned the sky as he walked. Brendon looked as well, but saw nothing. The stalagmites that marked their way appeared more solid now, more in focus, but Brendon felt dizzier, almost nauseous, as he had when he first arrived in Sedona. At the same time he was extremely excited, eager for the unknown to make itself known. The way led to the round building, but not directly; it swooped towards it in a great curve, forming a sort of whorl around the edge of the hollow. The drone had become louder and developed a beat as they descended. It seemed to clog his head and block out any other sounds, like a sinus cold. Dennis, if he perceived it, took no notice, in fact he seemed quite at home; his walk and demeanor were lighter and more confident than ever, as if he had finally been able to share the secret knowledge he had been hiding behind that smug smile.

A profound solemnity infused the air as they drew near the center building, a deep silence that was somehow cemented by the pulsing cadence of the drumming, as if thought were excluded by the beating heart of the place. Carved into, or added onto the temple, or kiva, if that's what it was, were enormous figures that seemed to be buttressing the huge round wall from which they were emerging. Brendon recognized them as kachinas, the pueblo people's spirit beings. Each was different; some bore feathers, some horns, some both. Their squarish, oversize, nonhuman faces had always reminded him of space helmets. They were positioned evenly, and stood hand in hand looking out at the village. They were not colored in the customary way, rather their smooth surface, and that of the entire kiva was shimmering like the stony stalagmites they walked between. Waves of mottled coppery marblings *circulated* around the sacred enclosure. The building itself did not seem to be moving; the giant kachinas did not shift, it was only the bright lustrous flow that ran over and through, into and out of the walls, like the northern lights – the aurora of the kiva of Palatkwapi.

Dennis continued to follow the way laid out by the whorl of markers, although Brendon wondered what would happen if they walked straight to the center of the basin, whether it was only ceremony and tradition that held them to this long process, or if there were other forces involved – forces Dennis did not wish to disturb. At last, when they had all but circumnavigated the kiva, they came to an opening in the ring created by the rambling pueblo houses. Tall, fretted, iridescent gates were drawn aside. When they had passed through, Brendon saw many forms in varying degrees of focus here and there, and maybe not there, so far as he could tell; people, or spirits, projections, memories, he knew not what to name them. Their manner of dress and measure of luminance varied; some were seated and still, others were in process – coming, going, or just spinning in their own whirlwinds, as if sustaining a specific velocity of rotation was their entire purpose. It reminded him of being under water in the pool, where the confused motions of wave shadows, refractions, and gleams of desert sun intermingled with suspended leaves and bits of gyrating debris. They appeared voltaic and fluid, glinting occasionally where their limbs deranged or obtruded on each other, knocking them out of register.

The sky seemed a deeper green now; Brendon kept one eye there, watching for a sign of whatever mysterious arrival Grandfather had alluded to, and one eye on the dizzying play of light around him as he was led to the focus of the basin, the great kiva. Dennis was apparently quite familiar with the place and its inhabitants; he smiled continually, and waved, which seemed to illicit responses from the forms around them. Some even joined them on the path, but there was no speaking; the drumming was too loud to accommodate that.

The kiva was comprised of three tiers. There were no windows or doors. A tall ladder waited at the end of the way. Dennis motioned for Brendon to go first. He climbed the ladder, which ended at a narrow ledge, where he waited. The drumming sound was louder than ever, and obviously came from inside the kiva. When Dennis joined him, he gestured, indicating that Brendon should help him raise the ladder up after them, which they did. They placed it securely on the ledge, and began climbing again. In this way they reached the top of the structure. There was no roof, only a walkway along the top edge, slightly wider than the ledges below.

The bright exterior and the dim depths inside the kiva competed for his peripheral attention; Brendon's sense of perspective failed him, vertigo set in. A nudge in the center of his back propelled him forward a fraction of an inch. He lurched backward involuntarily, almost losing his balance.

"Asshole," he muttered, for of course it was the grinning Brother Rose who had teased him with a faux shove. Dennis chuckled, said something, and winked.

"What?" The drumming now filled Brendon's head.

"Watch out for that first step," he shouted. There were in fact steps leading down into the shadows; the ladder remained outside. Dennis went in front this time. The stairs were not freestanding, but clung to the interior wall. Although they were very narrow, there was no railing. Brendon leaned against the curved stone as he began the descent, and thought perhaps he could feel the current of its coppery aurora, which was more pronounced on the inside because all was in shadow. A bright circle of light emanated from the bottom of the kiva, drawing them down toward it. The resonance of the drumming shook him to the core.

As they neared the floor, people took shape in the darkness. Many had the features and dress and the stalwart bearing of Native Americans. All were composed and focused. They ringed

197

the edge of the space, sitting silently, most with eyes closed. Two or three nodded at them to acknowledge their arrival. There was a large rectangular drum to one side; a separate group surrounded this, beating it in perfect unison. Their presence was strong; there was no flickering or wavering.

Dennis walked over to the circle of light in the floor. He got down on his knees and motioned for Brendon to do the same. The light source was actually an opening; perfectly round, an oculus on the world below; for it was now apparent that they were in fact suspended over a second ground. Together they surveyed the underworld. It was remarkably familiar, a place of meandering canyons and towering buttes. Here was Sedona, still in tact, still carrying on, the morning sun heating up the desert floor. Brendon was reminded of graphics programs on his computer, with their separate layers of color and transparency, because from the vantage point of this higher place, this *third globe*, other aspects of the ordinary world were perceivable, like overlays on the Sedona of his memory.

A sparse web of iridescent strands and glittering nodes like giant pearls outlined the red rock formations. The canyons glowed with dull phosphorescence, and the familiar dense, scrubby shapes of the junipers and cedars were overshadowed by towering bodies of Light. These were somehow conjoined with the trees themselves, interpenetrating them, engendering them, as if the Light was their subtler, yet truer form. It filled him with hope to see these spiraling, glowing beings populating that land which had previously seemed so barren to him. Crystal's words resounded – *they twist to assist the energy; they become the Path.* Now he could really see it, these illuminated entities looked like receiving funnels, investing the earth with spirit.

People, too, were discernible, hiking and walking their dogs in the early hours. From the new perspective, their shimmering auras were clearly visible, whereas their physical bodies appeared as shadows, the vacancy of form. Around each person, or what he assumed were persons, he saw other beings; fluxile, fulgurating, nearly manifest yet just out of phase. Their bodies refracted the surrounding space like a heat mirage. They hovered and followed the shades and shadows, the dense physical counterparts of the lower world.

Dennis tapped him on the shoulder.

"See, Arizona didn't go anywhere," he shouted in his ear.

"But how are we here? Why don't we fall?"

Dennis either didn't hear, or ignored the question. He tipped his head back and pointed. "There, the *merkaba*. It's time," he yelled, pulling him off to the side, away from the portal in the floor.

Brendon looked up and saw something golden in the celadon sky. It was fairly small and round with a nub or bulge above, much like the proverbial flying saucer. Its sheen dulled as it slowed, banked, and approached the opening of the kiva. He felt an unaccountable electric urgency; a need to leap into the air and convene with it, as if his volant heart had preceded him and the rest must follow or perish. Then his woozy mind put two and two together, Sedona below, UFO above.

"Are we on the mother ship?" he demanded.

"No," Dennis said, leaning close and speaking into his ear, "we are fully contiguous with the core, the root. Perception of the various density domains is dependent on the awareness of the individual. Metaphors, such as mechanical vehicles, are often more easily assimilated."

As Brendon struggled to make sense of what he had said, the interior of the kiva suddenly became brighter, almost crystalline. Refracted rays of green and blue formed vivid, open figures of geometric precision, which stretched across the space in overlapping layers. He watched the saucer lower straight down through the center of these laser-like polyhedrons. This sparkling framework was echoed in the structure of the *merkaba.* As it slowed its rotation he saw that its solidity was an illusion due to rapid rotation; there was no hull, or metallic panels. It settled just outside the portal to the underworld, at which point it opened, or rather, effloresced – bloomed. Its lines of light replicated, intertwined and coalesced with exponentially increasing speed, until they revealed, or became, a woman of golden proportion. The sight was jarring and bewildering, but Brendon at last understood that she *was* the vehicle. She was seated in *padmasana*, the lotus position; her protruding knees had formed the flat part of the saucer, her head the center nub. Her eyes were closed. Dennis remained at a respectful distance.

"She's going to need a minute or two," he observed. The drumming had ceased, as if it had been sounded to guide her to the place.

Brendon could not take his eyes off her. Her presence was magnetic, beyond mere beauty.

"But..." he protested vehemently, "She's not *real*. I mean, nothing here is, right? It's all just energy, and... vibration and whatever." Her arrival, her metamorphosis, her aura of divine grace, and his subliminal comprehension of *who* she must be; were wrenching at paradigmatic structures in his mental and emotional bodies. "This is all metaphor, like the rock Rune told me to find, it's just a dream!"

Dennis laughed heartily, "It *is* all a dream, but there are different levels of dream. She's real, Pearce, just as real as you or I, see?" He reached out and playfully slapped Brendon on the cheek, drawing his eyes away from her for a minute. "And of course it's all just energy. There is nothing else, never was. Matter does not constitute consciousness. Particles come and go, we breathe in, we breathe out, we eat, we excrete, we slough our skin, our bodies, our lives; consciousness remains. So it is with less dense beings. Particles come and go, flowing through their beings with ease, but the waveguide of consciousness remains. Forms are wrought on frameworks woven of rays and intent, here as in every globe, every density domain or plane of existence. The only difference is, here some forms are wrought and witnessed momently, out of time. Still, they are no more than convenient composites of standing waves in the universal pleroma."

"The what? Make sense, damn it."

Dennis chuckled again. "The aether, the plenum, the koilon, mulaprakrti, the matrix, akasha, the Bose-Einstein condensate, dark energy, God. You'll see. You'll know."

"You're so full of shit," Brendon said, but he was no longer certain of this, or who exactly Dennis was, or what he was doing in his dream, or whose dream it was. His attention returned to the resplendent woman. She was achingly familiar, like something precious long lost. The way her hair was dressed upon her head, her bare shoulders, and the golden bangles on her wrists and ankles gave her an Eastern air, and reminded him of that painting he had seen at the Orange Grove Gallery, that the handyman had referred to as the *dakini*.

"At any rate," Dennis continued, reaching out a hand, "My time with you is done, I've been reassigned," he said with that familiar wink.

"Oh yeah? Where to?" Brendon asked, taking his hand firmly, but looking past him at the beautiful being who had dropped out of the sky. Her roundish face bespoke a sweet temperament; her lithe hands, deft poise; her galvanic glow, profound power. Her eyes fluttered.

"I'm headed to Dinas Affaraon," he said, "Going to meet up with some druids."

"Okay. Well have a good trip, and don't forget to write," Brendon quipped, still unsure of when to take the man seriously, and feeling eager to have him gone.

"But you," he continued, "you're goin' to the big show." Brendon waited, holding a quizzical look, letting him have his dramatic pause.

"Shambhala."

He had heard the word; Rune or Carol had mentioned it. He took it to be another name for Shangri-la. Utopia. Heaven. Then we *are* dead, he thought, we'd have to be. Before he could put the question again to Agent LeRose, the good Brother had turned away. Brendon expected him to head back up the stair, but he did not. He chose a spot on the ground beside the *dakini* and sat with his back to the oculus. He crossed his legs and composed himself, taking deep breaths.

"Agent Pearce," he said, smiling his knowing smile, "allow me to introduce Agent Khandroma." The woman unfolded and rose; emanating an intrinsic radiance so bright as to obscure the form they had only just seen woven of rays and intent. Brendon knew he was seeing what Rune had seen, for she was shining like the sun, and he knew likewise that he did not, could not deserve her. 'Know always you are loved' Rune had related on her behalf. He loved her instantly, completely, and eternally.

"Her name means 'she who moves in space'. You may already know her as Skydancer. She will be working with you for the foreseeable future," Dennis concluded. Then he closed his eyes and was still.

When Brendon looked her way again, she was dressed in diaphanous robes, which happily dimmed her brilliant emission. He was speechless; a nod was all he could manage. Khandroma demurely bowed her head in return. He waited. She did not attempt to instruct him. She did not lead him anywhere or exhort him to any task. She only stood before him, smiling gently, a look of infinite kindness and understanding. Her glowing aura warmed and softened his guard; her pure frequency equalized the wave of his being until his perception of isolation was corrected. Eventually, despite the disturbing nature of all he had witnessed and felt since waking in the desert, he began to feel safe. He relaxed. Waves of emotion were freed. He smiled. Only then did Khandroma act.

She advanced, took his hand in hers, and moved away from the opening, toward the stairs. Out of the corner of his eye, he saw Dennis; if that was his name, lean backward into the sipapu and drop.

CHAPTER THIRTEEN

A WHIRLING gray mass, which Brendon took to be in some way his inscrutable winking friend, shot up through the portal and high above the kiva before veering and vanishing into the greenish sky.

"Thank you," he said to her, still looking after LeRose. Gratitude is the key to progress, someone had told him, and he had never been more grateful than to be in the presence of Khandroma. He looked back at her. She said nothing in response, but continued to smile lovingly at him. His mind could not help but replay all that had been attributed to her and wonder if she were truly the source of certain phrases: *she wants you to open your heart...I've got your back...*

"For being here," he clarified. Her hand was still in his. There was a palpable vibration flooding up his arm, as if she were trying to communicate with him through pure energy. He savored the memory and hope of that odd phrase: *I like Ike,* which by the ludicrous caprice of providence had come to mean, 'I hear your lowest vibration, I know all your basest desires, yet I love you still.'

"I mean, for inviting me," he continued stupidly. *Had* he been invited? Or abducted? It did not matter to him; he had fallen in love with her, like a schoolboy. Her receptive smile broadened, as if he had been foolish and she loved him for it, because of course – if Rune was to be believed – it was *he*, or his soul who had invited *her*. Miraculously, she had come. '*She asks nothing*

205

but that you embrace her, and allow her to embrace you', the little man had said. The longer he beheld her, clasped her with hand and eye, the greater his sense of gratitude became. 'You are right where you're supposed to be', he remembered, 'you are needed for the forward progression of events.'

"So what do I need to do?" he asked, eager to repay her for the gift of her presence, to somehow compensate her for lowering herself to his ignoble frequency.

Marry me, he heard – or was it merely one more replay, a words only in his head? She had not moved her lips, she gave no particular indication that she was trying to communicate with him, no squeeze, no finger movement, just enough pressure to maintain contact; so this proposal had to have been a reiteration, a memory of that previous delusive occurrence, that identical acousma experienced while painting, when he had thought the sound had come from Carol's mouth.

"What is this baetyl?" he inquired, recalling Rune's words, 'you are to find something. There is a baetyl.'

"Is it real? Where is it?"

"You will see," she said, taking his arm in hers. That propinquity caused his entire side to quaver, like all the cells within a certain range of her had changed their vibration to match hers. They began making their way up the stairway, out of the kiva. She moved fluidly, gracefully, with neither haste nor leisure nor the least sign of effort, the drape of her gossamer gown barely ruffled, as if movement itself was a deceit she played at out of necessity, a glamour the senses required to induce some particular awareness. His body ached to be nearer yet.

"Is it by the gate?" he asked, suddenly remembering the title of the print, View from the Gate, and thinking of the iridescent gates he and Dennis had come through.

"That is not the gate in question," she replied, "This is." Here she motioned with her other hand towards the inside of the kiva they were climbing out of, or perhaps toward the sipapu itself. But how did she know, Brendon wondered, what gate I meant, or what question I had in mind?

"I can see them, like colors in the wind," she offered.

"What?"

Thoughtforms which emerge and cling to you, she answered, floating a lithe hand in the air as if to mimic a process he could scarcely imagine. Her comely lips had not parted. They had reached the top of the kiva, where the strength of her emittance was equaled by the sunlight, and she looked more normal, solid, and womanly. He turned to face her, took her other small hand in his, and looked intently at her beautiful face.

Your lips did not move, he noted silently. Her big eyes flashed a spark of glee born of his astonishment; her smile enveloped him.

It is of no consequence, he heard without hearing. *I love you, Brendon Pearce. Marry me.*

The surroundings faded, blended, and blurred into her golden aura. Her gaze held him; there was nothing but her. He was grinning, returning her gleaming ardor with equal intensity. Her hands were softly receptive, her scent inviting, her eyes accepting; then his senses moved *beyond* the anticipated, the hoped for, the surface expectations. He saw her face morphing from Khandroma through Harmony, Sharon, Linda, Cassidy, Krista, Mother, Mary, Venus, Ishtar, Shakti... it was she he had loved all along, before he had seen her, before he had heard of her, before his birth into this or any past or future life, before consciousness, before existence itself, it was she he had sought. She was his soul. And still reverberating through the gelid

207

medium of his being, the persistent, inductive frequency – in words – *Marry me.*

Yes oh yes, he replied, pulling her to him. He kissed her; she responded without reserve, wrapping herself around him as though she had four, six, eight arms. He began to experience synesthesia, as she had described – seeing wafts of color and light associated with her touch, with thoughts he could not hear, then he found himself hearing the way she looked, smelling the way she felt in his hands, tasting the music of her spirit as his awareness moved into her. He knew truly requited love; she gave herself to him completely. He made no effort to resist his violent attraction to her, but abandoned himself to her, as the blue flame was kindled and roared up from the depths. He abandoned his *self* for hers, vacating with a great rush that which he had thought to be him, letting go of all control, surrendering. Yet as surely as the note was sounded at the base, so it rose rapidly, spiraling up the *nadis*, firing center after center, consuming his desire like rocket fuel.

Now Light poured into him from above to meet that which rose from below; he could feel it as an electric charge, a buzzing, a sounding working down from the crown of his head; yet he could also see it, for he was without, he was in her as she was in him, and whether he was feeling the Light coming into her body or his was a ludicrous, moot question, because each could feel and see both. By coming together, they had created a new path for energy to flow. It was more than copulation, more than making love; they were inviting love, conducting love. They were not activating a chakra; they had *become* the chakra, as forces poloidal and toroidal conjugating beyond differentiation, *marrying* to produce the vortical engine, the tube torus. As the Light was allowed in, so the sorrow and longing and darkness took the counterclockwise outward arc, rising in release, and as the sorrow and longing welled up and overflowed and washed away, so in turn the Light was sucked into the clockwise inward arc, and filled them with bliss, joy, and humor. In this way decades of frustration and resentment, which might have turned adoration to lust in their relentless quest for escape, fell away like so much slag from white hot steel, as if the passion, though originating in the old world of the fourth globe, could only exist here in the third as its higher harmonic, compassion. The depths were all but forgotten as overtone after overtone rang true and clear, and his beloved, who now dwelt in him, opened his crusty heart from the inside. His love of her was so great that he had become her, and she him. This he knew without thinking, without seeking, likewise that he had been able to rise, to let go of the dead weight of his personality, his ego, only because she had let go of hers, and his gratitude was everlasting.

Now Brendon sensed movement, the lifting of their convolving nexus from the solidity of the kiva. He realized they had transformed into the *merkaba*, the rotary vehicle of transport. The spinning was faster; they moved horizontally over the sacred space, hovering momentarily, then suddenly rushed upward as if they had been sucked into a pneumatic tube, and it seemed to him they had become as the fire of life coursing through nadis in the body of another.

The patterns of their energies melded and meshed as they opened to each other and exchanged their selves, like the puddles he had joined as a child. There was a calculus at play adding her wave to his wave, just as when two pools of water merge. Because her energy was the stronger, or purer, or because she had passed through more than he and her awareness was the greater, the bound of her being, the membrane of her egoic bubble was many times vaster than his own; her pool was deeper. Therefore, he felt a tremendous expansion, an increase in that which his 'I' compassed. His identity changed from what *he* knew and was to what *she* knew and was. Her love was of such volume and clarity that it raised Brendon to a pitch higher than he had ever experienced before, to a place where fear was funny and reason ineffectual for knowing; a vibration at which old ways of thinking and feeling could not maintain their form, so that, just as he had intended, he was repatterned, tooled to a new geometry which could withstand the shorter wavelengths. Lifetimes of habitual thought dropped like unneeded ballast. That which his mind had access to was multiplied. He reveled in it, as he reveled in her heart. She gave him answers before he asked, as she had given her love. He began to see as she saw, to feel as she felt, to hear as she heard.

Through his *dakini*, his beloved, Brendon began to understand the layers of form, the interpenetrating coherences of energy which as yet appeared both brumous and auroral, shimmering fogs of plasmic condensates surrounding features in the landscape, or flickering on their own like cloudy ghosts. He knew through her that the things he had seen since entering the stone spiral; the unusual fog, the triangle of whirling lights, the tunnel, Grandfather's vanishing headdress, the marbled glow of the Kiva, then the way Sedona looked through the sipapu, all the trees mirrored by towering light bodies, the iridescent strands covering the buttes, the hundreds of beings clinging to mortal men – he knew now that it was all real, that none of it was anyone's dream. He knew by Khandroma's knowing that subtle bodies were only subtle because of the equipment of evolving man, that the blurred, unstable qualities he now perceived were due to his newborn eyes, and that the clinging fire on the edges of things was a but a hint of the crisp hyper-colored focus he might expect to experience. He knew too that these layers, these different densities of phonons, photons, bosons, leptons, hadrons, fermions and on and ons, these different pitches in the voice of God were what made it possible for Khandroma to come to him, to speak to Rune and Dexter in the fourth globe, to appear to him and Dennis in the third globe, to move and work forms by intent.

As they rose, Palatkwapi was quickly left behind. They flew and whirled west over the desert, climbing in and passing through the celadon sky. Their rotational velocity increased, until all became white and fluid, a frothy flume of light. Brendon felt, kinesthetically, that they were moving higher and farther, through a channel in the diaphanous air. They were not advancing under their own propulsion, nor were there storm-like forces pushing them, but rather they were being guided along a preexisting pathway made and kept clear by repeated use, as if the habitual energetic action of the sky itself was pulling them to an appointed destination. It promised to be a place of great wisdom, openness, and power.

With a perceptible change of pitch, a shift to a new octave, the lovers came into a golden atmosphere where all the stars of the cosmos made white sparkles in the midst of day. Their rotation had slowed; vision began to return. They had risen in more than altitude and were now constituted at the vibration of the fifth world. Khandroma cheerfully informed him of the waters they had crossed, the deserts they had escaped, and the peaks they had conquered. Ahead of them the white particulates accumulated, the flume curled and fell away precipitously. Along with this coursing white light, they were being pulled irrevocably around and into a shadowy funnel.

This gyre brought them down amidst a ring of mountains, but these did not appear as expected, they were not snow topped, or verdant, or jaggedly shaped. They were smooth, faceted, free of vegetation and debris, and the color of smoky quartz. The valley of their destination seemed to be situated within a geode of colossal proportion. There the ground sloped down into a deep hollow or well, out of which rose an enormous circular formation of pillars and lintels, an ancient hypaethral temple or henge. It challenged the height of the crystal peaks amongst which it sat.

After hovering a moment, they lowered into the center of the henge, just as Khandroma alone had lowered into the Kiva at Palatkwapi. He could see now that the pillars were shaped in human form, giant gilt statues holding up a ring of stone, some male, some female, some old, some young, suggestive of various ethnicities. Each one was unique and portrayed with its own particular dress and accoutrements, but all were in a seated position, with a look of deep contemplation on their faces. The columns extended from the top of their heads and the base of their seats. These shafts were pellucid like the mountains, so that the figures appeared to be levitating several stories in the air. The edges of the lintels, those crowning slabs that linked all the pillars, ran with a pulsing fire.

The interior of the temple was wider than a football field, and concave like a great bowl. A palpable hum pervaded all, a low rumbling like Harmony's didgeridoo, only fuller, with clear high overtones. It had the timbre of a thousand voices chanting, and the continuity of a vast turbine or roaring cataract. Just as at Palatkwapi, there was an aperture in the center of the space, only this one was much larger. Brendon and his beloved settled on the sweet turf beside the portal. She let go of him; with a twinge of regret he felt the engine of their twining cease, and their beings separate. He watched Khandroma regenerate beside him, cohere into womanish form at this higher vibration, and marveled that here in the golden globe she was even more beautiful. Her radiant smile reassured him that their separation was temporary, was in fact an illusion, because they were forever

212

entangled – karmically, quantumly, soulfully. When he saw that she yet loved him, he could not believe his good fortune.

"Welcome to Shambhala," she said, motioning around her. He looked about the temple space. There were flowers and trees of impossible, Elysian shapes and colors, all blooming with gold and violet light; a stream purled mellifluously as it followed its coiled course around the temple, cascading at last through the central portal as an iridescent shower of blessing on the lower worlds. An immanent dynamism seemed to issue from the entire valley, as if the whole were quavering with excitement. The lustrous, diademed sky tasted of ambrosia, spring, and baby's breath.

"I love you," he said, still grinning.

"And I love you, my Smiling Bear," she playfully responded, rising and taking his hand. They bobbed barefoot along the bank of the stream, following its spiral outward from the oculus, spinning and skipping like children as they wound their way. Turning around the henge, Brendon counted seven major pillars, seven giant statues of bodhisattvas or gurus. Each of these was buttressed by seven smaller columns, including similar representations of saints and sadhus locked hand in hand or arm in arm, their gaze focused upward to the center of their particular group, and each smaller statue had its own cluster of adherents. In all there were seven tiers of this configuration.

The air dripped sunshine, moisture, sweetness. As birds, they opened their mouths to receive it. As honeybees, they tasted the flowers. As squirrels, they climbed the tittering, ticklish trees. As lovers, they rolled together on the velvet turf of the temple, laughing at the conceit of self. Their laughter echoed pink off the crystal mountains. The curl of the stream bed eventually brought them to the perimeter of the henge, and deposited them before a midlevel support of the temple, in which could be seen the likeness of a lama, life-size, seated in the lotus position, adorned

213

in saffron and maroon robes. He had a thin mustache, a high forehead, and eyes full of humor and compassion. Surrounding the base of his column, at their feet, was a ring of similar yogis and monks the size of garden gnomes, each with their own pillar, and below them were smaller figures in like attitude. The warm, golden complexion of the lama lent a noble quality to his humble visage.

Welcome to Shambhala, he said. The words were audible, yet not auricular, just as when Khandroma communicated with him, Brendon heard, but not with the ear. Those thin lips had not moved, yet he knew perfectly well that the statue had spoken to him. Only then did Brendon realize that the lama was not merely a likeness, but a living being, a man of the golden globe. As if breaking a spell, the sounding of this thought in Brendon's mind altered the manner of his percipience yet again; he had been waiting, as Dennis earlier said, for his sensatory capacity to come online. In rising to the frequency of the fifth world, they had crossed another perceptual limen, stepped into a harmonic where his sense mechanisms had never been. There was an issue of time involved, Khandroma explained, as well as his own dependency on form. He could now see that the column issuing from the lama's head was no more stone than he was, it was Light, a type of plasma, an influx of energy pouring down through him.

A smile slowly curled up from the corners of his mouth. Brendon's heart opened fully to this holy man, and he knew Khandroma's was open to him as well, either would do anything for him. Perhaps it was only overflow, his love of Khandroma being too much to contain, perhaps it was the hallowed nature of the place, the peculiar vibration of the henge, or perhaps the lama was of such purity and goodness himself that it could not be helped, but Brendon loved him, to his astonishment, every bit as much as he loved Khandroma, every bit as much as he had ever loved anyone. Then he realized that this was because once the heart is open, there is no greater or lesser love. There is no allotment, no singular or plural, no duration to eternity, no limit to infinity. The three of them stood grinning at each other.

Then the shape shifting began. The lama's face softened, blurred, and morphed into that of a kindly bespectacled matron. Her face rose out of the lama's head, and was replaced by the stippled and adorned visage of a Massai warrior which in turn rose, sort of pushing the face of the woman higher up the pillar of energy, then the head of an elephant appeared on the lama's body, only to rise and give way to a grizzled, bearded mountain man, a pale, painted geisha, a great white heron, a nun in habit, a turbaned Sikh, a sad-eyed Grey, a little laughing blonde girl, a lion, a wizened crone, a Satyr, a butterfly, a sphinx; faster and faster they appeared and took their place as totems in the mounting pole, and Brendon loved them all.

Marry us, they said. He and his beloved laughed, for surely they were already married, surely all are one. Without hesitation they embraced him – them, the lama and the parade of beings streaming from or through him – thus avowing their intent to cleave, to attune their hearts to the frequency of the ashram. In so doing, they were pulled into the current of Light, and quickly rose to the tier above, entering the body of the avatar, that is to say, their energy fields flowed into hers, circulating with myriad beings in cooperation with the now familiar roiling vortical flow of the everting torus, thus adding their lesser powers to the greater dynamo.

Here Brendon was privy to the minds of many, as if he had walked into an auditorium where a hundred conversations echoed; he caught snippets from this or that quarter, concern for particular kingdoms of nature, rumors of planetary etheric congestion, and the destruction of planetary etheric tissue. Elsewhere came cautions to expect disruptions when suppressed pain is released, as it must be in the first step toward healing. He heard exhortations to include all, and reminders of the importance of observing auspicious conjunctions, but from everyone he felt the excitement, the growing awareness at all levels, in all kingdoms, of the coming change. The anticipation was felt by all beings who at some time, in some way had their hopes tied to the evolution of the planet, including plants and animals, the Devas, the Seraphim and Nephilim, the Annunaki, the Lemurians, the Atlantians, the Greys, the Nordics, and all manner of stellar beings.

Despite all the new information at his disposal, or perhaps because of it, Brendon's confusion increased, he turned to Khandroma, his questions compounded; *What change? What conjunction? How can you love me? Where, when are we? Whose pain?*

She wrapped herself around him, kissed him, quieted him, and led him, at the correct moment of the cycle, into the current again, riding into the giant heart of a bodhisattva, where tranquility again held sway.

By virtue of his inclusion, Brendon now understood it was through conscious resolve and quietude that this guru, this master of energetic control, or rather energetic *allowance,* invited and guided rays of energy through his being. He had evolved beyond the static egoic bubble, beyond even the forging of the connecting bridge, the *antahkarana* vortex at the crown of his sphere. By the use of two seemingly opposing forces, Will and Love, brought into harmony through their conflicting directional applications (latitudinally and longitudinally) he was able – like the galaxy with its black hole center, and the electron cloud of certain molecules – to maintain the torus of his being in its open tube shape. He had become a superconductor of Light, a guide of the waves of Spirit following the inward arc, and of Matter being redeemed to Spirit. And Brendon perceived that all the columns of the temple were axes of tori, formed in the subtle bodies of these masters by the conscious will to love, by the opening of their hearts, minds, and souls; offering themselves as broadband conduits of cosmic power. It was an honor to know and contribute to that intent.

They; Brendon and Khandroma, the lama, the mountain man, the geisha, the heron, the nun, the Sikh, the master, the little blonde, the Greys and lizards and all the crowd of entities aggregated from all the tiers of the hierarchy below, were now married in the body of the bodhisattva, were now rotating and convolving as the helical winding of his torus. They had become the wheel of fire itself, the churning living waters, a chakra in a larger form, which was itself a nexus in a yet larger form.

They were very high above the valley now. Above them was the ring of lintels, a marvel pulsing with fire, the crown of Earth, built to build, calling and melding the energy of the seven giants into a supercharged waveguide, quivering with the sound it contained, the drone of the ages, the song of the cosmos. From this vantage point, he saw a web of white strands, like those he had seen on the buttes and mesas of Sedona, a vast matrix of light covering and interpenetrating the entire planet. This fretwork was relatively static. By the assisted recall of Harmony's words, *'the form of the dense body issues from a network of meridians which is in turn formed by the intersection of waves in the subtle bodies'*, he was given to understand it was structural in nature, a stabilizing influence. Khandroma, hearing him remember, gave him a resounding 'yes'. It was then clear that *this* – the lace of spectral lines and nodes spread out beneath them – this was planetary etheric tissue, an energetic armature to which matter

217

clung. This is what was in danger of destruction, and if destroyed the dense globe would become unstable. It was Earth's pain that must be released before healing could begin.

Like a bolt out of the blue, an idea was placed into his head, an indubitable understanding, a revelation: the Earth is not only alive, it is conscious. It is a being of age beyond comprehension, yet vital, evolving, and purposeful. It is not merely a parking lot for humans, not only a home, it is mother, father, sister, brother, friend, teacher, beloved. Like you, it is an individual, and it is a multitude. Like you, it needs the cooperation of all of its parts to thrive, to increase its capacity to comprehend, communicate, and love.

Brendon reacted to this revelation with compassion, and grave concern, plying Khandroma with questions, and remembering the task he had already been assigned.

How can I help? What, how, why is the baetyl? Where is the View from the Gate, when will I find it, why is the baetyl there, what is it, what will it do, what does it mean...

Again, holding him close, his beloved took him higher, where knowledge might be passed more readily. They entered the outward flow and became the observer, seeing the world from above the temple, the mountains, the sphere of golden light, witnessing from the darkness of space. To see, through her eyes, the planet as it truly was – a series of nested globes rotating at different velocities, constituting at specific densities, vibrating each to its appointed harmonic – filled him with gratitude and excitement. The different colored plasmas ebbed, flowed, and interacted with each other as they progressed along their various cycles. He watched these energies, the Earth's subtle bodies, twisting, flaring, arcing, joining, parting and joining again, all in an attempt to synthesize a balanced, coherent current across all layers, to maximize efficient flow. It was an incredibly beautiful display, and left no doubt that it was alive.

Outstanding in this display was a marked pattern of white light streams, flumes turning and spiraling into the hub of Shambhala. The phrase *lines of transmission* was dropped into him, triggering his recall of Dexter's reference to chakra petals. There must have been a thousand of these connective threads in confluence over the temple they had just departed, coming together from all over the planet. Taken as a whole, they looked similar to a spirographic diagram he had seen in Crystal's office titled *The Flower of Life*. It was by one of these pathways that they had arrived from Palatkwapi. It was via these nadis that Earth's chi, or prana, or *Élan vital* circulated. It was through these channels, and a complex process of stepping down vibratory rates, that the masters distributed Fohat, the synthesized primary cosmic energy, to all entities in the various kingdoms, and it was from this center of Shambhala, the receiver of Light, that all awakened beings received guidance.

By direct impress, he knew the masters were not there at Shambhala because it was a center; they were not pilgrims. The Light came to Shambhala because the masters were there, and they had chosen the place for its quiet isolation. With Earth's encouragement, they gathered to raise the local resonance. Their consciousness, their constancy, the temple they had become, set up a new eddy in Earth's subtle bodies which had evolved into the formation of a vortex, a portal through Earth's waveguide, formerly known as its ring-pass-not, or egoic bubble. In the fullness of time this would take on the geometric qualities of a tube torus, thus enabling Earth to become a radiant conductor of energy, a being ready to give not only within itself, but also without. Working together, the saints and monks and yogis functioned as Earth's head center, its crown chakra, holding the image and intent of its perfected form, receiving and synthesizing the seven rays into one, for the exaltation of the planet.

Further, he understood that just as he, Brendon, had sent forth supplication at the wishing wall by the Chapel of the Cross for his beloved to appear; the Earth, too, had requested contact. There was an instability. The various tori and centers of the several interpenetrating globes of Earth were out of alignment. As with any entity from subatomic to supragalactic, if the various bodies, (physical, emotional, mental, causal, etc.) are not integrated, but function as separate personalities with separate aims, their orbital resonances, the music of the spheres, will not resonate harmonically, but discordantly to the fundamental. This instability, if not corrected, will eventuate in the shattering of the form.

Yet, as he had learned from Dexter, a crisis is an opportunity. The anxiety felt by beings across the kingdoms over this tipping point was equaled by their excitement at the first tingling hints of an awakening, a growing awareness. In fact the anxiety itself was a harbinger, an anticipation of the coming divine spark, the nudge, as Dennis put it, the Application of the Rod of Initiation, the *response* to Earth's call, the inducement, the threefold plasmic jolt from the Solar Logos by which Earth would take its leap of faith, cross a broader perceptual threshold, and establish consciousness at a new frequency.

To Khandroma, who surrounded him, he nevertheless turned with new questions, only to learn that either way, crisis or opportunity, the entire entity of Earth, including all its inhabitants, *in all its globes*, will necessarily be affected. Yet he turned and turned again into her, asking, *How affected? What is happening? Why is it happening? Can't we stop it? Can I stay in you forever?*

Seeing that he had begun to slip into Doubt, to turn from the Path, they spoke into him a waveform, a frequency that might be translated as:

Peace, be still

Thus placing him with the power of vibration and intent at the center of all his windings, the critical point of the harmonic manifold, the place of zero curl, the irrotational moment, that silent infinity where things as coarse as words cannot form, where thought, being a motion like any other, must needs cease.

Om Mani Padme Hum

He watched the whirling of him slow, sag, and collapse to nothing like water in a blender when the motor is switched off. Unsupported by centripetal forces, the egoic membrane – the waveguide of individual identity – dissipated, burst, just like Dennis's water balloon analogy, leaving him everything, everywhere.

Nibbāna　　　*Ekénōsen*　　　*Fana Fi Allah*

Without emotion, without reason, without cause or effect, awareness dawned that the womanly body of his beloved was but a metaphor (created by sense mechanisms) for a crystalline body of pure light, which was in turn a metaphor for a set of wave-particle interactions, which, being fluid, were inseparable from all waves in the noumenal world, the Living Waters, the great cosmic soup, the plasmic pleroma; so that she was not only connected, but *indivisible* from him, and that both were in turn a metaphor for the greater light body of Earth, which was

221

therefore also his beloved, that in fact every numerable thing, the individualized multitude, all narratives and appurtenances thereto, was but an allegory of the Divine. He was, had been, and would always be, all in all, the indivisible singularity, despite being metaphorically known as Smiling Bear or Brendon Pearce.

As his attention returned to the name of his birth, so the rotation began anew, the membrane snapped back in place, he was separate again. Having thus quieted him, they reminded him of his part, his obligation through birth to his Mother Earth, to share with others his understanding so that all will have active intent to invite healing energy to the planet, to participate in the evolution of its consciousness, to let Light descend on Earth.

This he reaffirmed without hesitation, as they began to rotate clockwise now, to move from Spirit into Matter, to glide back toward the crystal mountains; but when they reminded him about the baetyl he was to locate, he balked.

"But I don't want to go *back*," he objected, "I can't." The idea of returning to the dark heavy world, to what he had been, was too much.

"Your work there is not yet done," she said.

"I will work from here, with you. We will guide those below together."

But it was not to be. The very weight of his desire to stay lowered his frequency like a balloon losing altitude. The Law was made clear to him. He would return, at one time or another, in one body or another, until his obligation was fulfilled. They did not reenter the henge of Shambhala, but curled away in a flume of light, crossing back into the fifth globe with its celadon sky.

"It's true form is hidden," she informed him, returning to the subject of the baetyl. "Many have touched, none have seen."

"Seen what? What is it?"

"A transmission whose time has come. It must be exhumed."

222

They seemed to be moving faster than ever; already they were over the luminous desert.

"But where is it?"

"During certain conjunctions, directly below the Gate," she replied, as Palatkwapi came into view.

"But I haven't been able to find that view," he protested. The sound of drumming again filled his ears, as the council beat out the oscillation that kept the portal open.

"Do not worry," she said, smiling, hugging him tightly, "Look for me and I will guide you."

Their revolutions slowed as they lowered rapidly into the kiva. To his chagrin, Khandroma released him. Without her, he felt he was falling, and dropped right through the sipapu, leaving his beloved behind. Facing downward, for the first time he noticed a silvery cord, stretching from his head down to the desert floor. This magnetic rope, the sutratma, was pulling him, retracting him, all the way back into his cataleptic body.

CHAPTER FOURTEEN

"PHIL," he said aloud, chuckling, "You look fabulous!" The words sprang spontaneously from his lips, as naturally as if he were speaking to Cass. The green sheen of the ficus in the morning light filled him with joy and gratitude, and he saw someone to love – not some *thing*, in need of care, but some *one,* a friend, a fellow traveler, a companion sharing the day.

"I guess Michael has kept watch over you in my absence." Phil quivered his leaves in response. There was a time Brendon would have dismissed any such movement as the effect of a stray air current or a heavy truck passing, but now he *knew*, and knowing made him smile more broadly at brother Phil, and rest his gaze there, admiring his beauty, sharing with the plant a moment of communion, of simultaneous recognition of the presence of Spirit in one another, and the interconnectedness, the inseparability of their beings. *Namaste.*

He rose to a sitting position. There was a woozy feeling, a bulging or swollen feeling outside his skull, but it troubled him no more than the tingling he felt at the top of his head. He thought of it as another sign of connection, better than a reminder of oneness, a sensation of it.

Beside him on the nightstand, the rhodochrosite glowed its deep magenta.

"And you, Rhoda, are more beautiful than ever. I am so honored to have you here with me," he added, with complete sincerity. He did not remember everything about where he had been, or at least he didn't *think* he did, but there were certain realities that had changed for him, things he perceived differently now. For instance, he understood clearly what a blessing the lucent cluster bestowed on him, and that because they have arranged their molecules into the form of platonic solids, crystals hold the most coherent vibration of any stone. They are the most attuned, the most evolved, the best conductors of spiritual energy in the mineral kingdom; they are Masters, inviting and allowing the rays to move through them. This is why they are healing. They do not keep the energy for themselves, but pass it through.

"Thank you for your generosity," he said, touching the stone gently, observing the depth and hue of each facet, sure in the knowledge that it was, in some way, registering the love, the exchange of Light that was the truth of all interactions.

There was a soft knock at the door; his voice had been heard.

"Come in," he called.

"You're feeling better," Crystal surmised, entering the room with her familiar, life-affirming flounce.

"I am," he agreed, rising. "Never better, I think."

"I'm so glad," she said with a light embrace, which he returned a bit more robustly. To his surprise, he found he was completely devoid of his usual awkward self-consciousness, despite being in only boxers and a t-shirt, knowing his hair was probably sticking up and he smelled of sleep. It was laughably unimportant.

"I can never thank you enough, Crystal," he said, still holding her hands. "I mean that." He suddenly felt great affection for her, and embraced her again.

"Whatever for?"

"For inviting me. For creating this place."

"You're most welcome, Brendon."

Behind Crystal, peeking her head through the door now was Harmony, her long hair wet from the pool. He grinned at her, went to her, and hugged her tightly, overflowing with love. He felt the warmth and softness of her body, acknowledged its supple sensuality, yet the energy, the tingling, began in his heart and rose to his head.

"So good to see you," he said, though he had seen her briefly the day before, when he had come home from the hospital.

"You too," she admitted, coming further into the room. He chuckled, because there was no craving, no longing, no consuming desire — for who desires themselves? You can only desire what you do not have, he thought, what you believe you *are* not, and Brendon, knowing they were one, found consumption, possession, consummation no longer necessary. Simply loving her, opening his heart to her was a far more powerful communion, and he rejoiced in it.

Behind her came the gaunt, severe face of Rune. Seeing him, perhaps because of that moment he had seen Skydancer in those eyes, made Brendon tear up, for there again was the beloved. He moved forward and embraced him as well, feeling the very same open heart to open heart. Soon Michael and Carol had joined them and received their hugs in turn; so all of them were there together in that small room. Brendon sat on the bed, overflowing with joy at having his friends around him, seeing the beloved radiating from each one of them, and marveling that only a few days earlier nothing would have made him more uncomfortable than for all of them to be there in *his* space, which he now knew, along with all the worlds and planes of the multiverse, was *their* space, together, because there was, after all, only One space, only One life.

"Are you okay?" Carol asked as she sat beside him, because his face was leaking even though the smile would not budge.

"I think so," he said.

"It's not your fault," Michael observed, referring to Dennis, who had died out there in the desert. There was not time enough to save both of them, Ben had said. He had been struck too, but somehow had not lost consciousness. He was nearest to Brendon, and had performed CPR successfully, but Dennis was already gone by the time he reached him.

"No, I know."

"We're all going to miss him," said Carol. Everyone's eyes showed concern, because they had gone through this trauma as well, and had not been able to say goodbye.

"I'm sure he's in a better place," Harmony added.

"Oh, no, it's not that," Brendon assured them. He felt no sorrow, only gratitude, joy, and a certain astonishment. "I mean, I'm going to miss him too, but I saw him there..." He paused, uncertain what he had seen or where he had been, "...on the other side, or... wherever we were." He laughed out loud. "I *know* he's in a better place. He was happy. To be moving on. His next mission, I think he put it."

"Then what is it?" asked Carol.

"I just never expected... I never thought change was real. I mean I'm not sure what happened out there. I remember, but I don't remember. I think I may have been abducted," he chuckled.

"*Inducted*," Crystal corrected, smiling softly, "Initiated. It is plain to see. Your face shines with agape."

"Oh, yeah, anyone can see that," Michael declared, "You've been bathing in the paramatman light."

"Yes! So much light, and... like fire. But even more than that. I had this strange experience. I was like everything, everywhere. Dennis knew."

"The Kundalini awakening," Harmony said.

"Just you wait. The changes have just begun."

228

"You have been illumined with shakti," noted Carol.

Brendon began to leak again, overwhelmed with emotion. "I want you to know how grateful I am to all of you, for including me, teaching me."

"Don't be silly."

"You're welcome, dear."

"Now you must pass it on."

"Thank *you* for teaching us."

"What of the baetyl, Smiling Bear?" Rune asked pointedly. For a moment, the room dissolved. The name returned Brendon to the place of quavering air, the hum of the henge, the voice of the Masters, the arms of his beloved, and he wondered if he had ever left, *could* ever leave, could ever know where he was again. He felt unsure of what he was *supposed* to be seeing, hearing, or experiencing. Then focus returned to his rented room in Sedona.

He nodded, smiling broadly, acknowledging her in Rune, as well as Rune's awareness of her. The others looked at the little man quizzically because they were still unaware of the task she had bestowed, and they had no notion why Rune had suddenly pinned such a colorful appellation on him.

"I think I know where it is," he said, rising. He took the print from its place on the seven-drawer chest, held it up so all could see, and poked the plastic with his forefinger. "It lies at this point of view."

"And where is that?" Rune demanded.

"We'll find it. She'll show me."

"What kind of beetle is it?" Michael asked.

"It's not an insect, it's a stone, a meteorite," Crystal informed him, "and this particular baetyl has been waiting – for us – for quite some time." Both Brendon and Rune looked at her in astonishment.

"What? Do you think I fumble in the dark?"

229

* * *

"You absolutely must meditate first."

"Yes, but... all right, you're right," Smiling Bear acquiesced, smiling. He, Rune, Harmony and Michael were preparing to go out in search of the sacred stone. He had gone to Crystal's office to let her know they would be leaving shortly. She was in the process of adding one more piece of paper to the collage of images and words covering her walls. This one was a conception of the Sun, with its magnetic fields described, rising far above the poles, twisting around in the familiar vortical pattern.

"Did you know the Sun rotates once every 27 days?"

"No, I didn't."

"That is why the energy travels in a spiral. Rotation begets cycles. The surface of the Sun vibrates with sound coming from deep within the core."

"Huh."

"There are many waves coming to us from the Solar Logos."

She taped the paper up next to the one of the sun flare, the *Coronal Mass Ejection*, with the added caption: *Rod of Initiation*. Something surfaced in his mind, something he had learned while he was away, about the coming divine spark, the *response* to Earth's call.

"So, you knew, you know that Earth is going through an initiation?" he realized.

"Of course, dear. This has been understood for quite some time. The shift is fast approaching now. Why do you think so many of its inhabitants are doing the same? Here," she said, pointing to a smallish paper on which was a quote:

230

"When that is the case, the initiation of his own Planetary Logos takes place, and consequently he (as a cellular body) receives an added stimulation along with the other sons of men." – the Tibetan, through A.A.B.

Although the terminology was unfamiliar, Smiling Bear thought he understood.

"But I mean, something bigger. Faster. You know... a real jolt of kundalini, to give it that nudge, make it leap."

"Yes, I do know. And it is coming, but will only occur when both are ready. Divine timing, remember," she chided, thrusting her chin at him, "Willingness, openness, acceptance. It is only when the frequencies synchronize and vibrate in unison that the greater light can enter. Do you not see? *We* are the *antahkarana* of the Earth. It is our task to enervate the center – awaken humanity to its role as conduit, transfer agent, as Earth takes initiation. Only then will the globes pass through to greater frequency and join the sacred planets as a conscious participant in the body of the Solar Logos. Only when all the kingdoms are attuned will we take the next step along the Path, which will eventuate in the realization of the perfected crystalline form of each of the globes. Until then we must work for peace. A new pattern cannot take shape in turbulence."

"Peace, be still," he recalled aloud.

"Exactly. In order to utilize the inherent plasticity of the matrix, the old pattern, the current waveform, must first be halted. Then the seed thought can propagate."

"I feel like I've been living with my eyes closed."

"You were asleep, now you're awake. There are many levels of awakening, many veils to pass through. Come, let's gather everyone and meditate before you go out."

In the great room, he took his place with the others on the circular couch. Sunlight was streaming in through the tall windows, bathing Guanyin, Buddha, St. Francis and Ganesha in gold. Everybody was smiling as they closed their eyes.

"We are so grateful for this time together and the work we embark upon," Crystal began, "Allow your body to relax. If thoughts intrude, let them pass through. Become the observer..."

Smiling Bear relaxed. He heard Crystal's words, but did not register them. He had thoughts (of the heat outside, his water bottle, where to park), but did not hold them. His forehead began to tighten and register pressure. A shiver went up his spine, followed by strong tingling at the top of his head. He felt these sensations, but did not dwell upon them. He left the body in oblivion and rose to become the observer. He saw the circle of friends from above. Their varied shapes and sizes blurred. A pinkish mist circulated around them as they sat. One of them began to glow. This raised the question in his mind: who? It was not Crystal, Carol, Harmony, Michael, Rune, or Brendon. It was a seventh. The figure, whose radiance now obscured the other participants, tilted her head upward and he saw into the eyes of his beloved. They grinned at each other, she rose to meet him, he sank into her light, she wrapped arm after arm around him.

Just as their rapture began to remove him entirely from the fourth globe, Crystal spoke.

"Gently, softly, return to the room. Feel your body grounding. Wiggle your hands and feet. Breathe deeply, knowing you are fully prepared for today's excursion, and you have been given all you need."

It couldn't possibly be over, he thought, she just now told us to relax. Skydancer was still there; he could still see her. She was no longer sitting on the couch, but was standing in the hall with one arm outstretched toward the front door, smiling. He smiled back, rose, and followed her out of the house. He was vaguely aware that the others were scrambling after him, calling him, gathering their water and snacks, but he didn't dare look away from the beloved, for fear she would vanish, even though he knew she was there in Rune, in Harmony, in Phil and Rhoda and Carol and Michael and Crystal and even in himself. Seeing her beautiful face and her golden aura was a pleasure he would not willingly release, not yet. And he knew she had come for a special purpose, to lead him to the baetyl at last.

He nearly lost her in the sunlight, it brought the Sedona rocks up strongly in his vision, but then he sensed the grace, the 'high energy' Rune had spoken of, as if because her vibration was purer or clearer than what surrounded her, her passage made a ripple in the day, leaving a catroptic trail for him to follow. He knew she was pleased that he was able to perceive this, and he chuckled as he walked past the parked cars to Soldier's Pass Road.

The plan of the group had been to drive to and hike Sterling Pass, which they had all agreed seemed the most likely place to start the search. It was one of the few trails Brendon had not already attempted, and Rune had a premonition about Vultee Arch. Now Harmony, Rune and Michael were following him down the street, as he followed Skydancer. She led him to the trailhead just yards from the house, the place he had hiked on that very first day. They were giggling together over it, quietly, to themselves. As they went along, he began to hear again the drumming, the haunting sound he had asked the others about. Now he realized it was the drone of Palatkwapi he had heard that day, and was hearing again, the Elders maintaining their vibration in the kiva. Somewhere above was the Gate, the oculus, the wormhole. Somewhere ahead was the baetyl.

They came to the fork in the trail where the tall cairn stood sentry. Hints of the beloved light glided to the right. He followed, winding through brush and twisted junipers, and then clomping

233

over dusty, naked rock toward Brins Mesa where caves and arches hid in the ancient layers of sediment. There was a sign on a feeble fence reading *Wilderness Area;* he crossed it without hesitation, to keep up with the quavering image of Skydancer. They turned away from Brins and began a slow incline toward other, far off buttes and mountains. The morning passed. For a while there was a trail running like an old habit through the scrub, a hint that others had passed that way before, but it was soon absorbed into the belly of the land, into the conscious community of cacti, succulents, conifers, shrubs and grasses. Brendon did not pause to calculate the miles or location; he knew Michael and his app-rich phone had accepted that task. Rune walked directly behind him, presumably assisting him to keep his vibration high. Harmony mothered the men about their water intake, urged rest periods, and hummed occasionally, matching the pitch of the drumming which continued to grow in strength. Brendon agreed to pause once, but kept his eyes closed, held the beloved's smile in his mind, spoke to no one. His head was heavy, yet floating, reaching upward. When his friends spoke to him, he found it impossible to listen or respond while maintaining the connection, holding the *antahkarana* in place.

At last, Skydancer stopped, hovering like a beacon above a spot in the crumbling face of another nameless cliff along the Mogollon Rim. The party approached the looming sandstone, and Brendon began reaching upward and scuffing the rock with his feet, searching for a grip or a foothold. He pulled himself up, maybe a yard, and slipped down to the ground.

"Let the others climb," Michael said. Brendon nodded and stepped back, simply pointing upward to where he saw her shimmering radiance, while his friends busied themselves looking for a way up the escarpment.

"Here," Harmony suggested, having discerned a likely avenue with better footing.

"We should come back with proper equipment," Rune recommended.

"What if he looses sight of it?" Michael protested.

Brendon steadied his breathing, released their words, set free all thoughts breezing through him, and focused on that feeling of blowing into the flute, of flipping up an octave, of raising the frequency of his oscillation to that place whence the light of the beloved issued.

"I think we can manage it free hand," Harmony decided, and began scaling the wall. Rune followed her while Michael stayed with Brendon at the foot of the formation. Brendon closed his eyes and looked for Skydancer's smiling face. She was still there, now brighter than before, sitting in the scaffold of white nodes and spectral lines, the etheric body of the cliff.

"To the left," he shouted up at the climbers, "Like twenty feet to your left."

They adjusted their course accordingly, expertly picking their way in the soft stone, rising slowly but surely toward something they could not yet discern.

Brendon's head opened and he slipped out, rising to meet her, passing the shadowy climbers and slipping into her open arms. Her embrace was warm and loving as ever; he flooded her with gratitude, she held him and turned him to look within. Then he could see it – not on the cliff face, but inside; not as the world would see it, a lump of ataxite bearing intricate markings, but in its perfected form, all the bodies of its complete being – the exact trapezohedron of its pearly lattice, the flaming diamond of its center, its gleaming crystal facets and the precise convolutions of its flow, the patience of millennia, the gift it was from others, the gift it gave of itself.

"You're almost there!" Brendon shouted. "Look for a dark spot in the rock, about the size of a baseball. That's all that's exposed, the rest remains interred." Because he had to speak, the light of the beloved slipped away. His friends were shadows no longer; the vision of the flaming, glimmering crystal vanished.

"Here?" Harmony reached out her hand and touched a smooth, rounded bulge, which was noticeably shinier and darker than the surrounding sandstone.

"That's it!" he exclaimed.

"Are you sure?" She found a nearer foothold and pulled herself closer to it.

"That's it. You can't see it, really, it's much larger than that."

Harmony was able to brush away dust and loose fragments with her hand, enlarging the exposed area to grapefruit dimensions.

"We're going to need a shovel," she noted.

"No," Rune countered, "It's got to be done properly. Crystal just wants the location."

"Should I mark it with something?" Harmony asked.

"No, we don't want it to be any more obvious." Rune answered. "Have you got the location, Michael?"

"Yeah. I've got it."

"Make a note of any distinguishing landmarks directly below her. Or above, if you can see any."

"I did. We're good."

What just happened, Brendon wondered momentarily. He felt like something had been taken from him, he had only just located the buried treasure, and it was already someone else's baby. But exhaustion was taking hold of him. He didn't really care what Rune or Crystal had in mind for the stone, incredible gift that it was. They would do right by it, there was no question. He had done his part. The drumming in his mind's ear had ceased.

236

He looked for the light of the beloved, but saw only a dusty trail. He slumped to a sitting position and sucked on his water bottle.

"Is there a quicker way out of here?" Rune, who had already climbed down, asked Michael.

"Maybe. If we head east we can pick up the Mt. Wilson trail. We should be able to get Carol to meet us by Midgely Bridge."

"Are you alright to go several more miles?"

"Yeah," Brendon answered. "I just need to sit for a minute."

* * *

"Were you followed?" Crystal asked.

"No, I don't think so," Michael reported.

"Any helicopters?"

"No."

"Good, good. There are those who would suppress this information."

"So let's go back right now and dig it out," Harmony suggested. Brendon groaned and flopped onto the sofa. All this anxiety and conjecture struck him as silly; there is no intrigue in love.

"It's a bit late to start something like that," Michael pointed out.

"No, it must be professionally excavated," Crystal insisted, "It must be dated and documented by scientific authority, so that all might believe."

"Anyone who gets involved will be dismissed as a quack," Carol warned, "It will ruin someone's career."

"Nevertheless, it must go through its paces. I've already made some calls. The right person will step forward to help bring this to light."

"I can't wait to see it!" Carol exclaimed.

Harmony sat beside Brendon, her knees twitching anxiously to get back on the trail.

"Where do you get so much energy?" he asked.

"The energy is all around us for the taking, you know that," she answered.

"Then why do I feel spent?"

"You should rest," Rune said warmly, "You've been through an awful lot in the last week."

"Hey, where's that print of yours?" Harmony asked, fiddling with her phone, "I took a picture from up there."

"How the heck did you manage that?" Brendon wondered, leaning over to look at the image.

"Yes, that's it. See, there's that one spire sticking up on the right. It's on my nightstand."

"I'll go grab it, you stay there," she said, and returned a moment later with it in her hands. "The photo shows a little more than the print, but it's definitely the same," she concluded.

He would have responded, but he was already asleep. They removed his shoes, covered him, and left him on the curving couch for the night.

CHAPTER FIFTEEN

IT WAS unnerving at first, to be there where Dennis died.
They had gathered for a twofold ceremony, and brought Dennis's
ashes with them. The authorities had been unable to locate
any relatives of his. Crystal had commandeered his laptop and
confirmed that there was indeed a lengthy manuscript on it, but
that it was unfinished. She had said that the right person would
certainly come forward to complete the work, but that it would
remain in her care until the 'moment of divine timing' arrived.
Brendon had agreed that the combined Earth ritual and memorial
service was a great idea; he had not hesitated; yet now that they
were all there, anxiety began to creep in. Rune touched his back,
held his hand there over the heart chakra for a minute.

"Is it that obvious?"

"I'm sure there is a great deal of trauma still associated with
this place for you. No one would blame you if you preferred to
leave."

"Oh, no. I'm okay. It's just... I guess I expected her to be
here."

"But she is," Rune assured him. "She is there over the center
of the spiral, even now."

"Really? But I don't... I saw her so clearly the day we found
the stone. But after that, she just disappeared."

"Now you've upset her. She wants me to assure you she is
still there with you, always."

"If you say so. Of course she is. It's not that I doubt her, I just... miss her face."

"Don't worry," he said, "You will see her again. Telopsis is cyclic just like everything else. You have only just acquired the instrument, you cannot expect to have mastered it so soon."

"You're right. I'm being ungrateful. And I know her face is everywhere, in everything. But I still wish I had a photo or something," he chuckled.

"I suspect you're trying too hard. Remember, it's not about reaching, it's about allowing. You cannot lose her now. You are forever entangled. You are married."

"Thank you," Brendon said, turning to hug his friend.

"Do you need this?" he asked, holding out a climbing hammer.

"Oo, yeah, thanks." Brendon took the tool, and knelt again over the dimple he had made in the hard desert ground. The little trowel he had brought had simply bent.

"Okay everyone," Crystal's voice rang out, "I believe it's time. Does everyone have their hole prepared?"

"No!" came the nearly universal reply. Most of the thirty people spaced around the spiral laughed and bemoaned the inadequacy of the bulb transplanters, garden spades, and spoons they had brought.

"Alright, alright. We'll take a few more minutes. Perhaps those of you with better implements could help those who are having trouble. The holes only need to be four or five inches deep, now, just so the weather doesn't expose them, all right? But don't plant them yet, we must all do it together."

There was more laughter as each confided to their neighbor their inability to dig a four-inch deep, four-inch wide hole. There was conferring, advising, and giving. There was joy, Brendon thought, a good start.

The idea for this event, this ceremonial planting of intent, had come through Harmony, when she had heard about their stone spiral, when she got Ben to bring her to the place when Brendon was still in the hospital, and she had sat in the center of it in the lotus position for an hour, meditating and calling on the local deva to heal her friends on either side of the veil. That's when the idea came to her, she said, a little ritual to reiterate the energy the three of them had instigated that night, to build up the course, the groove in the matrix before it dissipated, to heal by completion. She, Michael, Rune, and Ben had completed laying out the stones. Carol and Crystal had composed the invitational email and dealt with logistics; transportation, refreshments, and of course, the acquisition of thirty to forty similarly sized quartz points. Brendon had gladly submitted to their directive to rest. Now, with his knees in the soil and his head swimming in thoughts of Palatkwapi, it seemed to him that the idea had come through Harmony from Grandfather.

"Now are we all ready?" Crystal inquired again.

"Yes!"

"Okay, everyone get as comfortable as you can. Take your crystal in your hands. Close your eyes. Relax. Breathe in deeply. Exhale. Breathe in through the heart. See your heart connected to the hearts of all those present. See a strand of light connecting all our hearts at the center of the spiral, connecting all of the crystals. The quartz is conducting the Light perfectly, as it moves from one to the next. Now see that Light following the spiral, in, and out with each breath, contracting, expanding, vivifying. Now see that spiral as one plane of a great sphere. As we breathe in, the flux dilates and rises; as we exhale, it contracts and falls. With each breath, the circumference increases... wider... and wider. Now see that when it rises, it flips on itself, so that the contraction falls within the expansion. Each pulse is both an expansion and a contraction, which moves down through the top of the sphere. See that dimple on the top of the bubble, it grows and grows and becomes a vortex, whirling down inside, where it flips and becomes the expansion, the pulsing spiraling energy, which continually rises and folds in on itself, pushing the funnel ever wider, until the torus is open, inviting the Light of pure love to flow through it. Our group heart has become a perfect conductor. With this breath it expands to fill Sedona, pulsing with the toroidal flow, becoming a balancing point, a great node which completes energy circuits along the ley lines, the meridians in Earth's etheric framework, its energetic armature. In this way, we repair the grid, and heal the Earth.

"Now I want you each to take your crystal, which we have impressed with this energetic pattern, and plant it in the soil. Be sure to set them with the point up. Cover them firmly. We do this silently. We maintain our intent. We see the Light of Love descending to Earth via the node we have co-created. We hold this in our consciousness. Now we are going to continue to see the pulsing of this energy center as we rise and begin walking the spiral. Everyone move to your left. You may be moving further in, or you may be moving out of the spiral. When you reach the center, or the entrance, simply continue to the left along the stones, and you will then have reversed your course. So you see we are moving both in and out at the same time. Continue to visualize the open torus, the perfect flow, the engine of group intent. We are habituating the energy, creating a pathway for it to follow. As we walk, we know that our intention never ends. This pathway will remain as long as it is needed. The entire planet is aligned with these little seeds. This node will continue to hold this energetic pattern, to conduct the Light where it is needed, which will assist in the balancing of the globes, the alignment of

Earth with the Solar Logos, and the construction of the planetary *antahkarana*."

They continued the walking meditation for quite some time. Afterward, Dennis's ashes were sprinkled around the spiral. Harmony, Carol, and Ben wept. Crystal spoke of his generosity, his sincerity, and his compassion. Brendon had a hard time keeping the smile off his face, remembering the last time he had seen him, that flickering, fulgurating swagger, and the joy he had taken in being an 'agent'. He saw no cause for sorrow; he knew full well that Brother LeRose would remain in their dreams forever.

* * *

The baetyl was excavated in due course. By then, Brendon had left Sedona. Carol left before him; she moved to Seattle to spend more time with her grandchildren. Harmony seemed to be going through something or other, she saw hardly any clients for a couple weeks. He had offered to lend an ear, but she said she was fine, and anyway, Rune was always there for her. The house got even quieter, despite the general excitement about the buried treasure stone. There seemed little reason to stay, now that his 'mission' was accomplished. He missed the ocean. He missed Cass. He had written lengthy emails attempting to describe his experience, but her responses had been so short and generic that he wondered if she had even read them. She had indeed met someone as predicted by the artist in Ojai, a guy by the name of Derek, who was 'incredibly hot' and 'insanely sweet'. Fortunately, Derek had gone to China on business for a fortnight, so Brendon was able to stay with his sister for a few days. They had a good time. She couldn't get over how different he was, how much he smiled now, how at peace he seemed. He agreed. They had hugged a lot.

There had been an email from Michael. His dad had had a stroke, and he was moving back to Akron to help out. He was worried about Phil and the rest of his friends. A woman named Karma was taking Carol's old room; he was hoping she had a green thumb. Poor Karma, she had no idea what she was in for. She had probably responded to the very same ad, word for word, under the apartments heading, still with no mention of Crystal's intention that her household would function as a group mind. Harmony was doing better, Michael said. Crystal was the same as ever, plotting the consciousness revolution, holding her head high. She had been on local television, talking up the importance of their find. Rune had received some tangential recognition and was benefiting from a surge in clients.

Attached to Michael's email were the first pictures of the baetyl. It was quite large, about the size of a kitchen trashcan. It was ovoid, dark, and shiny in places. On one side of the stone was a diagram, deeply engraved to a precision beyond the capability of modern technology. Its fine lines depicted a complex series of tori, nested within one another, and completely open through the center. The sight of it made him shiver, and grin. The initial determination was that the layer of rock in which it lay was 250 million years old, but the arguments had just begun over its authenticity. Although the stone was being studied and kept at the university, Michael had noticed a number of black hummers and white vans driving slowly by the house lately. He said he was glad to be leaving.

Brendon remembered this concern of Michael's while driving route 150 from Santa Paula. He reflexively checked his rearview for large paramilitary vehicles, then laughed at himself. Let them come, he thought, I've got connections. I'm with Shambhala.

As if on cue, he spotted the sandwich board just off the shoulder of the highway, the one that promised *Spirit Paintings*.

He parked and strode anxiously into *ORANGE GROVE GALLERY.* At the little jingling sound of the shop bells, the psychic artist turned her chair to face the door.

"Oh, I'm so glad you're still here," Brendon exclaimed, going to her and bending down to hug her in a spontaneous display of gratitude. "Thank you so much," he said.

"You're welcome," she said, hugging him back.

"Do you remember me?" he wondered.

"You look familiar, but..."

"A few months ago you gave me a print of Sedona," he explained.

"Sedona?"

"Yes, the red rocks? It was titled *View from the Gate.* And there was a message from... a friend."

"Oh, right!" she said, grinning happily. "That was such a clear transmission. She was so determined."

"Well I certainly appreciate that you took the time to pass it on."

"It was nothing. I'm just the mouthpiece."

"It made all the difference," Brendon assured her. He turned and looked to the little niche in the far wall, holding his breath. There was the beloved, tucked away beneath the arch of light, looking back at him, waiting for him.

"So that was Sedona? I never knew where that came from."

"Yes," he affirmed. "Actually, I have a photo of that exact view on my phone, would you like to see?"

"Really? I'd love that."

Brendon flipped through and found the picture Harmony had emailed him, and then handed the phone to the artist.

"Oh my gosh. Honestly, I've never even been to Sedona."

"If you had told me that a few months ago, I wouldn't have believed you, but now, for some reason, it doesn't surprise me at all," he chuckled.

"Did you hear about the meteorite they found there?"

"Yes. And that's exactly where we found it," he revealed with a grin, "from where that picture was taken."

"*You* found it, you're kidding!" she cried, bouncing in her chair with excitement.

"If it hadn't been for you, it would still be hidden."

"Oh my God. That's so awesome. Spirit never ceases to amaze me."

Someone else entered the gallery and began looking at the work.

"Believe me, no one's more amazed than I am," Brendon assured her, taking his phone back. "I would love to tell you the whole story some day, when you're free. I'm going to be living here now, for a while anyway."

"That's great. Stop by anytime."

"I'd like to buy this painting," he declared, walking over to the portrait of the *dakini*. She was just as he remembered her. All the kindness, understanding, and beauty that Skydancer was sprang forth from the canvas.

"Oh, wonderful. She'll be so happy to have a good home."

"May I take it down?"

"Sure, go ahead. Can I help you with anything?" she asked the newcomer.

"Just looking," was the reply.

Brendon carefully removed the painting from the wall, and handed over his credit card.

"Are you the artist?" the browser inquired.

"Yes."

"Aren't they incredible?" Brendon remarked.

THE ROAD TO SHAMBHALA

"I love them. They're so spiritual."

"Take my advice – ask for a reading," he advised, smiling at the stranger.

"Oh, are you psychic, too?"

"Well... sort of," she admitted, "I mean I don't really tell futures. But sometimes I can get in touch with those who want to get in touch with you."

"Ah. Well I'll think about it. It certainly seems you are in touch with something."

"Yeah," she replied with a giggle, then handed Brendon his receipt. "Thank you so much," she said. "You made my day."

"Thank *you*. You've made my life. We'll talk soon," he said, turning to the door. He held up the *dakini*. "I will treasure her always," he concluded.

With the painting beside him in the passenger seat, Smiling Bear continued on his way. After a few more miles, he turned right, away from the highway, down a winding road where orange groves were interspersed with immaculate front lawns of modest multimillion-dollar homes. After a mile or two he came to a sign that read *DEAD END,* and kept going. Here and there overarching oaks shaded the narrowing pavement, their massive trunks blocking the view beyond the next twist in the road. There was a pressure and tingling on the top of his head. He could not escape the sensation of *entering into* – something hidden, charmed, expectant. Another slow mile passed, another sign: *END OF ROAD.* He kept going, smiling now, his heart warm and open. He could hear the silence coming. Then the trees parted, the sky opened up, and the Light engulfed him, as he began his ascent of Meditation Mount. It seemed the hairpin turn would lead him off into nothingness, but there she was, his beloved, smiling, beaming her radiance, guiding him to the summit. Rune had been right, she had returned at long last. His impulse was to chide her, but he could not. He knew, feeling her love streaming down, that it was he who had found his way back to her, not the other way around. She was always there, loving all. It was she who patiently waited for him to open up to her, for his senses to come on line, for him to observe her, and know the truth.

He parked beneath a grand eucalyptus, a towering transmitter of Light, and thanked him for the shade. As he got out of the car, and was walking toward the main building, a guy was heading the opposite way, preparing to leave. He looked familiar. Brendon smiled, his new Smiling Bear smile.

"Hey, how's it goin'," the fellow said, and with a preliminary uptick, he nodded, wagging his wavy forelocks. Just as he passed by, he winked. Brendon turned to look, almost reached back and grabbed the man's arm, but realized at the last moment that he was mistaken, of course it was not Dennis, this man was bald. Then he chuckled, under his breath, rejoicing at how fluent of form Agent LeRose had become.

The beloved waited, floating above the sweeping, uplifting roof of the auditorium. His whole head vibrated, rising to meet her. Here was a nexus of long standing, a node kept open by the constancy of those who had worked at and visited the Mount for decades, by the energy invited at each full moon. Here was a bridge between above and below, a place where those who aspire might mingle with Masters of Form, Light and Love.

In the breezeway were flyers of upcoming events. One was titled *JOIN THE NETWORK*, and called for participants in an Induction Ceremony, inviting one and all to bring a quartz point to Soule Park, the proposed site of a new stone spiral. 'Join us in planting the seed of intent to heal the Earth', it read.

"Wow," he said softly to himself, "Crystal moves fast."

He dropped a twenty in the donation bowl, strode up to the big, sound door, and opened it. A woman was inside, arranging chairs. Her friendly face looked surprised.

"Yes?"

Brendon, smiling, asked, "What can I do for you?"

About the author:

GERALD Stanek has written numerous children's books, several of which have been illustrated by his wife, intuitive artist, Joyce Huntington. The couple lived for a decade in Ithaca, NY, the setting of Gerald's recent novel, *Skirting the Gorge*. An artist in residence stay in Sedona and many hours spent in meditation inspired *The Road to Shambhala*. He now resides in Ojai, CA.